'There is something about t
its gentle, melancholy watchfulness, that grows inside
the reader rather than knocking them over the head.
No fireworks, no wordy dazzle: just the slow, determined
explication of damaged lives and thwarted hopes.'
Geordie Williamson, *Review of Australian Fiction*

'A truly miraculous writer.' Philippe Chevilley, *Les Echos*

'Turning his back on the preoccupations of most
of our current novelists, Chambers taps into several rich
seams…Chambers's voice is distinctive and individual.'
Andrew Riemer, *Sydney Morning Herald*

'There's a lyricism in the language and a depth to
the emotions laid bare here that's utterly irresistible.'
Diane Stubbings, *Canberra Times*

'An author not only in possession of an authentic feel for the
ordinary but also blessed with a well-developed understanding
of personal turmoil.' Eileen Battersby, *Irish Times*

'Chambers plays with the density of things left unsaid,
with awkwardness and silence, as one would a musical
instrument: without sadness, but with a hint of elegy.'
Liliane Kerjan, *La Quinzaine Littéraire*

'Chambers writes very powerfully about the sadness of memory.'
Kate Saunders, *The Times*

'Jeremy Chambers writes in a parched, tight prose.
His words are like sun-blanched stones.'
Eric Neuhoff, *Le Figaro Littéraire*

'Chambers is a great writer. He's the real thing.' M. J. Hyland

Jeremy Chambers is the author of *The Vintage and the Gleaning* (2010), which was published to much acclaim. *Suburbia* is his second novel.

jeremychambers.com.au

SUBURBIA

Jeremy Chambers

TEXT PUBLISHING MELBOURNE AUSTRALIA

textpublishing.com.au

The Text Publishing Company
Swann House
22 William Street
Melbourne Victoria 3000
Australia

Published by The Text Publishing Company 2017

Book design by W. H. Chong
Cover image: Bill Henson, Untitled 52/144, 1985/86, type C colour photograph, 128 × 100cm
Typeset by J&M Typesetting

Printed in Australia by Griffin Press, an accredited ISO/NZS 14001:2004 Environmental Management System printer

National Library of Australia Cataloguing-in-Publication entry
Creator: Chambers, Jeremy, 1974–, author.
Title: Suburbia / by Jeremy Chambers.
ISBN: 9781922079572 (paperback)
ISBN: 9781922253651 (ebook)
Subjects: Bildungsromans. Life change events—Fiction. Australia—Fiction.

This project has been assisted by the Australian Government through the Australia Council, its arts funding and advisory body.

This book is printed on paper certified against the Forest Stewardship Council® Standards. Griffin Press holds FSC chain-of-custody certification SGS-COC-005088. FSC promotes environmentally responsible, socially beneficial and economically viable management of the world's forests.

To my mother and father

THE HILLS ROLLED from north to south and they were steep on the south-facing side while the other side rose gradually. The suburb of Glenella lay east of the city and was not really known for anything: people lived here, but that was all. Once these slopes had been forested and the creek etched its way through gullies of ferns. Its banks, in those places where the water coursed shallow and sluiced through rocks, had long been home to a people. Then a new people came and they cleared the forests and told their own stories. Plum trees grew well in the claggy soil, so there were many orchards. The rest was given over to grazing land and apiaries and there was a brickworks with a kiln, the chimney of which rose very high and was for many years the only landmark, a monument to the burgeoning town. The first artists of the nation also came here, because it was so beautiful, and mostly they painted the landscape: they loved the enormous eucalypts with their sloughing bark, its mottled textures, and the falling pastures in the sunlight. The inhabitants, when they did appear, were often depicted as dreamers.

Graham and Joyce Arthurson first moved here in 1982 with their seven-year-old son, Roland, and baby daughter, Lily. Glenella was then populated chiefly by former servicemen and their wives, who had moved into the neat developments of cream-brick veneers that had been built here after the war. Each house had its allotted front lawn, a low brick fence with a decorative iron gate, and a generous backyard where the owners planted lemon trees and put in Hills Hoists. Everyone had a camellia bush somewhere. There were older houses as well—Cape Cods, California bungalows and iron-roofed weatherboards—but they were now like islands in a sea. The places were kept immaculate by women who raised children and spent most of their lives indoors. The men mowed the lawns obsessively and had their clubs for drinking and bowls. It had been a hard, dirty war, a long time ago now, but they still expected recompense and were given it here in the suburbs. This was their earthly paradise, their utopia: these grids of airy streets, this order and cleanliness, this sameness that bespoke similar lives, which was a comfort, the quietness that sometimes, in the heat of summer, could make the place feel forlorn. Houses were still being built—now it was brown-brick veneers—on what remained of the paddocks and orchards and areas of bush; new owners and developers tore down old weatherboards, the last of the farmhouses and bushmen's shacks.

The Arthursons were not the only young family in the area and one day Graham stopped at a house on Creek Road, five doors up from his own, to talk to a man his own age as the man washed his car in the driveway. Graham had recognised him from the gigantic illuminated sign that hung above the car yard on the nearby highway, on which the man's likeness appeared, crowned by bold capitals, a sort of heraldic scroll unfurling underneath—'Reg Noble Auto' the sign read. 'Your No.1 Eastern Suburbs Car Dealer'—his plump face grinning and winking at the passing traffic. The man was indeed Reg Noble; his wife's name, he mentioned in passing, was Colleen. Joyce suggested to Graham that they invite Reg and Colleen to a party they were throwing the following weekend.

It was a mistake, she realised on the night. The other guests were old friends from teachers' college: men with beards, wine enthusiasts, educated women. In their youth, they had protested against the war Reg had fought in, or had at least denounced it at parties. Reg was the only clean-shaven man in the room. Clutching his glass of beer, his belly already beginning to swell beneath his shirt, he regarded the other men with disdain. Those bearded men couldn't take their eyes off Colleen, who was dressed all in white: seamless pants that clung to the taut curves of her buttocks, a top that showed off her heavy, tanned breasts, and stiletto heels that Joyce would later discover left dents in the linoleum floors. Her hair was long and peroxided. A small heart hung from a chain around her ankle.

'She's so gauche,' one of the women whispered to the others, milling about irritably while their husbands leered.

In time, those old friends disappeared, while the Nobles remained, visiting the Arthursons every Sunday afternoon, Reg carrying the esky, his gut ballooning as the years passed, Colleen in her high-heeled sandals. Their daughter, Cassie, was the same age as Roland, a bright, sharp-featured girl, who on her first visit had remained sitting on her father's lap while eyeing Roland with a hard, quizzical stare. The next time she came, they were friends.

They went down to the nearby creeklands, where they played hide-and-seek and other games Cassie devised in the moment. She was expert at hiding: Roland would find her sometimes flat on the dirt beneath an impenetrable bush, or secreted among beds of wandering Jew, or so still behind some thin tree that he would pass without seeing her. They waded in the water of the creek and tried to swing from the cascading willows, and went to where the stream widened and was shallow and scrambled over the rocks. Cassie turned over a flat stone. Water splashed, the colour of rust.

'Look,' she told Roland.

A yabby scuttled and froze on the slimy underside of the stone, an ugliness and wildness in its claws and rustling legs and the bristling of eggs beneath its tail. Roland was horrified. It was as though some unconscious thing had emerged, some atavism, something that should have long been banished by the neatness and order in which the children had grown up, wiped clean with fragrant chemicals, subdued as all irregularities had been subdued in that husbandry of flowers and tonsured shrubs and lawns, in right angles and concrete edges and streetlights.

Cassie squatted down, reaching towards it.

'No!' Roland cried. 'Don't touch it!'

But she did, grabbing the yabby as it snapped its claws. Its tail flipped and the rows of legs waved. Cassie squinted up at Roland as she crouched there, clearly delighted by the fearful expression on his face as she held the thrashing creature out to him.

He watched as she returned the yabby to the water and was up again, off across the rocks, her pink thongs flapping, her skinny legs a joy of movement. Her laughter tinkled over the sound of the rushing water. He followed. He felt so slow, so dull when he was with her. She seemed already to know things, to understand what Roland was only beginning to become aware of. He was always struggling, always trying to keep up.

Their parents sat outside at the Arthursons' garden table, talking and drinking. It was a late summer's afternoon dripping in soft sunshine, a spiritless warmth that would be swept away in the dusk, a knife edge to the breeze. The children whispered in the shadows while little Lily staggered towards them through the spangling of vinegar flies in the hanging golden light. Colleen was telling her and Reg's story.

'We were at school together,' she said. 'At Nunawading High. We didn't know each other while we were there, although Reg always says he did notice this little blonde thing bobbing about. I was just starting the year he left. We didn't actually meet until he got back from Vietnam. I was modelling for a knitting magazine. It wasn't as glamorous as it sounds. Reg was working for his father. He saw me walking past the car yard one day, didn't you, Reg?'

'So, that was your father's car yard?' Graham asked Reg.

'That's right,' said Reg, reaching to tap his cigarette over the ashtray. 'Prestige Motors Quality Second-Hand Cars. I was only twenty-four when I took it over. I sold the same sort of cars as my father for a while, but then I started doing my own thing. It was Colleen who convinced me to start selling new cars.'

'It certainly was,' said Colleen. 'I said, "People like new cars. They don't want to be driving around in these old bombs."

I said, "People are proud of their cars." And I was right, wasn't I, Reg?'

'You were.'

'And I got him to change the name. The sign and the window stickers were my idea as well. I said, "People like to put a face to a name." Reg was worried about what his mates would say. I said, "And what have your mates ever done for themselves?"'

'So, you're the woman behind the man,' said Graham with a grin.

'I am,' said Colleen, cackling, banging the table with her palm. 'That's exactly what I am.'

When Graham asked Reg about Vietnam, he said it was the best thing that ever happened to him.

'It gave me the kick in the pants I needed. Before that, I was wasting my life, hanging around with my mates. Chasing birds. I went over there and saw how hard those little bastards worked. For nothing. A bowl of rice. It was a real eye-opener for me. I came back here and I'll tell you what, I appreciated everything. Every little thing. Indoor plumbing. Electric heating.'

He counted the things he appreciated off on his fingers.

'Refrigerators. Air conditioning. Flush toilets. Hot water. None of them had any of that. Not out in the villages, the rice paddies. Where we were. My father said, "Well, it's fine to talk that way, but you've got to prove yourself, boy." And I did. I worked hard. I worked bloody hard. Everything I've got, I've worked for it. No one ever gave me any handouts.'

'Well, they're all over here now,' said Colleen, shrill, drunk, her drink tilting in her hand and almost spilling as she gestured. 'We're becoming foreigners in our own country.'

'The Americans didn't know how to fight a war,' Reg told Graham. 'Used to smoke marijuana before they went out on

6

patrol. Wandered around the jungle yapping their heads off. None of them could shut up for five minutes. What we did is we found a path, we set up an ambush and we waited. The Americans could have won the war if they'd stuck to ambushes and kept their mouths shut.'

'What about the Viet Cong?'

'They were all right. They did set up ambushes, but they weren't very good at it. The only time any of us were afraid, I mean really fearing for our lives, was this one time when we lost about four blokes in the space of a week. So, we went out looking for whoever it was setting up these ambushes. You know who it was? Bunch of kids. I would say not one of them over twelve years old. Kids with Kalashnikovs.'

'So, what did you do?'

'What do you think we did, Graham? We did our job, didn't we.'

He lit another cigarette. Colleen and Joyce were looking at something in the garden. Colleen, barefoot, her glass in her hand, stepped on a prickle and stood balanced on one leg, picking it out with long painted fingernails. Joyce was wearing a flowery Indian-cotton dress, a relic from her hippie days, its shapelessness concealing her slim figure. Her hair was tied with a purple scarf and fell, a dull wheat, to her waist. The breeze brought the faint whiff of meat and burning charcoal from a far-off barbeque, the bubble of conversation.

'I mean, we weren't social workers,' Reg said to Graham.

Lily came to adore Cassie in the years that followed, and Cassie started to spend more and more time at the Arthursons' house. She would appear at the back door every day after school, slinging her schoolbag down by the kitchen bench and running off to play as though she was in her own home. The girls would giddy about, laughing at everything, falling against the walls as if on a ship in rough water as they sent each other into fits of shrieks and giggles. They dressed up in Joyce's cast-offs and put on fashion shows in the lounge room, Cassie striding and pouting and jutting her hips as Lily bounced about. They made up dances and performed them to Top 40 songs that Cassie had taped from the radio. In games of make-believe, they acted out imagined adult lives. On the weekends, Cassie often stayed over and the two girls would talk until late and wake themselves to shuffle bleary-eyed to the kitchen for much-anticipated midnight snacks. Although she was older by seven years, Cassie's enthusiasm for Lily's companionship did not wane as she approached her teens; she seemed more content than ever with tea parties and Barbie dolls and imaginary worlds as she teetered on the edge of new things. Her growth spurt happened early, while she was still in primary school, and the change did not go unnoticed by Roland. They suddenly became awkward with one another, tongue-tied under each other's gazes and embarrassed at what they did manage to blurt.

Sometimes, when she came around, Cassie seemed more enamoured of the parents than the children. She would spend her afternoons in the kitchen, chatting to Joyce as she prepared dinner. Joyce would give her vegetables to chop and peel, dishes to wash, tasks the girl would perform with earnestness, almost reverence. She would tell Joyce about her day, a succession of names and those frighteningly astute observations that are the preserve of girls: subtleties that adults might observe but are loathe to utter. How much easier to be a boy, Joyce found herself thinking during one of these conversations, glimpsing

Roland as he threw a tennis ball about in the backyard. Running around. Unaware of the complexities, the hidden aspects.

At other times, Cassie would come to the house quiet and shy in that delicate, mournful way of girls in the first painful blush of adolescence. After dinner, as she sat watching television with the Arthursons, she would snuggle up to Graham, clinging onto his arm or squeezing his hand.

'Are you all right, pet?' Joyce would ask her. Cassie nodded solemnly but said nothing.

'I don't mind her being here at all,' Joyce said to Graham one night as they were preparing for bed. 'She's such a sweet girl. But Colleen could at least ask if it's okay with us. Or thank me. She's never thanked me. She's never even mentioned it. Not once.'

When Roland and Cassie were twelve, the two families holidayed together in a house among the scrub and hot roads of the peninsula. Every morning they trooped out to find a space on the beach amidst the towels and pitched umbrellas, the sunbathers and crackling radios, women in high-hipped bikinis, fathers playing cricket with their sons. Children ran in front of the crashing waves, shrieking, their footprints marked only briefly on the sheen of the wet sand. Roland sat sulkily, watching Cassie as she pranced through the roiling water with Lily and Reg, who splashed the girls, making them scream, or grabbed them and tossed them into the waves as they broke and surged. Colleen sunbathed topless, sprawled out on her back with her eyes shut. She was lathered in baby oil, every part of her bronze but for the shock of peroxided hair and the silver V of her bikini bottoms. Reg came swaggering up from the water and shook his wet hair over her gleaming bare breasts, scattering brilliant droplets onto her oiled skin. Colleen screamed, then laughed, trying to push him away.

'Stop it, Reg!' she shrieked. 'Stop it! Stop it, Reg! Stop it! Reg, stop it!'

In the evening, the two families sat on the balcony of the Surf Lifesavers' Club, watching the last of the beachgoers below as they shook out their towels in the silver light. Figures stalked the shore: tall, perfect silhouettes, looking out onto the fractured water, drying themselves like limp birds or gathered in still, observant tableaus. The children ate fish and chips, served with tartare sauce and lemon wedges, the cook ringing a bell as he slid the plates onto the servery from the clatter and noise of the kitchen. Graham and Reg drank pots of beer. Reg let Cassie taste the froth from his and she made a face, holding her tongue out.

'I'm so envious,' Joyce said to Colleen.

They were comparing arms: Joyce's was pink and freckled, a little burnt; Colleen's was a golden brown.

'I did get burnt as a girl,' said Colleen. 'I just pushed through it. You burn, you peel and then you tan. I was very disciplined. Out there every day in summer with my alarm clock. I think my skin has just got used to it.'

'And lemon juice in your hair,' Joyce said. 'Did you do that?'

'Of course,' said Colleen. 'I used to iron mine. Every morning. And wearing your jeans in the bath, do you remember that? To make them tight.'

The two women laughed. 'The things we used to do!'

After dark, Roland and Graham went out with a torch to look at the nightlife in the rock pools. The tide was coming in, the ocean roaring from the darkness, the lines of the breakers lit by the moon. The wind off the water was icy. It bit and howled and turned the night cool. The mad heat of the day was forgotten.

In the pools, they found strange life forms: scuttling crabs, trapped stingrays, toadfish, a blue-ringed octopus—sensing their presence, the rings turned neon, they seemed to burn. Sea anemones waved in the still water, their delicate tentacles drifting, and schools of whiting flashed and surged. Gulls roosted in the cliffs above them, silent among the ledges and patches of grass. Their feathers fluffed, white in the light of the torch.

'Your mother has asked me to have a talk with you,' Graham said to Roland as they crossed the dark squall of the headlands. The rocks stretched out like musculature, slippery under their feet. 'You're paying a little bit too much attention to Colleen. You've got to stop staring at her breasts.'

'I'm not!' Roland said. It was shameful to even refute it. 'I never even looked.'

'Don't argue. Your mother has seen you, so it has to stop. You're embarrassing your mother.'

At that time in his life, Roland was unhappy, miserable at school. He often felt lonely. Sometimes he searched his memories, looking for some sort of meaning, some configuration of moments that could presage his life and tell him what he should strive towards, but he found nothing. He was at an age where lucid thoughts often gave way to something rawer, a sort of pounding animal feeling, intimations of that deep and inexorable drive towards sex. It confused him, and he was ashamed. Understanding, which had always seemed dulled, seemed dulled even further; things were obscured, as though a curtain of gauze was fixed across his eyes. He was ready for it all to happen, waiting for it, but he did not know how it began. He wandered alone sometimes out along the sinewed rocks to where the waves hit and burst with a great noise, rising into the air, white for a moment, and then splattered down like heavy rain. Spindrift flecked his face in the whipping winds. He closed his eyes to it. It was the elemental violence that he liked, this fury of nature: in it, he could somehow lose himself.

At the end of January they all drove back to Glenella and another year followed, much the same as the last.

THE COCKATOO COUGHED. There was movement in the pittosporum. The two girls laughed and delighted in the sun and the coolness of the grass—this long afternoon that would never descend into shadows and glare. Cassie Noble brushed her cheek against her knee as she painted her toenails with long, tender strokes, bending forward now and then to blow on them. Lily wriggled her toes as she waited for her turn, her flowery sunhat perched jauntily on her mass of blonde curls. Away in the shade of the wisteria that cascaded over the back fence, Roland sat reading, watching Cassie as she lingered. She paused to admire her work, the paint blood-viscous and glistening in the hot, bright sunshine.

Next door at the neighbour's house, the screen door opened with a whine. Maurice came out onto the tiled veranda, his squat body moving with surprising speed and deftness, his pudgy child's face scowling. He picked up a broom and hit the cockatoo's perch with the handle. The cockatoo squawked, lifting its wings.

'Shut up!' yelled Maurice.

At the garden table, the ashtray was piled high with cigarette butts. Reg Noble's gold necklace glinted in the sun. Empty UDL cans sat in a line: bourbon and cola for Reg, vodka and orange for Colleen. Graham and Joyce drank Lindeman's Riesling from the perennial cask in the fridge. A packet of chips lay gutted, split down the seams, the burnt flecks scattered with salt on the brilliant foil. Colleen's shoes lay kicked off on the grass, her legs up on Reg's lap. He stroked them as she talked, her long hair drifting and white in the sun. She was telling a story about a friend of hers.

'You think you know someone,' she said. 'But you don't know them.'

The cockatoo wheezed. 'Christ!' it gasped. 'Jesus Christ!'

Maurice hit the perch again. 'Shut up!' He glared at the cockatoo through thick, steel-rimmed glasses, a wrinkled Band-Aid wrapped around the bridge. His face was flushed, red to his balding, sunburnt pate.

The bird's eyes boggled. It lifted its chained talon and sidled away from Maurice, watching him with one swivelling eye. Its round tongue moved mute within its open beak. The sulphur crest lifted and unfurled. It coughed.

'Shut up! Shut up! Shut up!' Maurice yelled, hammering the perch.

'She accused me of chasing her husband,' Colleen said. 'I said, "I have my own husband, thank you very much."'

Reg grinned and lit another Winfield Blue. Colleen's laughter pealed through the vacant afternoon. Cassie was languid, sullen, lazy in her movements. She painted Lily's toenails the same visceral red as her own. Lily squealed.

'Stop moving,' Cassie said. 'Sit still.'

'But it tickles.'

When Cassie finished, Lily fanned her toes and skipped up to the table to show her parents. Next door, old Jack shuffled onto the veranda in his worn dressing-gown, carrying his transistor radio. Through the crackle there was the sound of bat on ball, a roar from the crowd, excited voices. He rolled a cigarette.

'What's all the fuss?' he asked the cockatoo.

The cockatoo edged over to him, its head cocked, one pebble eye on Jack's face. It opened its beak, its tongue rolling.

'He's not bothering you, is he?' Jack called over the fence.

'No, he's all right, Jack,' Graham shouted back.

'He's just trying to say hello,' Jack said to Lily, who had run up to the fence and suddenly turned shy. She waved Cassie over and climbed up on the crossbeams, folding her arms against the planks. Cassie got up slowly and brushed down her shorts. Jack smiled at Lily as she peered over at him.

'How are you, darling?'

'Um, can you tell my friend his name?' Lily asked in a tiny voice.

'His name's Cockie,' said Jack, lighting his cigarette.

'He's a cockatoo and his name's Cockie,' Lily whispered to Cassie. 'Why?' she asked Jack. 'Why do you call him that?'

'Suits his personality,' said Jack, the smoke drifting around him.

Lily looked over at the garage, shading her eyes with her hand.

'Can we see Maurice's new chicken?'

'Maurice!' Jack called out.

Maurice came out of the garage carrying his poor ragged

rooster by the legs, the one he kicked around in the mornings.

'He's a killer, this one,' said Maurice, holding up the rooster.

'No, not that one,' Lily said to Jack. 'The other one. The big red one.'

'This one's a killer,' said Maurice. 'Watch out for this one.'

He took a piece of wire out of his shorts pocket, wrapped it around the rooster's feet and hung it upside down from the Hills Hoist. The rooster lifted its head to the side, flapped a little and dropped down, stunned, as the clothesline turned and creaked. Maurice went to the garage and came out with the Rhode Island Red in his arms. Cassie and Lily reached over the fence to stroke the blazing feathers, the bright comb. They watched its quick movements. Lily looked at Cassie, as entranced as she was by the wondrous bird.

'I'll tell you a secret,' Colleen was saying. 'She's tight with money. I didn't even know it until the other day. Reg wasn't surprised, were you?'

'No,' said Reg. 'Not at all.'

'But, of course, I always see the good in people, don't I? That's why it comes as such a shock.'

Birds scuttled. A twig cracked in the heat and fell through the rustling foliage; leaves and branches waved and fluttered in shadow across the lawn and the hot concrete. There was a shrill, piercing pulse of cicadas. Lawnmowers had been droning all afternoon, starting up here and there like stunted voices, joining in harsh choruses across the endless stagger of paling fences. The regularity of the shifting pitch and volume was somnolent, hypnotic.

'Tiffany Pellegrini is Cassie's best friend,' Colleen told Joyce. 'She's a gorgeous girl. She and Cassie are the most popular girls at their school.'

'Really?' asked Joyce.

'Oh, yes. All the other girls want to be friends with them. And the boys are chasing them already. They wait for them outside the gates at the school every afternoon and then they all go to the McDonald's in Camberwell. It's where the trendy kids go. Reg isn't happy about it, are you, Reg?'

'No, I'm not,' said Reg, stony-faced.

'Reg doesn't want his little girl growing up is what the problem is,' said Colleen.

'It's the boys I'm worried about,' said Reg. 'You can't trust boys that age. I should know. I used to be one of them.'

Joyce laughed.

'Well, I'm glad you find it funny, Joyce,' Reg grumbled. 'Because I don't. Not when it comes to my daughter I don't. I mean, look at her,' he said, nodding at Cassie as she lay on the lawn with Lily, the two girls lost in their own conversation. 'She's a beautiful girl. She's tall. She's blonde. I know what those boys are thinking. I know exactly what they're thinking.'

'The Pellegrinis have this amazing house in Doncaster. It's practically a mansion,' said Colleen.

'What does he do?' asked Graham.

'Bernard's a builder,' said Reg. 'Does a lot of concrete work.'

'And he imports these marvellous tiles from Europe,' said Colleen. 'He's been getting contracts for the big office buildings in the city. He does their bathrooms. He's made an absolute fortune.'

'I tell him he hasn't done too badly for a wog,' said Reg, lighting another cigarette, the smoke unfurling in the sun and breeze.

'Not to his face, I hope,' said Joyce.

'Why not?'

'But that's an insult, Reg. You've probably insulted him.'

'I give him a hard time about it. If he's too sensitive to take a joke that's his problem.'

'The Pellegrinis go out at least once a week,' said Colleen. 'If Evelyn doesn't feel like cooking, the whole family goes out for a meal when Bernard gets home. Just like that. Even on weeknights. It's what Europeans do. We went out with them one night and Bernard bought a seventy-dollar bottle of wine. I said, "Bernard, this is wasted on me. I couldn't tell the difference between French wine and cask wine. I really couldn't. It all tastes the same to me." And Bernard said, "Trust me, just try it." And do you know what? I could tell. I said to Bernard, "Normally I don't like wine at all, but this one I like." I said, "You're spoiling me, Bernard. You're going to give me a taste for it."'

The girls stood up and began clapping their hands together, left palm against left, then right against right, then both together, clapping their hands in between. They chanted.

My name is,
Al-i Al-i, Chickle-i, Chickle-i,
Oo-i, Oo-i, Bok Bok Bok
Chinese Checkers, Cheese on Toast,
Wally Wally Whiskers. Poke, Poke Poke.

As they chanted the last line, they poked each another, Lily shrinking away and turning to jelly as the older girl tickled her. They collapsed on the lawn, exhausted from the hilarity, and sat there whispering, glancing conspiratorially towards the table. Lily got up, ran over, and tugged on her mother's dress.

'Can we go to the pool now?'

'You can,' Joyce said. 'And you can take Roland with you as well.'

'Why?' Roland protested, closing his book.

'It will do you some good. You should be running around, not sitting there reading all day. It's not normal for a thirteen-year-old boy.'

'But it's for school.'

'Well, take a break. Honestly!' she said to Colleen. 'He'd rather be stuck here with a book.'

'Ruining his eyes.'

'Yes.'

'You don't want to end up wearing glasses,' Colleen told Roland. 'My brother Barry wore glasses when he was your age. He loathed them. Absolutely hated wearing them. Big thick things.'

The children walked to the pool through the sunlit empty streets, the miles and miles of concrete and bitumen, the rows of identical brown-brick houses that lined the rising hills, their orange-tinted windows blinding in the sun. The grass on the nature strip was lush from sprinkler hoses that ran all day long, thin sparkling arcs dampening the footpath and trickling down the dusty gutters to the stormwater drains. The road melted, seethed; it turned to black liquid. It shimmered in the distance and made mirages at the rounded peaks and hollows. The children's thongs slapped the footpath, echoing like rifle shots. Lily stopped chattering to concentrate on the quick stride of her legs, several paces to each of Cassie's steps. She puffed. Cassie wore a pair of men's Ray-Bans, too large for her face, her orange fluoro bikini visible beneath an oversized white T-shirt.

A car swept past as they reached the highway. Men yelled out of the open windows, their words lost in the roar of the engine. Brief glimpses of bare tanned skin, hard faces, fluttering hair, tattoos faded to a burnt verdigris. Cassie watched with interest as the car slowed and turned at the chicane. The children continued through the gravel carpark, the joyous clamour from the pool amplified through the fence and metal turnstiles. There were Reg Noble Auto stickers on the back windows of the cars, Reg Noble's face grinning and winking at them as they passed. Light flashed across the glass as though winking at them also, as though all the world was likewise roguish and cheerful.

They spread their towels on the gentle rise of grass by the outdoor pool. The shallow end was a frenzy of splashing children, their shrieks echoing off the concrete. At the deep end, a lithe girl dived from the board while groups of straggly-haired boys watched through mirrored sunglasses. They flexed their biceps, lit cigarettes, argued with the lifeguards and traded insults with other groups of boys, shouting across the lawns and getting up to swagger among the people on the towels, staring at the sunbathing girls and women. Tattooed men growled at them as they passed. The women sat up and rubbed baby oil into their already tanned skin. The boys joined the line to the kiosk along the cracked concrete path and came back with sausage rolls, pies, chips and soft drinks, sucking on icy poles and Sunnyboys.

Roland watched as the girls went down to the pool, Cassie checking her bikini, tugging at the material and the straps and looking down at her breasts as she walked. Lily, plump, still a child, ran boisterously alongside her. She jumped gleefully into the water and was soon lost among the other frantic children.

Cassie paused at the edge, dipped her toes into the water and looked around. A group of boys walked past and Cassie smiled at them, sweeping her hair back. Lily yelled to her from the pool, 'Cassie! Cassie!' through the shrieking and the splashing. One of the boys gave Cassie a cigarette and lit it for her and she blew the smoke into the air over her shoulder, holding the cigarette between two straight fingers, close to her cheek like a movie star. The boys crowded around her, puffing out their chests and tensing their stomachs and making large gestures with their arms. Cassie went to sit with them on their towels.

Lily got out of the pool and ran over to Cassie and the boys, her wet feet spotting the pebble-dash. A lifeguard shouted at her and she slowed. Cassie looked up and shooed her away. Lily's face reddened as she turned around again and wandered slowly back to the pool with her head down. There was exuberance in the water behind her; it boiled, rough wavelets flashing. The divers speared effortlessly from the boards. One boy leaped, holding his knee, and hit the water with an echoing splash. The water flowed over the mass of heads as a lifeguard leaned over the blocks and yelled. Lily began to shudder and cry, wiping her face with the back of her hands. Her wail swelled like a siren. Cassie went over to her and hugged her, stroking her hair. They walked back up to where Roland was sitting, Lily letting out long, woeful sobs, her head against Cassie's chest.

'Poor Lily. Poor darling. I didn't mean it like that.'

The two girls went to the kiosk and came back with salt-and-vinegar chips and cans of creaming soda. Cassie wordlessly held out the open packet of chips to Roland. Lily was bright again and chattered as she ate. She slurped her drink and belched, laughing. When she had finished, she jumped up and started to run down the grass.

'Watch me!' she shouted to Cassie.

'I am,' said Cassie, waving.

Lily paused at the edge of the pool, looked back and leaped into the water with her arms and legs splayed out. She bobbed joyfully. Cassie put her sunglasses on.

'What are you reading?' she asked Roland.

He showed her the cover of the book.

'*King Lear*,' she read. 'Can I see?'

Roland handed her the book and she flicked through the pages.

'Do you understand it?'

'Yeah. Most of it.'

She stopped at a page, concentration furrowing her brow. 'I wish I was smart.'

'I'm not smart.'

Cassie looked at him through the dark lenses of her sunglasses, puzzled.

'But you are,' she said. She bit her lip. 'You know you are.'

Down at the pool, everything was noise and movement. Roland felt lost among the shrill calls and splashing, surrounded by bodies, bright bathers, indolence: a rolling acre of sunlit skin. The smell of the chlorine, drying on the concrete, mingled with the odours of hot skin and damp hair and the coconut scent of tanning lotion, the clutter of fragrances kindling Roland's memories of near-forgotten days, summers that were all so alike to the senses that they bled into each other in amorphous sunlit images, heaving with heat and water. The pages of the book were dazzling, the words erased by brilliance—when Roland closed his eyes they continued to burn. He was aware of Cassie beside him, of her slow breath and movements. She stretched, sighed for no reason, took off her sunglasses and lay on her stomach, her head nestled between her folded arms. Nearby, a man got to his feet with a groan. He was sunburnt, bright red across his chest and sagging belly. He picked up his towel and shook off the leaves and twigs and gumnuts, the towel waving like a flag in the warm, gusty breeze.

Lily came running back, her hair dripping.

'Did you see me?' she asked Cassie.

'Yes,' said Cassie drowsily.

'Did you see me when I dived deep, deep down and stayed there for *ages*?'

'Yes. I saw.'

'Did you really, though?'

'I saw everything, sweetie. Of course I did.'

They walked home through the hazy light of the late afternoon, the sun trembling across the terracotta roofs. It lapped at the bricks and paling fences, making patterns of brightness that moved like smoke or vapour. The tinted windows glittered and burned. Cars turned into driveways, their doors slamming loud through the quiet and the thickening air, and televisions murmured from within the houses, a blue flicker of light behind the curtains and the scrim. Lily hopped through the long-angled shadows of trees and peaked roofs, elaborate arrangements of aerials, the black line of the telephone wire slicing diagonally across the road. She threw her towel into the air, catching it as it flared out and fell. Cassie went wearily, the day's heat lingering on her skin. They sat on the footpath outside the house in the shade of the tall swarming roses. Cassie inspected her knee and picked at the peeling skin, discovering white patches on her thigh.

A motorcycle came thundering up the hill. It slowed and stopped, shuddering, its engine strafing. Cassie sat up, brushed back her hair and straightened her sunglasses, which stared blankly at the boy on the bike. Light burst from the spokes and the big chrome belly; the petrol tank gleamed. The grinning boy squinted at Cassie through the glare. He revved the engine and continued up the road.

MAURICE AWOKE BEFORE dawn and walked past the sleeping cockatoo to the garage. Inside, the chooks started squawking: there was a frenzy of wings and dull thuds as they hit the asbestos walls. Next door, Graham woke, swore, and turned over. The bedsprings squeaked and groaned. Maurice returned to the house with efficiency in his stride and thick countenance: the air of important duties, a steel bowl full of eggs. The hysteria in the garage subsided.

Lily was also up early in the blueness and silence before first light, before the singing of birds. She was a tiny thing, six years old. She dressed herself, tiptoed through the dark and sleeping house and went out into the cool air in a sun frock sewn with ribbons, her feet bare, a basket swinging from her arm. She greeted the morning singing and pattered down the drive to the ramshackle California bungalow next door. Clutching four speckled eggs, she returned and climbed into her parents' bed to show them each one, turning them under the lamp and marvelling at this small miracle.

Next door, the cockatoo started coughing with the birds: it was a smoker's cough, a morning cough; the bird hawked and spat and wheezed. Old Jack shuffled onto the tiles in his worn dressing-gown and rolled a cigarette, man and bird coughing together. Graham got up and went outside for the paper, greeting Jack and Maurice over the fence. It was school holidays, and Graham was spending them in the garden, planting banksias and fuchsias and Japanese camellias that would one day produce delicate, ruffled flowers with petals so fine they would seem to glow from within. He worked shirtless, sunburnt, covered in dirt, pausing from time to time to stand and look with quiet satisfaction at what he had done.

Tilly Johnson arrived at around ten-thirty with her two fat, pampered dachshunds. She tied them to the patio railing and let herself in the back door. Her shoes were sturdy, her cardigan buttoned tightly. Although the day was hot, she wore lisle stockings, thick and beige. 'Yoo-hoo!' she called, bustling into the kitchen. She found Lily playing games at the kitchen table with her peg dolls, speaking for each of them in tiny voices. They were fiery characters, caught up in some desperate melodrama. Lily bounced them across the Laminex while they argued and pleaded.

'No, no, no, no, no, no, no,' piped one of them.

'If you don't love me then I'll kill you,' said another in a growl.

'No, please don't kill me!' the first squealed. 'I love you! I love you! I love you!'

The two dolls kissed, knocking their wooden heads together.

'Go and get your mother, dear,' Tilly said. She put her handbag on the table and sat down.

Lily paused in her game, aghast at the interruption. She eyed Tilly suspiciously before returning to the dolls, who canoodled and chattered to each other. Lily's eyes were large and blue; her curly hair was like fleece.

'Go on,' said Tilly, clapping her hands briskly. 'Chop chop!'

Lily fled the room, her dolls clutched to her chest, and trotted down the hall. Joyce was lying on her bed, reading a book and listening to a Seekers' record on the portable record player. 'Mum! Mum!' Lily cried. 'That *woman* is here again!'

Joyce closed the book and got up with a sigh. She turned off the record player and went to the kitchen, where she immediately switched on the electric kettle.

'Well, it looks like George Kyriakides has done the dirty on me again,' Tilly said to her. 'He's got more tenants in that house of his.'

'Really?'

'He certainly does. Despite what he promised me. I said to him after the Ponsfords left, I said, "Renovate it, sell it or knock it down. But please, no more of these awful tenants."'

'You know, I don't think I ever spoke to the Ponsfords,' said Joyce. 'I don't think I ever even saw them.'

'Well, no one did,' Tilly sniffed. 'The only time I ever saw Angie Ponsford was when she took her bins out. Late. Always very late. Cigarette hanging from her mouth. She used to leave them out there for so long I had a good mind to bring them in myself. Never saw him at all. Len. Heard him coughing away inside, but never saw him. And of course the boys used to sit there all night on those old bombs they left out on the front lawn. Drinking and smoking with their mates. Using the most foul language you can imagine, believe you me. Used to hoon around the streets at three o'clock in the morning.

Drove right up over the footpaths. Churned up all the nature strips. But George Kyriakides knew all of this. I told him. I said to him, "Carlington Street is the premier street in Glenella. The Ponsfords are not Glenella people." But he didn't take any notice, it seems.'

'So, who's he let it out to now?'

'Some woman and her boy. Another hoon, by the looks of things. Has his big motorcycle parked out there.'

'Oh, dear.'

'George Kyriakides promised he'd do something with that house,' said Tilly. 'He swore it.'

Graham was looking for a tape measure. He came into the kitchen in his shorts and terry towelling hat, an anticipatory grin on his face.

'I was talking to George Kyriakides a little while ago,' he said to Tilly. 'He'd come to mow the lawn at his house. Smoking that big pipe of his, like he does. We were talking about the state of the world and so forth and the subject got onto the banks. George doesn't think much of them. Doesn't trust them. So he took me over to his car, that battered old Kingswood, and opened up the boot. It was full of money. Banknotes, all stacked up under a plastic tarp. Must have been tens of thousands of dollars there. I said to him, "Aren't you worried about getting robbed?" He says, "You think anyone is going to steal this car? Look at this car."' Graham imitated the accent, making effusive hand gestures. '"And me?" he says. You know, pointing to his beard, those daggy old tracksuit pants he wears. "Who's going to rob an old man like me?"'

Graham left, chuckling. Joyce brought two mugs of tea over to the table and sat down. Lily came back in, draped in plastic necklaces, an old handbag of Joyce's in the crook of her arm.

'I'm off to see Cassie,' she said matter-of-factly, waving at them as she passed.

'All right, but if you're going to stay there, make sure it's okay with Colleen,' Joyce called after her. She picked up her cup and blew on it, cradling it in one hand. Outside, Tilly's dachshunds whined and panted, their tongues hanging out. The cockatoo cleared its throat and coughed.

'Colleen says Cassie's already becoming interested in boys,' Joyce told Tilly.

'Well, that's just like her mother. She was running around with boys at that age.'

'I can imagine that.'

'It's true. Believe you me. Marjory White told me just the other day that she was talking to a woman who knew the family. Apparently, Colleen was very wild when she was growing up.'

Tilly shifted in her seat and sniffed again.

'Father couldn't handle her. He was too soft on her when she was a girl. Spoiled her. Never said no to her. The mother had problems with her nerves. Well, she reached a certain age,' Tilly said, nodding knowingly. 'Seen driving around with boys in cars. Sneaking out at night. Right under her parents' noses, but they were none the wiser. She acted like butter wouldn't melt in her mouth, apparently. Pulled the wool over her father's eyes.' Tilly paused meaningfully. 'Got herself into trouble.'

'No.'

'Oh, yes. When she was fifteen years old.'

'Oh, dear.'

'Yes, indeed,' Tilly said. 'The mother took her to Sydney before she started showing. Had it up there and adopted it out, presumably. And then she just traipsed back home and carried on like nothing happened.'

'I'm sure it wasn't like that,' said Joyce. 'She must have been devastated. Having to give up a child. It would tear you apart, surely.'

Tilly nodded, her eyes wide and her cheeks sucked in. 'That's how it was. That's what I've heard. Went around like she didn't have a care in the world, showing off all the new clothes the mother had bought her in Sydney.' Her lips tightened. 'Got up to all her old tricks again.'

She craned her neck to look out the side window, frowning in the direction of the whining dogs and the coughing and spluttering coming from next door.

'Oh well,' she said, as she sipped her tea. 'I suppose it's none of our business, is it? All in the past, of course.'

The conversation turned to other things. Bill Worthy, who owned Worthy's Supermarket down at the Glenella shops, had just bought a new car, Tilly informed Joyce. 'Very flash,' said Tilly. 'Showing off his money.' She kept Joyce up-to-date with the continuing saga of Trevor Conner, a neighbour who had been thrown out of the house by his wife after she discovered he was having an affair with Val Kelly, a single mother living down the road with a rabble of boys. Val's husband, a plumber, had left her for a younger woman.

'And she got her claws right into Trevor Conner,' said Tilly. 'The man didn't stand a chance. She's a tough one. A real gutter-fighter. Not a thing he could do about it.'

'You don't think maybe it was some sort of romance?'

'Oh, no,' said Tilly. 'She needed someone to look after her and her boys. Someone with money. I'd say she had a good look around and took her pick. You're lucky your husband's only a schoolteacher, otherwise I'm sure she would have made a play for him as well.'

In his room, a mathematics textbook open in front of him on the desk, Roland listened to the women talk. Trevor Conner was the stout, hearty man who owned the local shoe shop. Every year just before the start of school, he measured Roland's feet with a Brannock Device, before going into the storeroom and producing a pair of black Clarks shoes, one or two sizes too big. 'There's no point getting him a perfect fit now,' he would say to Joyce as he checked for Roland's toe, 'because he'll have grown out of them by tomorrow.' When he was younger, Roland would spend the first months of school slipping around the schoolyard in the big shoes, falling and grazing his knees so often that they were stained red from all the iodine.

He tried to imagine Trevor Conner having an affair with Val Kelly, but couldn't. How had it happened? he wondered. Whose idea had it been? It had never occurred to him that a man like Trevor Conner was capable of love or sex or any sort of life really, apart from being pleasant to customers and greeting his neighbours as he mowed his front lawn on the weekends. He thought about Trevor Conner's daughters, two girls he used to see playing in their front yard, dark hair plaited and tied with ribbons. What did they think about this? What had their father told them?

He had been reading through the introduction of the textbook, but couldn't concentrate, turning pages before realising he hadn't absorbed a word of it. On the first day of the long summer holidays, he had promised himself that he would start his reading for the upcoming school year, but somehow it had never happened. The holidays were almost over and he had barely begun.

He had been putting it off, enjoying the hot weather, reading fat novels he borrowed from the library, or sometimes taking the train into the city, where he wandered around, daydreaming and going into shops that took his interest, trying to decide how to spend the money his grandparents had given him for Christmas. He loved the city, the faded grandeur of it, those parts of it that still seemed to be turned—a grubby, graven face—towards its more glorious past. He loved the networks of small lanes, passages flecked with guano, derelict arcades with cracked marble floors. Shops that seemed to hold little more than dust and shadows. And the grimy subways with their barber's shops and shattered newsstands, the realm of old men in suits and hats, the wayward, rough-tongued drunks who seemed native to the city during the empty sunny daytime—shouting, drinking from bottles wrapped in brown-paper bags, spitting on the footpath, sprawled under architraves—before the disgorgement of the afternoon. All there to be explored, all the treasures it seemed to promise.

He visited coin shops and stamp shops and military antique shops, huddled along the cramped, narrow lanes. Antiquarian bookshops in glass-walled alcoves, or along the defunct passageways of jaded office buildings, up a flight of worn stairs. Examining, under the glib fluorescent lights, ancient Roman denarii, colonial stamps, bayonets that he imagined once beaded in blood, a leather-bound book with gilt lettering and marbled end papers. Newspapers from the days of the French Revolution. In the windows of the pawn shops were trumpets and electric guitars, paperweights with scorpions frozen within the resin, a hookah made from silvered bronze and delicately etched glass that was as green as the green of boiled lollies.

In the end, the money was spent on an executive organiser that he found at the Glenella newsagent's in one of the sale carts they put outside the shop on Saturday mornings. The organiser was marked for the ending year and reduced to five dollars. It was a deluxe model, faux leather, hefty, the pages bound by two metal rings, like a folder. There were several sections: a daily planner, personal financial records, contacts, to-do lists, a business-card holder and blank pages for notes. He loved the feel and weightiness of it, the idea of planning every-thing in his life, of making lists and ticking things off as done. In the notes section, he began to gather certain thoughts that had meandered in his head for some time now, and in writing them down, he felt, he was committing himself, in some way ensuring that these things would one day happen.

'Self-Improvement,' he titled one section.

Listen more when people talk to you.
Do at least twenty push-ups every night before bed.
Try not to think or say bad things about people.
Be more confident.
Try to talk more to girls.
Learn how to fight.
Eat healthy food.
Study for at least four hours every night and sixteen hours over the weekend.
Read the biographies of great men and try to be like them.

The other sections were titled: 'Ideas', 'Things to Learn About', 'Goals', 'Books to Read' and 'Miscellaneous'. He spent hours poring over the organiser in the evening, pen in hand, thinking up possibilities: imagining a future as bright and glorious as the passing summer days. He dreamed and dreamed, his window open to the fragrant night and its songs, the insects flittering and buzzing and crawling across the flyscreen, attracted, as they were, to the light.

Now, images from the previous day at the pool arose involuntarily, slithering into Roland's consciousness as he tried to concentrate: the dazzling sunshine, the chlorine reek, the tanned bodies of the sunbathers. Cassie. The faint scent of her sun-kissed skin, the gentle rise and fall of her breath as she lay so close to him. He imagined what it might be like to touch her—the smoothness and the softness of her, everything familiar, a comfort—to kiss her, and for her to smile at him, speaking his name softly. Ideas about love. A suffused yearning, a slow-burning longing flared and swept through him, and he was at once weakened and spurred, so exhilarated that he felt a ringing blissfulness. And at the same time, he felt so desperately unhappy that he thought he could die.

He was always this way after seeing Cassie; this was the form her absence took in the stultifying aftermath, in the wake of the thrill of her company, and it worried at him in the manner of a deep-rooted illness. Long periods of melancholy were riven with expectation, a wild excitement, a need for action, although he did not know what form that action should take. He felt it in the pit of his stomach, like a terrible, gaping emptiness.

Just after midday, Joyce sent Roland to the Nobles' house to tell Lily to come home for lunch. He walked down Carlington Street, past the neat cream-brick veneers, their perfect gardens sweltering in the full sunlight, the crescendos of the cicadas so loud they drowned out thought. The birds were silent apart from the occasional bell note, a moment of clarity bursting through the drowsy, shimmering streets. The breeze was hot. He passed the Kyriakides house, a slumping weatherboard in the shade of a towering white gum tree, its foliage swarming against the unerring blue of the sky. The motorcycle was sitting on the overgrown front lawn, radiant as a vision in the sunlight.

THE FOLLOWING WEEKEND, the Nobles threw their annual Australia Day barbeque. Carrying Tupperware containers full of meat and salad, a wine cooler swinging from Graham's arm, the Arthursons walked through the midday holocaust to the big two-storey house at the top of the hill, the glazed windows of its triple frontage gawping onto the street. The guests were still arriving, family groups walking from their cars. Children skirmished as they skittered and hopped, barefoot, along the lacework of sun and shade on the hot footpath. Their mothers hissed, tearing them apart. The fathers called 'G'day' to the other men as they saw them, their bleak domestic visages washing off them in a moment as they saw their line of escape to the group massed around the smoking barbeque in the backyard. Their legs were bare, tending to fatness, their shorts short and their shirts already beginning to stick with sweat. They carried six-packs, wine casks, polystyrene containers piled with sausages and mince patties, chops and steaks oozing blood beneath the cling wrap.

Inside, Reg tended the bar, which stood in the corner of the living room. Hanging on the wall behind him were his medals and ribbon bar, mounted in a frame, next to a knife in a leather sheath: a thin, deadly dagger with a nickel-plated handle and a skull crusher at the pommel. He poured beer on tap for the men and made cocktails for the women.

'How about Sex on the Beach, Carol?' he asked a woman with short, streaked hair and large plastic earrings. 'Or would you prefer a Slow Comfortable Screw?' The woman laughed, sitting on one of the barstools, her elbows on the counter.

The younger children tore about the house in a pack, directed by Lily, whose small voice chirped above the others. They alighted upon a bowl of Twisties, taking handfuls and chewing industriously, their fingers and lips stained orange. Seizing bottles of Fanta and Coke and Marchants Lemonade from among the beer and wine in the ice-filled bathtub, they competed in skolling drinks until they felt sick. The sugar turned them into shrill lunatics, chattering and scampering around at double speed. Roland moped about near his mother, who was talking to a group of women. He glanced at Cassie, who also stood with the adults, politely answering their questions as she pressed a hand against her back to straighten it. She had a tendency to slump and was making an effort to appear poised. Lily ran up to her.

'Can we see when your dad was on television?' she asked.

In one great hurtling rush, the children swarmed the brown velour lounge suite and the thick cream carpet, waiting restlessly while Cassie went through the video tapes. The television had been left on, showing the broadcast of the bicentennial celebrations, which consisted of a lot of aerial shots of boats. Cassie put in the tape and a gameshow came on. 'Let's look at our prizes,' said the quizmaster at the start. The announcer ran through them as golden-skinned models waved their hands. There was a lounge suite, a diamond bracelet, a holiday in Fiji, a television in a cabinet. At the end, he announced, *'A new car!'*

A gleaming car turned on a revolving floor, two models in sequinned dresses gesturing at it. 'Valued at thirty-five thousand dollars,' the announcer enthused. 'This car features a turbo-charged, six-cylinder, fuel-injected engine, front and rear disk brakes, active suspension and power steering. Windows open at the press of a button.' One of the models demonstrated with an immaculately manicured finger. 'Pure driving pleasure. Courtesy of Reg Noble Auto, your number one eastern suburbs car dealer. The lowest prices guaranteed. Why not come on down to Reg Noble Auto and test drive a car today?'

'You see?' Lily whispered to the other children. 'I told you it was true.'

They watched to the end of the episode, when the final question was answered correctly by the carry-over champion. Confetti and streamers spilled from the ceiling, trumpets blared and the quizmaster and the winner walked over to the revolving car. Reg Noble stepped proudly out of the wings, shook the winner's hand and presented him with a key. 'Enjoy,' he said. A bevy of long-legged models rushed out to join Reg, the contestants and the quizmaster in front of the car, putting their arms around each other and waving to the camera as the closing theme music played.

A number of adults had also gathered in the living room and were watching the television from behind the couch. A man with a dimpled chin leaned against the bar, joking with Reg.

Colleen whispered to a group of women.

'It cost me a bit,' Reg said when it was over. 'I just hope the publicity was worth it.'

'Of course it was, Reg!' exclaimed Colleen. 'Everyone knows who you are now. The whole world knows!'

Cassie was pouring Cokes for Roland and herself. She took a packet of chips from the pantry and they climbed the carpeted stairs to her room. It was immaculate, still a little girl's room with its frilly pink bedspread, dolls and stuffed animals lined up on the shelves. There was an open jewellery box on the dresser, the pirouetting ballerina surrounded by mirrors. No desk, no books. When he was in primary school, Roland had occasionally been invited to the house of a boy who had older sisters—contemptuous, volatile creatures—and had caught a glimpse of walls papered with posters of bands and movie stars, clothes strewn across the floor, bras hooked over the handles of wardrobes and open drawers overflowing with hair ties and butterfly clips and crimping irons and baubles. Doors were always quickly slammed shut on these intriguing vistas. There was no such chaos in Cassie's room. To Roland it seemed sterile, unlived in, like a picture from a catalogue or the room of a girl in a soap opera. The smell of lemon-scented washing detergent, coming from the bedsheets, was overpowering. Through the window you could see all the way to the city, its distant towers shimmering under the blueness of the sky.

'My friend Sharon pierced her own ears,' Cassie told Roland as they sat down on the floor and opened the chips. 'Her parents wouldn't let her so she did it with a compass.'

Colleen, Roland remembered, had Cassie's ears pierced when she was eight. His mother had been horrified. 'She dresses her up like a doll,' she had told his father.

'Sharon is meant to be my best friend, but sometimes she's so mean to me,' said Cassie. 'Some days she just won't talk to me, for no reason at all. And she goes and hangs around with this girl Elise, who thinks she's so ace. And when I go over to talk to them, they're really rude, like they don't want me there at all, and Elise says all these horrible things to me. It's so childish. I just say, "Whatever." I don't care.'

'I thought Tiffany Pellegrini was your best friend,' said Roland.

'Why do you think that?'

'Your mum said. The other day.'

'My mum just wishes I was best friends with Tiffany because she's in love with Tiffany's parents. She thinks they're so good just because they're rich. She's such a snob. All she cares about is how much money people make. I'm friends with Tiffany, but not best friends or anything like that. I don't think I have a best friend anymore.'

'I don't really have any friends,' said Roland.

Cassie dabbed at the corners of her mouth. Her lips were pale, rough with flaking skin she had gnawed on until they bled.

'Why not?'

'They're all idiots at my school.'

She screwed up her nose, looking sceptically at him.

'They can't all be idiots.'

'I suppose I just don't fit in there.'

'Yeah,' said Cassie thoughtfully. 'I know what you mean. School sucks.'

'Yeah,' said Roland.

They ate the rest of the chips, licking the salt from their fingers. Cassie opened one of the dresser drawers and took out a pile of magazines.

'Hey, have you ever read Dolly Doctor?' she asked Roland.

'No.'

'It's so funny sometimes. Some of the letters are so gross and embarrassing. Listen to this.'

She flicked through one of the magazines and began to read.

'Dear Dolly Doctor. I have been going out with my boyfriend for nearly six months now. The other day I was getting with him on the couch and he told me that it hurts him, because I make him get "blue balls". I am not ready to have sex with him yet, but I cannot stand to think that I am causing him pain. I really love him. What should I do?'

Cassie laughed, flipping through the pages. She pushed one of the other magazines over to Roland.

'Here,' she said. 'You find one.'

They took it in turns reading. Roland was fascinated and horrified at the same time.

'Dear Dolly Doctor, am I still a virgin if I use a tampon?'

'Am I still a virgin if I let my boyfriend finger me?'

'Is it wrong to let my boyfriend finger me?'

'Can I get pregnant if my boyfriend fingers me?'

'Can I get pregnant if my boyfriend ejaculated while we were pashing?'

'My boyfriend wants to have sex with me, but I am worried it will hurt.'

'Will I get pregnant even if he pulls out?'

'Should I tell my mother that her boyfriend touches my breasts?'

'Should I let my boyfriend touch my breasts?'

'I want my boyfriend to touch my breasts, but he doesn't. How do I let him know?'

'How do I let my boyfriend know that I want to have sex with him without seeming like I am a slut?'

'Is it wrong that I have already had sex with four different boys and I am only fifteen?'

'Is it wrong that I have used a cucumber for sex?'

'One night on a sleepover, I practised kissing with my best friend. It was meant to be a practice kiss for a guy she has a crush on at school, but I really liked it. What do I do? Is there something wrong with me?'

'Dear Dolly Doctor, sometimes I think I am not normal. I feel like everything is wrong with me.'

There was a knock on the door, Lily's voice calling from behind it. Cassie and Roland collected the scattered magazines and put them back in the drawer, looking at each other breathlessly. Cassie's face was flushed. The door opened, Lily draping herself from the handle.

'Cassie,' she whined. 'I'm bored.'

'What about all the new friends you've made?' Cassie asked her.

'I'm bored of them. I want to do something with you.'

They went back down to the living room. The air was grey and acrid with cigarette smoke, and the eyes of the adults were beginning to glaze over. On the television, the sound turned off again, Prince Charles was making a speech. The sliding door opened and closed as women came back and forth with dirty plates and cutlery. They clattered them into the sink. Graham was sitting at the dining-room table talking politics with another man.

'All this government's doing is giving our taxes to the Aborigines,' the man said to Graham. 'And the dole bludgers.'

'Well, I don't know that I agree with that,' said Graham.

'I think they've done a number of good things.'

'And what would you know, Graham?' said Reg, sitting at the end of the table.

'I read the papers,' Graham said. 'I follow the issues.'

'Yeah, but what do schoolteachers know about the real world?' Reg said. 'You go to school, you go to teachers' college, and then you're back at school again. You've got no life experience. You don't know anything about the real world.'

Graham began to protest.

'No,' said Reg, waving his hand, a cigarette between his fingers. 'You don't know.'

Cassie went to Reg and whispered into his ear, hanging off his arm poutily. Reg took his wallet out of his shorts pocket and gave her a twenty-dollar note. He pointed to his cheek and Cassie leaned over and kissed it.

'Thank you, Dad,' she said.

The three children left the house and strode wearily along the footpath in the pounding heat of the sun, little respite offered by the wisps of shade thrown by the paperbark trees along the nature strip. As they passed one house they heard splashes and cries and the thump of water against the walls of an above-ground pool, but otherwise everything was empty and mute but for the birds twittering on the telephone lines and the relentless choral scream of the cicadas. Reg Noble's cheery face grinned and winked from the back windows of the cars parked in the driveways, looking onto gardens of ferns and succulents and juniper bushes among beds of quartz stones that were as white and smooth as eggs. A glass beer bottle lay smashed across the footpath, the fine shards glittering like an apparition.

'How come your dad gave you twenty whole dollars?' Lily asked Cassie.

'I asked him for it,' said Cassie, shrugging.

'Is that your pocket money?' Lily asked her.

'I suppose.'

'I think maybe you're rich,' said Lily.

'Why?'

'Well,' said Lily. 'Roland doesn't get that much pocket money.'

'How much pocket money do you get?'

'I get six cents because I'm six,' said Lily. 'And Roland gets fifty cents because he's much older. But you get twenty dollars, so I think you must be the richest person in the whole world!'

Lily shouted the final words, throwing up her hands. She was skipping as she talked, trying to avoid the cracks in the footpath.

'Also,' she said. 'You have a video.'

A bell tinkled as they opened the door to the milk bar. Inside it was cool, the air conditioner growling, the confectionary sweetening the air. Music poured out of the tape player on the shelf behind the counter: a wild tangle of accordions, saxophones, drums and wailing voices. Advertisements plastered the walls. The owner, sitting behind the counter, looked up from his newspaper.

'Hello, my young friends,' he said absently.

Lily ran up to the counter, nearly tripping on her sandals. She surveyed the boxes behind the glass, each one brimming with a different type of lolly, everything from acid drops, spearmint leaves, musk sticks, milk bottles and Marella jubes to wrapped Redskins, Choo Choo bars, boxes of Fags and bags of Wizz Fizz. In the corners were liquorice straps, folded over themselves.

'How is your day today?' the milk bar owner asked Cassie as she approached.

'All right,' said Cassie with a grimace. 'We're having an Australia Day party.'

He nodded gravely.

'You like this day? Australia Day?'

'It's all right,' said Cassie.

'Good to have some holidays,' he said. 'But not for me. I have no holidays here. Every day I work.'

'Really?' asked Cassie.

'It's true,' he said with a gracious nod, tilting his head. 'Six o'clock in the morning to ten o'clock at night. Every day.' He was wearing a crisp white shirt, the cuffs fastened with onyx cufflinks, a slim gold watch showing underneath the stiff lines of cotton. His dark hair and neatly trimmed beard were speckled with white. Through the open doorway behind him, his teenage son kicked and boxed at a punching bag that was hanging in the small backyard of cracked concrete slabs and yellowed grass. He was wearing a pair of black and gold shorts with a roaring tiger on them.

'I love this country,' the milk bar owner said to Cassie, the music rising exuberant behind him. 'But it is not a good place to live. A good place to work, certainly. But for living, I would go back to Cairo. If I could. Here, they do not know how to live. It's true,' he said.

'Umm,' said Lily, pointing to the lollies. The man produced a pair of tongs and waited patiently as she made her choices. In between the volleys of kicks and punches and grunts, the son turned to glower at them through the shock of hair that had fallen over his face. Roland looked away, bowing his head.

'And could I also have a pack of Alpine Lights?' asked Cassie. 'They're for my father,' she added.

The man picked out the cigarettes from the rack on the wall.

'Your father smokes these menthols?' he asked, amused.

'Yeah. And a lighter.'

He looked through the tray of Bics and carefully chose a pink one: bright, hot pink.

'You think this lighter?' he asked. 'You think your father will like this colour?'

'Yeah.'

'He likes pink? This is his colour?'

'Yeah, he'll like it.'

'Okay then,' said the man, smiling to himself as he went to the cash register.

They spilled out into the sunshine again. A group of sparrows scattered into the air like a handful of tossed rice and then came down again, hopping. Lily and Roland followed Cassie past the video shop. BMX bikes leaned against the window and boys in Metallica T-shirts played the arcade games inside. One of them stuck his head out the door. He had long messy hair, the ends licking at his shoulders. He leered at Cassie. 'Hey, blondie!' he shouted after her. Cassie turned and looked at him, but kept on walking. 'Those guys are morons,' she told Roland. They continued past the RSL club, where Cassie turned into the laneway.

'Why are we going up the lane?' Lily asked her, passing the bag of lollies from one sweaty hand to the other. Dogs barked as the children walked past the back fences and snuffled at their feet under the gates.

'Just a different way to go, that's all,' said Cassie. 'Don't you think it's fun to go a new way?'

'Yeah,' said Lily, walking wearily, her head and shoulders slumped. 'I suppose.'

'Aren't you going to share your lollies?' asked Cassie.

'I don't want to eat them now,' said Lily. 'I want to save them.'

'All right,' said Cassie. 'If that's what you want to do.'

'I want to count them first, before I eat them,' said Lily, growing enthusiastic again. 'This is the most lollies I've ever had.'

As they came to the old people's home, a long whitewashed Besser-block building with step-like cracks in the masonry, Cassie stopped and put on her sunglasses. She examined her reflection in the glass door of the back entrance, then lit a cigarette and posed with it, jutting out her hip and taking on a cool, uninterested expression, her lips pouted. They continued on to Carlington Street. Cassie stopped again as she came to the slumping fence of the last house, which was the Kyriakides house.

The boy was in the backyard with his motorcycle, a canvas tool roll spread out on the grass next to him. He was polishing the bike with a chamois, carefully buffing the chrome handle-bars and the headlight. Cassie took in a deep breath of smoke, blew it upwards in a plume, and leaned against the fence.

'Is it broken?' she asked the boy.

He turned around, still crouched by the headlight, and squinted up at her. He was wearing a grubby blue singlet, tight, faded Lee jeans and a pair of scuffed desert boots with an oily patina that sheened like the coat of a horse. His sandy hair splayed out wildly at the crown and fell down his neck in a tangle of long locks that turned upwards at the ends. He had delicate features and would have been almost pretty were it not for the acne scars that made his jaw look worm-eaten and thick, as rugged as a man's. One of his incisors was chipped. His eyes were so pale they seemed almost transparent in the sun.

'What's that?' he asked her.

'The motorbike,' said Cassie, beginning to blush. 'I thought maybe there was something wrong with it. I thought you were fixing it or something.'

The boy straightened up, grinning.

'Nah,' he said. 'Just fine-tuning it. Making it go faster.'

Cassie ran a hand through her hair.

'Do you want a smoke?' she asked the boy, gesturing with the lit cigarette in her fingers.

'Yeah, all right,' said the boy. He came over to the fence, nodding at Roland. 'How are you, mate?' he asked.

'All right,' said Roland.

The boy looked at the packet of cigarettes Cassie was proffering to him.

'Are those menthols?' he asked her.

'Yeah,' she said. 'I only smoke them so my parents don't find out. Otherwise they'll smell it on my breath and that.'

'That's all right,' he said. He went over to the motorcyle and took a soft pack of Peter Stuyvesant from the pocket of a flannel shirt lying across the seat. He tapped a cigarette out and lit it, then walked back over to the fence.

'Hey,' he said. 'Do you want to come around and sit down? I feel like a bit of a dickhead leaving you out there. Not very sociable, is it?'

'Yeah, all right,' said Cassie, throwing her cigarette butt onto the ground and grinding it out with her thong. She sauntered around the fence and went into the backyard through the tumbling carport. Roland and Lily followed. They sat down on some old kitchen chairs arranged around the motorcycle, the ring pattern faded on the weathered linoleum.

'You want a beer?' the boy asked Roland, heading towards the house.

'Okay,' said Roland.

'I'll have one,' said Cassie.

'All right,' said the boy. He glanced at Lily.

'I'm only six,' said Lily.

'All right then.'

While he was inside, Cassie adjusted her shorts and combed her fingers through her hair again. She tossed it back with a shake of her head and fluffed up her fringe.

'Thanks,' she said as the boy came back with a six-pack of Victoria Bitter. He opened a can and handed it to her, then threw one to Roland.

They sat there in silence. Lily put her nose into the bag of lollies and inhaled noisily, looking around at the others with a satisfied smile. Roland sipped the beer. It was bitter. He struggled to swallow the mouthful, trying not to let the distaste show on his face.

'I like your bike,' Cassie said to the boy.

'Yeah?' said the boy.

'Is it a Harley?'

'Nah. Triumph. I was going to buy a Harley. I was down on Elizabeth Street, all set for it, and then I saw this one. And I said to myself, "I've got to have it."'

He turned and looked proudly at the motorcycle.

'When I went into the shop, the guy there asked me if this was my first bike. I said, "Yeah," and he said, "You don't want this for your first bike, you'll drop it." He said I should buy some Jap crap and thrash it up, then come back and buy this one. I said, "Mate, I'm not going to drop it." And I haven't. I haven't dropped it once.'

'So, are you really into bikes?' asked Cassie. 'Like, is that your thing?'

'Well, I bought one, didn't I?' said the boy.

49

Cassie blushed. She took a swig of beer and choked on it, coughing and wiping her mouth with the back of her hand. She smiled helplessly as she blushed even deeper.

'Nah,' said the boy, grinning at her. 'I'm not really into them like some guys, you know, buying bike magazines and going to all the meet-ups and everything. I know some guys like that, though. Hanging around Elizabeth Street on a Sunday arvo and everything. Doing wheelies down the tram tracks. I'm not into that sort of thing. I just thought I'd like to have one. Just get out there, wind in your hair and everything. Take it out to the country somewhere and go full bore. That sort of thing.'

He looked at the dazzling motorcycle again.

'You know. Just being able to take off any time you want. Having your freedom and everything. All that bullshit,' he said, smiling at the children. His eyes crinkled.

Cassie had regained her poise. She took another sip of beer, careful this time. The boy was sitting with his limbs spread out, one arm over the back of the chair. He held his cigarette loosely between his fingers. His gaze lingered on Cassie's long, tanned legs.

'I'm Darren, by the way,' he said to them.

Many of the guests had left by the time they returned to the party and the adults who remained were well and truly drunk. Cassie, Roland and Lily passed through the living room, where men were sitting bleary-eyed in front of the television, watching a news summary of the bicentennial celebrations. Outside, on the lawn, children were dashing through the sprinkler, shrieking, stripped to their underwear or entirely naked. Lily immediately threw off her dress and rushed to join them.

'I don't think I'd ever go back to teaching,' Joyce was saying to the women sitting with her at the garden table. 'I am planning to go back to work when Lily's finished primary school, but not teaching. I just want to be able to go out there and be myself again, have an actual adult conversation for once. I mean, I love being with the children all day. It's just that sometimes I feel like I'm suffocating, stuck in Glenella all the time. It's still a long way off, of course.'

'What sort of work would you do?' asked one of the women.

'Oh, I don't care. Waitressing or working in a shop or something. Anything.'

'You'll ruin your legs,' Colleen advised from the other end of the table. 'All that standing around. They'll swell up and you'll get varicose veins. I should know. My mother worked in a dress shop all her life. Used to come home and give her feet a mustard bath, every single night. I certainly wouldn't be going out and getting varicose veins for six dollars an hour, or however much it is they pay you. Even if I wanted to go back to work I don't think Reg would let me, anyway.'

Reg, standing with a group of men around the barbeque, overheard her and turned, frowning, as he opened another UDL. Although it was only just approaching evening, the insects had already begun their night-time chorus with the lazy late warbling of the birds. Reg had been drinking steadily all day and his movements had slowed, his face red.

'Bullshit,' he said to Colleen. 'I don't bloody well care what you do. If you want to work, go ahead. You might even lose some weight,' he said, swilling his UDL. 'My wife's getting fat,' he told the group of men, who grinned nervously.

'You say that,' Colleen shouted across the lawn. 'But who's the one who gets grumpy if his dinner's not on the table the minute he gets home? Whinging and moaning if everything's not exactly how you like it.'

'I could always go to the pub and get myself a counter meal,' said Reg. 'Be better than your cooking anyway.' He turned sluggishly back to the men, his eyes unfocused. 'She can heat up a frozen meal,' he said. 'I'll say that much for her. Open a tin.' He barked with laughter that seemed too loud even among all the other loud voices, and guzzled his drink. Some of the men shifted away from him, starting other conversations, muttering into their beer cans.

'You have no idea how much I do around the house every day,' yelled Colleen. 'You have no idea whatsoever. And besides, what about Cassie? She wouldn't survive one minute without me running around after her. A girl needs her mother,' she told the women. 'Children need their mother. I believe that. I never put Cassie in crèche. I never put her in afterschool. The idea of my child being brought up by strangers makes my skin crawl. I would never let it happen. No. Not a chance.' She turned back to Reg, a quaver in her voice. 'You have no idea how much I do for that girl.'

'Well, my kids never went into crèche either,' Joyce said quietly. 'I didn't even think about going back to work until recently. I might not be there in the afternoons when the children get home from school, but otherwise things are going to be exactly the same. I know plenty of women who do it.'

'Don't believe it,' said Colleen, regaining her composure. 'You'll see. Children need their mother.'

At dusk, the mosquitoes came out, attracted to the plump flesh and soft wet skin of the children as they continued to tear through the sprinkler, their voices piping, the spinning head throwing water about like rope. Colleen brought out a can of

Aerogard and the mothers called their kids to the table. They sprayed them and sent them running off again. The little bodies were vellum-pale in the gathering darkness, seeming to glow. Pink streaked the tombola glassiness of the sky, incandescent above the silhouettes of houses and reaching trees. The aroma of spilt beer, the lemon fragrance of the insecticide and the chlorophyll mustiness of the grass were cloying in the still, hot air. Graham and Joyce made their farewells and went to catch Lily, who had eaten the big bag of sweets and subsequently gone haywire, frolicking about the backyard naked and trilling meaninglessly. Joyce searched for her clothes.

'I mean, the nerve of that woman,' she said to Graham as they walked home. 'Trying to put a guilt trip on me. As though I was neglecting my children. For Colleen to say that, of all people.'

THE FOLLOWING SUNDAY was the last day of the holidays, a pall over Roland as he anticipated the grind and loneliness of the coming year, the relentless bullying of the emerald grounds and roaring cloistered halls of his school. Outside, the day slumbered, blanched by the intensity of the sun. From his room, he could hear his parents talking to Reg and Colleen at the garden table. Colleen crowed away, apparently unaware of his mother's curtness: Roland knew she was still angry about what had been said on Australia Day. The girls had been in Lily's room earlier, talking excitedly before they left the house in a flurry of whispers and giggles and flicking thongs. Cassie, he had noticed, was wearing lipstick.

'So, my news,' Colleen was saying, 'is that I've had a falling-out with Evelyn Pellegrini.'

'Well, that's a shame, Colleen,' said Joyce dryly. 'And you were such good friends.'

'I know,' said Colleen. But it just goes to show. You really can't trust anyone. It turned out that she'd been saying some very nasty things about me. Talking behind my back. About my family. And, well, I look after me and my own. You do not want to cross me. And if you do, watch out! I will come down on you like a ton of bricks. My friends are always saying, "But you're such a lady, Colleen. You're so well mannered." And it's true, I am. My mother brought me up very well. But you do not want to get on my bad side.'

'What was she saying?'

'Oh,' said Colleen, with a wave of her cigarette. 'That's not the important thing. It was all lies and there's no point dwelling on it. The main thing is that she said it. And she did admit it when I confronted her. I'll say that much for her. I just wonder whether it was something Cassie might have said to Tiffany. You know, Tiffany repeats it back to her mother, Evelyn gets the wrong idea and here we are. Not even talking to each other anymore.'

'But what would Cassie have said?'

'Well, Cassie lies,' said Colleen. 'When she gets excited or upset, she can tell the most hideous lies about people. And I say to her, "I will not have that from you, missy. If there's one thing I can't stand, it's liars. That is not something I will put up with in my house." But who knows what she says when my back's turned. I have no idea what sorts of things she might be telling the world about me and Reg. I hate to think.'

The girls were gone for hours before Roland heard them come back inside and romp into Lily's room. Their talk was rapid, all at once, rippling with laughter. There were loud thumps as they pulled the bottom drawer out of the dresser to raid the secret cache of chips and chocolate bars hidden in the space beneath. Joyce knocked on the door.

'It's time for Cassie to go home,' she told them.

The light was fading; there were clouds to the south. Next door, Maurice muttered by the fence, his chooks clucking and scraping under the junipers in the gloom. The voices of Joyce and Graham, farewelling the Nobles, seemed distant. A door slid open. Lights were switched on.

'My friend Darren Wilson has a motorbike,' Lily announced at dinner.

'Who's Darren Wilson?' Graham asked.

'He's going to take me for a ride,' Lily said. She was contentedly stirring her Neapolitan ice-cream into mud.

'Only if you wear a helmet,' said Joyce. 'And tell him he has to come and talk to me first. I'm not letting you on a motorcycle with someone I've never met.'

Lily continued stirring the runny ice-cream. She watched as it poured off her spoon.

'Darren Wilson doesn't wear a helmet,' she said.

'I don't care what this Darren Wilson does,' Joyce said. 'You're not getting on anyone's motorcycle without a helmet. You tell him your mother said that.'

'But that's not fair,' Lily protested.

'It's not about whether it's fair.'

'Is anyone going to tell me who Darren Wilson is?' Graham asked again, yawning.

ROLAND SAW CASSIE again the following afternoon on the train home. Students from the private schools packed the carriage, gathered about the doors and sitting on the carpet, their backs against the metal and the wood-grain laminate. They were hot and bored and restless. A group of girls took turns to draw on their legs with a biro: flowers and peace symbols and looping signatures, games of tick-tack-toe. Boys watched, nudging one another. One of them had wedged himself between the automatic doors so that they could not close and the wind ruffled his hair and churned the fabric of his shirt, sweeping hot and dry down the aisles. The train clattered loudly; its wheels squeaked on the rails. They passed rapid successions of pylons and bitumen-floored stations, graffitied walls, ditches overgrown with brambles, the baked rise of scrubby embankments, drenched in sun. Everything seemed close and sudden through the open doors.

Cassie was standing against a handrail in her gingham school dress, the hem taken up so that it sat high above her knees and showed off her tanned thighs. Roland had overheard Colleen telling his mother that she had it done at the tailor's, even though it was against the school rules. 'It's the fashion,' she had said. 'It's what all the trendy girls do.' Cassie was talking to some boys from Roland's school.

'How was your weekend?' one of the boys asked her.

'Shithouse,' Cassie said with a giggle, her voice rising.

'Why? What did you do?'

'Nothing. There's nothing to do where I am. It's so dead.'

'Yeah? Where are you again?'

'Glenella,' Cassie said, making a face.

'Out in the sticks.'

'Yeah.'

Cassie ran her hand through her hair as she talked, sweeping it back and playing with it, gathering it up into a ponytail and letting it fall. She smoothed down her skirt, leaning her hip against the handrail, and laughed when the movement of the train made her unsteady. One of the boys spotted Roland.

'Hey, Arthurson,' he yelled. Roland stared out the window, feeling the heat rise up his face.

'Hey, Arthurson,' the boy shouted again. 'You're a loser, Arthurson. You're a faggot.'

The other boys chortled. 'Loser,' they jeered. 'Dickhead. Faggot.'

Cassie turned to look at Roland and quickly looked away again. Colour spread across her neck and cheeks. She's ashamed of me, Roland thought to himself. She's ashamed that she knows me.

Coming up from the station, he saw Todd McKeon crouched over the footpath outside his house, scraping a big survival knife across the concrete while his four dark-eyed sisters stood watching from behind the fence. They were odd, silent girls who were rarely seen apart: Roland sometimes caught sight of them walking down Creek Road to the tennis club in a dour gaggle, carrying small-headed wooden rackets over their shoulders like soldiers performing close-order drill. Their clothes were always threadbare: the younger three wore sun dresses and knickerbockers and pleated shorts handed down from the eldest girl, which, by the time they reached the youngest, were thin and grubby and years out of fashion.

Todd showed Roland the black knife with its saw along the spine. He unscrewed the bobbing compass at the pommel and took out a bundle of matches wrapped in crinkled wax paper. They were waterproof, he told Roland, displaying the fat green tips before stuffing them back into the hollow handle.

'It's a good knife,' he said, running his finger along its edge. 'I took it on holiday with me. Got some use out of it.'

'Where did you go?' Roland asked.

'Up to Echuca,' said Todd. 'We go and stay in the caravan park there every summer. My dad goes fishing on the river. Whenever he caught a carp, I cut its head off with this,' he said, chopping the knife in the air. 'You can't eat them and you can't throw them back 'cause they're a pest. So he let me cut them up.'

He swung the knife in the air again, and made stabbing motions.

'No one's going to mess with you if you've got a knife like this.'

He was a small, chubby, freckled boy with a mop of brown hair. The tie of the local Catholic school was loose around his collar, the top button of his shirt undone. Nearby, the Hayes brothers were taking it in turns to skateboard down the hill. They went at thrilling speeds, sweeping from one side of the road to the other, passing fearlessly through the two intersections before they reached the dip at the bottom. As the skateboard slowed, they jumped off, stamped on the tail and flipped the board, catching it as they ran. The others sat waiting on the nature strip, their feet in the gutter.

'Hey,' Todd said to Roland. 'You want to go down the shops?'

'All right.'

'Have you got any money?'

'No,' said Roland.

Todd scraped the knife against his cheek. He inspected the blade.

'I know where we can get some,' he said.

Roland hefted up his heavy bag and the two boys walked through the dappled shade of Plunkett mallees and yellow gums and the sparse angry bristles of the paperbarks, Todd slashing at the roses and ferns that jutted from behind the castellated fences, their flowerbeds reeking of blood-and-bone in the baking sun. They went through the lane beside the milk bar and crossed the road to the long lawn outside the station, where schoolkids sat in groups ringed by schoolbags, cigarette smoke draping the hot air above them as they nibbled at potato cakes in brown paper bags, translucent with grease, or scooped up handfuls of hot chips from slim cardboard boxes. Coke cans sat on the grass, girls bending down to suck on the straws as though too lazy to lift them. Couples were shamelessly entwined, kissing, their faces flushed, hands exploring bodies over the thin cotton of uniforms dampened with sweat, a girl occasionally slapping her boyfriend's hand away as it crept under her skirt or grasped at her breasts. The boy would groan and kiss the nape of the girl's neck and she would squeal while her friends rolled their eyes and flicked their fringes and gave each other glances. Other boys unbuttoned their shirts and put their heads under the tap by the shrubs. They shook their wet hair like dogs as they ranged about, glaring at the languorous figures on the lawn. Roland looked around for Cassie, but she was not there.

Todd went over to a gangly, older boy in the lollipop blazer of the special school, who stood in the shade of the wattles and she-oaks beside the railway. He was watching the couples with his arms folded, his shoulders hunched.

'This is Pete,' Todd said to Roland.

The wolf-faced boy nodded at Roland, stroking the downy hair on his cheek.

'Gudday,' he said thickly.

'Hey, Pete,' Todd said. 'Don't you feel like some chips? Couple of dollars' worth of chips? Chips and a Coke? What do you reckon about that, Pete? You feel like some chips and a Coke?'

'Yeah,' said Pete, his eyes flitting, still distracted by the frolicking and caresses on the lawn.

They went back across the road to the fish-and-chip shop. Pete waited at the counter, rapping his knuckles against the jar of pickled onions as the owner flattened hamburgers on the hotplate, his teenage daughter standing sulkily over the deep fryer with her back to the customers. Todd took his knife from under his shirt and gouged at one of the Big M posters on the wall, twisting the tip of the knife into the crotch of a woman running along a beach in a white bikini.

'Hey, Pete,' he said, over his shoulder. 'How about some

dim sims? You feel like a dim sim? Nice fried dim sim?'

'Yeah,' said Pete, stroking his cheek.

They ate the chips and dim sims on the lawn between the library and the tennis club. Pete skolled his Coke in one go and held the empty can up in triumph, panting with the effort of his feat. He dropped the can onto the grass and stamped on it repeatedly before loping over to the en-tout-cas court and pressing his face against the fence as he watched two girls playing tennis. One of them hit a ball at him.

'Piss off, spastic,' she yelled.

Pete howled in anger, shaking the wire, and stuttered abuse at the girl, who coolly picked up another ball and resumed playing. He ran across the lawn to the line of pines by the railway tracks and furiously wrenched off a low branch, then galloped back and hurled it at the court. It bounced off the fence and fell onto the lawn. A silver-haired man came out of the club house.

'Oi!' he yelled, striding towards Pete and pointing at him. 'You!'

The boys ran through the pines and onto the tracks, Todd holding up his middle finger at the man as he scowled at them through the dark row of trees, his hands on his hips. They began walking down the line, Roland and Todd stepping from sleeper to sleeper while Pete stumbled through the stones.

'Give us a ten-cent coin, Pete,' Todd said, stopping to inspect a thin, precise split in one of the rails. He placed the coin over it.

'Watch this,' he said to Roland.

'What?'

'You'll see. We have to wait for a train first.'

They cut back through the pines and sat on the steps of

the library, Pete tittering with excitement. The boom gates went down and a train rattled past, slowing as it approached the station. After it left, the gates stayed down, continuing to flash and clang. Lines of cars built up on both sides of the crossing, their exhausts pumping fumes that shimmered in the hot air. A man got out of a panel van and slammed the door. He shielded his eyes from the sun as he walked up to the gates and stood there with his arms folded, peering up and down the tracks. Another man got out of his car and the two of them talked briefly, shrugging their shoulders before they returned to their vehicles. The panel van turned out onto the other side of the road and drove up the queue of cars, pausing at the gates before weaving through them. Others followed hesitantly from both sides, the lights still pulsing, the bell continuing to clang stridently. Pete was convulsed with laughter, slapping his legs as he looked from the crossing to the faces of his companions.

'How often do you do that?' Roland asked Todd.

Todd shrugged.

'All the time,' he said.

STEAM WAFTED DOWN the hall from the bathroom and brought a cosiness to the house, warm as it was and mingled as it was with the familiar fragrances of English Leather and Chanel No. 5 and the earthy sweetness of Joyce's make-up as she put it on. These were scents that lingered deep in the children's consciousnesses, existing in the darkness of their formation, a reminder of that paradise before thoughts and words. Lily stood beside her mother, watching, fascinated, reaching up to touch the black sequinned jacket Joyce wore over her dress. She was telling a story about an incident at school that had begun faithfully, but, as she had gone on, her mother listening, she had felt a duty to continue when there was no more story to tell, and had wandered off into the realms of fiction.

'And then, Miss Carlyle said, "You're all going to get punished for this," and she grabbed Gemma by her pigtail and pulled it so hard I thought she was going to pull it right off!'

'Did she?' asked Joyce absently. She leaned over the sink and looked at herself in the mirror, tugging on her eyelid as she blackened the rim with a pencil.

'Yes,' said Lily. 'And we were all saying, "Don't! Don't hurt her," because Gemma was crying. But she didn't care at all!'

'Did that really happen?'

'Yes! Well, it nearly happened. She was pretty angry anyway. And also—'

'Have you told Roland about Cassie?' Joyce asked Graham as he came down the hall, wearing slacks and a checked cotton shirt, the material still redolent with the singed smell of the hot iron. His hair was brushed, his beard newly trimmed.

'No, I'll tell him now,' said Graham.

'What's Dad going to tell Roland about Cassie?' asked Lily, reaching up to stroke the sequins again. She pinched one between her fingers and tried to turn it.

'Cassie's going to babysit you tonight,' said Joyce. 'But you have to be very good and do everything she says, otherwise we won't ask her again.'

'So is Cassie coming around here?' Lily asked, her eyes wide.

'Yes, but she's not here to play.'

'I don't care!' said Lily, throwing her hands up in the air. She scampered out of the bathroom and ran down the hall, whooping.

Roland was outraged.

'Why can't I do it?' he asked his father. 'Why do you have to get a babysitter at all?'

'Well, you have to prove that you're responsible enough to be left on your own,' said Graham. He was taking the ice packs for the wine cooler out of the freezer, banging them against the sink to knock off the scales of frost.

'But I am responsible,' Roland protested. 'I'm far more responsible than Cassie.'

'That's not true. Every night when I come home there's some sort of drama going on. Until you and your sister can learn to get along without fighting, I'm not confident that I can trust you.'

'She's not here to babysit you,' Joyce said as she came in. 'She knows that. Besides, do you really want to have to put Lily to bed?'

'But it's not fair. She's the same age as me.'

'Girls are more mature than boys at your age,' said Joyce.

Cassie arrived and Joyce gave her the emergency phone numbers and showed her where the tea and Milo and biscuits were.

'Lily needs to be in bed by eight,' she told her. 'Eight-thirty at the latest. You can read her a story, but not for too long.'

Lily danced around ecstatically, ululating. Joyce grabbed her by the arm and she went limp, putting her head against her mother's belly and singing nonsense.

'Now you have to do what Cassie says,' Joyce told her. 'You go to bed when she tells you. Is that understood?'

Lily looked up at her, *tra-la-la*ing even louder. Joyce shook her arm.

'Do you understand?'

Lily went cross-eyed. 'Yes!' she shouted.

Graham was standing in the doorway with the wine cooler, looking at his watch.

'We're going to be late,' he said.

Graham and Joyce left, the girls farewelling them from the patio. Roland went into the lounge room and turned on *Golden Years of Hollywood*. The film was *Calamity Jane*. Doris

66

Day strutted about with violent, jerky movements, belting out songs. The girls came in and lay on the carpet in front of the television. Lily was bored, fidgeting and glancing at Cassie, who seemed to be no less restless as she shifted her position on the floor. She sat up and untied and retied her ponytail.

'Hey,' she said to Roland. 'Have you ever tried rocket fuel?'

'No,' he said.

'Really?' she asked in exaggerated surprise. 'You should try it. I'll make us some.' She got up. 'Where do your parents keep their alcohol?'

Roland took her to the good room, which was sparse and immaculate, something chalky about the air inside. It had a sunken floor, white carpets, white velour furniture and a framed print on the wall of wild horses running in the moonlight. The windows, behind scrim, faced the road. It was never used by the family, except when Graham and Joyce held their occasional dinner parties, and the children had been forbidden from entering it such a long time ago that most of the time they forgot it was even there, although it appeared sometimes in their dreams in weirdly magnified forms. Roland felt the thrill of transgression as he and Lily followed Cassie tentatively across the threshold. The tall girl went confidently to the bottle-lined shelf, took down three tumblers and began pouring small amounts of the various spirits and liqueurs into each of them.

'What you do is you just mix everything together,' she told Roland. 'It gets you *really* drunk.'

She handed one of the glasses of dark liquid to him and another to Lily, then picked up the third.

'Cheers,' she said, clinking glasses with them. She watched Roland over the rim of hers as she drank. Acting as though she was already intoxicated, she staggered to the stereo and turned it on, moving through the stations on the tuner. When she found a song she liked—'No Say in It'—she began to dance, swinging her hips as she drained her glass and put it down on the coffee table.

'Come and dance,' she said to Roland, taking his hand.

'I don't know how to,' he said.

'I'll teach you,' said Cassie, pulling him towards her. She put his hands on her waist and grasped his shoulders, tossing back her hair. She swayed. Roland shuffled clumsily against her, the material of their tracksuit pants swishing. He could feel her leg against his, the firmness of her hip, and immediately there came the leadenness of an erection. He tried to twist away, but it seemed that Cassie either didn't feel it or, he supposed, didn't know what it was, as she did not pull away in horror and disgust as he imagined she would. They continued to dance across the carpet in this awkward way, Roland's hard penis heavy against Cassie's belly. His hands slid down her hips as he pressed himself against her. Cassie laughed, a high, melodious arpeggio, her arms tight around his neck.

Roland looked up and saw Lily, perched on the edge of the couch watching them, open-mouthed. It seemed to Roland that she knew exactly what was going on, that everything was in plain sight. He pulled away from Cassie and ran out of the room, his hands over his groin.

'Where are you going?' Cassie's voice followed him. 'Oh, come on, Roland!'

In his room, he sat down at his desk and opened his books, trying to concentrate on the weekend's homework as the stereo continued to blast from the good room. He was dizzy from the rocket fuel and the page in front of him was blurry. Odd, feverish thoughts came into his head and he tried to push them away. The bewildered expression on his sister's face kept returning. He was still awed, left dumbfounded by the feeling of Cassie's body against him, and there was something like an unquenchable thirst, that familiar hollow ache in his gut. The house reverberated with the thump of feet as Lily and Cassie danced. Then, after a time, the joyful voices become suddenly hysterical. There was running in the direction of the bathroom, the sounds of Lily throwing up into the toilet.

'You have to promise you won't tell!' Cassie shrieked above Lily's sobs and loud vomiting. 'Because if you do, I'll never be able to babysit you again. Ever!'

'I won't,' Lily wailed, continuing to retch. 'I won't tell. I promise.'

After things calmed, Cassie took Lily to bed. The stereo was turned off. Roland came out and peeked into the good room, where Cassie was on her knees with a bucket next to her, laving the carpet with a Wettex. Her back was to him, but he could see that she was crying, her body shaking as she scrubbed and scrubbed at vomit stains that would never entirely come out. He retreated to his room.

A TUMID WAVE of heat broke over Roland as he opened the front door, the sizzle of insects as deafening as a jet engine. It took a moment for his eyes to adjust to the sun, the world turned to bone by its brightness. Todd McKeon was standing on the patio, his Mongoose BMX lying on its side in the driveway. He was watching Pete, who was riding up and down the footpath wearing a piece of PVC piping over one of his arms like a cast. He hit the piping against the fences and letter-boxes as he passed them. It made a hollow sound, a resonant *whomp whomp* tolling through the listless morning.

'Get your bike,' Todd said to Roland.

Roland got his ten-speed Malvern Star racer out of the garage and followed Todd and Pete along the road as they drifted from one side to the other, trying to pull wheelies and jumping their bikes onto the nature strip and then back onto the road again. Pete's back wheel hit the gutter and he nearly came off; the PVC piping fell off his arm as he struggled for control. It rolled across the bitumen. They stopped outside Todd's house and Pete and Roland waited while Todd went into the garage. He came back carrying a can of engine coolant. They rode down to the creek and stopped on the bridge, where Todd poured the coolant into the water. Then he chucked the can in. It bounced off the rocks and settled half-submerged in the stream. The boys gathered some stones and threw them at it. Nearby, a group of little girls sat in a circle under a row of conifers, playing some intense, secretive game. They threw hostile glances at the boys as they passed.

'Hey, Pete,' said Todd. 'Show them your dick.'

Pete swaggered over to the girls and undid his fly. He waved his hairy penis at them and they ran away, crying. The boys rode down the path, pedalling furiously until they were carried by their own momentum, until it felt as though they were flying, the trees and bushes whipping past them. Todd was breathless with laughter.

'Oh, man, Pete. I can't believe you actually did that!'

They stopped at the Scout Hall, which had a recycling depot behind it. Beer and wine bottles were stacked neatly against the pebble-dash wall and the cyclone fencing, glowing amber and green where they were caught by the slanting sunlight. Pete climbed the fence and slid down into the yard over a stack of longnecks; the bottles clanked and a few fell with him onto the tamped earth floor. He passed them over the fence to Todd, who hid them in the bushes behind the hall.

'Give us some wine bottles,' said Todd. 'See if there's any big ones.'

Pete found a box of champagne bottles. He upturned them before passing them to Todd, trickling the dregs into his mouth.

'Aw! That's disgusting, Pete!'

Todd concealed the rest of the bottles in the thick profusion of onion weeds that choked the rising banks of the creek. They spiced the air around them, mosquitoes droning about the dank and darkly verdant shadows, coolness sweeping off the water. Pete straddled the fence, swigging from a Carlton Draught stubby. He drained it and threw it against the wall and it smashed, glass tinkling as it rained onto the bottles. He jumped down and joined the others.

'All right,' Todd said. 'We meet here tonight. Midnight. That's a pact.'

He looked at Roland sternly, blowing his hair out of his eyes.

'What are we going to do with them?' Roland asked.

'Chuck them at people's windows,' Todd said.

Roland did not go to meet them at midnight, although he was still awake, lying in bed with the lights off. At half past twelve, he heard bicycles whirring down his driveway, the skid of tyres as they braked, Todd whispering, 'Come on, come on. Where is he?'

The following day, Tilly Johnson brought all the local news.

'That McKeon boy's got himself in trouble with the police again,' she told Joyce as she spooned sugar into her tea. 'He's been leading that spastic boy astray, it seems. Had both their parents down at the Nunawading station at some ungodly hour.'

'He's a bit of a problem child, is he?' Joyce asked her.

'Oh, yes,' Tilly said. 'A complete delinquent. I'm sure he's doing it for attention. It's the mother. She completely neglects those children.'

'Is that right?'

'Oh, yes. Too wrapped up in her own world. Had the husband take her overseas last year. To Europe of all places. While those girls are wearing hand-me-downs. All of them sleeping in the same room. The boy as well.'

'Really?'

'I've seen it myself. The two older girls have put clotheslines around their beds for the privacy. Sheets hanging over them. Looks like the Black Hole of Calcutta in there.'

'But it's such a big house.'

'She gives them nothing. She's a very strange woman. Selfish. But then again so's the husband. With his flash cars. Yes, it's no wonder.'

The Nobles came around later that afternoon and Cassie and Lily disappeared again, although today their absence was brief. At dinner, Lily sat scowling.

'I hate Darren Wilson,' she said.

PETE AND TODD were waiting for Roland as he came home from school, sitting on their BMX bikes outside Todd's house. The afternoon was ablaze, a hard edge to Roland's shadow as it bobbed beside him on the marigold of the hot concrete. He watched as it merged with other shadows, lost itself and then returned. The boys dismounted when they saw Roland and stood on the footpath watching him as he approached up the hill. Pete was hunched over in his grey woollen pants and blazer. His arms were folded, a film of sweat across his brow. Todd blew at his fringe. Roland crossed the road and they also crossed, meeting him on the other side. As he tried to pass them, Todd knocked his shoulder hard into Roland's, throwing him against a fence.

'Where were you last night?' he demanded. 'What happened to you?'

'I fell asleep,' said Roland. 'My alarm didn't go off.'

'Bullshit,' said Todd, pushing him against the fence again.

The two boys struggled. Pete joined in, grabbing Roland in a headlock. He laughed maniacally as Roland tried to pull away.

'Where were you, hey?' he said in his garbled way, dragging Roland by the neck. Roland's nose was forced into the stench of his armpit, the wet animal smell of the sweaty wool. He continued to struggle. Todd went over to the bikes and came back with his knife, holding it against Roland's throat.

'I ought to cut you,' he said.

They were waiting for him again the following day. Roland doubled back and went around the block, coming up to Carlington Street via the lane. As he passed the Kyriakides house, he saw Darren Wilson working on his motorcycle in the backyard. Again, he was polishing it, sitting on the grass next to the back wheel as he rubbed the chamois over the lattice of the spokes. He peered up at Roland.

'How's it going?' he asked him.

'Good,' said Roland.

'Come on round,' said Darren. 'Pull up a pew.'

Roland walked around the fence and went through the carport into the backyard. Darren got up, wiping down his jeans, and took his cigarettes from the pocket of the flannel shirt on the chair. He put a foot up on the seat and lit a cigarette, leaning over his knee and squinting at Roland through the afternoon glare.

'So, is your sister pissed off with me?'

'I think so.'

'Yeah,' said Darren. 'I feel sort of bad about that. She was coming around here all the time. Kept sitting and watching me while I was working on my bike. I mean, that's all right, I suppose, but I'm not running a kindergarten here. She came around the other day when I was hungover and I just couldn't hack it. I told her to piss off. Told her to go home and play with her Barbie dolls.'

'She can be pretty annoying sometimes,' said Roland.

'That Cassie girl came around and told me off about it yesterday. Told me I was mean. I said, "I know I'm mean. I know that. I know I'm an arsehole. Doesn't mean I don't feel bad about it." She was pretty angry with me. Sticking up for her friend and that. Well, good for her, I suppose.'

He smoked meditatively, flicking the cigarette butt over the fence when he had finished, and went back to polishing the already shining motorcycle.

'How old's that Cassie bird, anyway?' he asked Roland.

'Thirteen.'

'Yeah?' Darren said, squatting down to examine the neat grooves of the cylinder. He wiped them with his finger. 'Thirteen, ay?'

When he came up the lane the following day, Roland saw Darren sitting in the backyard with two other boys, beer cans at their feet. One of them watched him from under the peak of a dirty Mobil 1 Racing cap as he approached. He had a hard face, a steely stare.

'Faggot!' he yelled at Roland as he came close.

Darren turned around.

'Oh, come on, Troy,' he said to the other boy. 'That's Roly. That's my new friend Roly. Jesus, Troy.'

He waved Roland over and offered him a chair.

'Yeah, well, I'm sorry, mate,' said Troy. 'But you walk around dressed like that, you're asking for it, aren't you?'

'It's his school uniform,' said Darren. 'He's got no choice about it.'

'Yeah, well, somebody's having a laugh then.'

The other boy had long, golden hair and wore a singlet that showed off tanned, enormously muscled arms. 'Curl just lifts weights all day and sunbakes,' Darren told Roland later. 'It's all he does.'

'You go to a co-ed school?' Curl asked Roland. 'Or all boys?'

'All boys,' Roland said.

'Fucking hell,' Curl said. 'That's just cruel.' He took a swig of beer. 'You know any of those little private school girls that hang around down at the station?' he asked Roland. 'Those long white socks,' he said to Darren and Troy, grinning and shaking his head. He turned back to Roland. 'You tell some of them to come up here one day. They can come sit on my lap.'

The afternoon was hot, the cicadas loud. The motorcycle sat by the garage, its headlight glittering like an eye watching them. Darren and his friends started talking about someone they went to school with.

'So this guy Adam,' Darren said to Roland. 'What would happen was him and his girlfriend would get on a bus and she'd go and sit next to some guy, sitting there on his own. And she'd be all over him. So, then Adam would come up and he'd go, "What are you doing with my girlfriend?" And he'd beat the shit out of the guy. Just some poor bloke taking the bus home or whatever. He was a complete psychopath. Well, both of them. Both psychos.'

'She was all right, though,' said Curl. 'Had a really decent body.'

'Yeah, I didn't say she wasn't,' said Darren. 'Whatever happened to Adam, anyway?' he asked Troy.

'He's in jail,' said Troy.

'I'm not surprised.'

'But it wasn't his fault,' said Troy. 'He was living with some guys in Croydon and they had all these stolen video players and stuff in the garage, and mull plants. Then one of them had a fight with his girlfriend and she dobbed them in to the cops. Adam was already on about three good-behaviour bonds.'

'Well,' said Darren, lighting another cigarette. 'I can't say I'm sorry.'

'What about his girlfriend?' Curl asked Troy. 'I wouldn't mind seeing her again. Crazy girls,' he said to Roland, winking at him. 'They fuck like anything.'

Roland began to stop off at Darren's house every afternoon. Troy and Curl were usually there with him—although on Tuesdays, Troy would leave early for his karate class—and Roland would sit and listen to them as they talked. They told stories of a world he had never even suspected, existing in the suburbs around them, its empty landscape: in the streets and shopping centres, on the trains, in nightclubs, pubs and pool halls. Within the faceless houses, it seemed, there were unknown lives. Wild lives. The people in the stories seemed out of control, to go about as though possessed. Roland could not fathom their thoughts and he sometimes wondered whether they thought at all. They seemed to be vessels of pure action, bundles of muscle and instinct. Their violence frightened and astounded him. Boys were punched, kicked, knocked out, stabbed, hit with star pickets and baseball bats. Ribs were broken, heads caved in. They seemed to stagger on. One boy was caught by some Greeks in Springvale, cornered in a carpark.

They took turns to bash his head against a towbar. Now he was brain damaged; his mates made fun of him. He spent his days wandering around, looking for Greeks to bash, getting into more fights and becoming more messed up every day. Others got rolled by skinheads, surrounded by bikies, jumped by their own friends and beaten senseless for a laugh. Roland was amazed these characters were still wandering around, that any of them could be bold enough to walk down the street, to catch a train, to leave their houses at all. There seemed to be gangs of boys everywhere, swaggering about, looking for victims.

There were girls in the stories as well, but these were entirely different stories. They seemed elusive, flitting through this same dangerous world with a strange self-possession, afraid of nothing. Darren, Troy and Curl listed off their names, grinning, for each one a comment. They had tight pussies; they had amazing tits; they didn't wear underwear; they gave you head jobs in the cinema. Everything there was to know about them, it seemed, was gleaned in the darkness, in someone's bedroom at a party, in backyards and laneways, the back seats of cars, on the couches of nightclubs. They appeared, they showed their nakedness, they submitted and then disappeared again, mysteriously, it seemed to Roland, leaving few clues to their own minds and feelings. On some evenings, groups of boys and girls gathered together to watch a video in someone's lounge room. They drank beer, smoked bongs, ordered pizza. They paired off and had sex, all in the same room, with the television still going.

'If you go out,' Troy told Roland, 'and you don't get a root and get into a fight, then it's not a good night.' His voice was measured, serious. He was giving him sound advice.

*

79

On Friday afternoons, when Roland came up the lane, he would find Darren alone in the backyard, the motorcycle locked up in the shed. The two of them would sit and talk, Darren smoking thoughtfully, until he went inside to shower at around six. While he was in the shower, Roland made polite conversation with his mother as she prepared dinner, which always seemed to consist of grilled chops, potatoes and frozen three veg.

A towel wrapped around his waist, Darren spent what seemed like hours with his hair as he chatted with Roland through the open bathroom door. He brushed it, sprayed it, spread gel through it, teased it with a comb. The result was spectacular. To Roland it looked like a lion's mane, as though the wind was through it constantly. He dressed in an olive-green suit with wide shoulders and pleated trousers. When he had examined himself thoroughly in the mirror and was satisfied, he and Roland would go outside again and Roland would watch as he rolled joints, cutting up the thick wads of bud with a pair of kitchen scissors.

Troy and Curl would arrive sometime later, Troy in a glaucous double-breasted suit that looked too big for him, his slight, fist-hard body lost in all the cloth. Curl wore a paisley shirt, the top buttons undone and a cowrie-shell necklace nestled under the collar. His hair shone with gel in the amber light of the evening. All three boys were doused in aftershave and it filled the air with a muggy sweetness. They passed around joints and drank beer and there was a lot of joking and laughter, an eagerness that they tried to hide behind a guise of cool reluctance as they sprawled out on the chairs as though settled in for the night. They wondered out loud whether they could be bothered going anywhere at all and got up almost wearily as the light started to fade.

'Yeah, sorry we can't take you with us, Roly,' Darren said as he got into Troy's car, dragging a last curlicue of smoke out of a damp roach before he threw it in the gutter. Troy blasted the horn as they drove away.

The same ritual was repeated on Saturday night, although Roland was rarely there to see it. He had Monday tests and assignments due and spent the day at his desk. The following afternoon, while the Nobles sat with his parents at the garden table, Cassie playing with Lily, he would leave unnoticed and find Darren, Troy and Curl sitting bleary-eyed in Darren's backyard, resting like warriors after battle. They chuckled and yawned and talked sparingly, smoking what was left of the marijuana and retelling their exploits from the previous nights, their comments often too cryptic for Roland to understand.

'Yeah, I don't know, Roly,' Darren said to him one day. 'Don't think we're having such a great time as we make out.'

It was late in summer, a chill in the air. Vinegar flies swarmed in the patches of soft light, disappearing into the quivering lines of shadow. Troy and Curl had gone home.

'You know, we go to all these clubs,' Darren said. 'We go to Chevron, we go to Chasers, Inflation, Metro. We never get into those places. They don't want people like us. They only let us in if it's a really shit night and there's no one there. Never when it's good. You know, when there's all the people you want to meet there. We always end up at the fucking Tunnel, every fucking night. But I tell you, Roly. Some of those girls you see in the queues. I saw this girl last night outside Chevron. Just beautiful. In this long red dress. I swear, she could've been right out of a magazine or something. I was standing there thinking, if I could just get in and talk to her for five minutes. I mean, I look at a girl like that and, you know, I could marry a girl like that.'

He was smoking a cigarette, drinking his last beer, and he looked tired, sapped of energy by the two nights out, the joints he had been smoking all day. It was another weekend over. He leaned back, his pale eyes searching the sky.

'You're smart, aren't you, Roly? You're good at school, right?'

'Usually.'

'They give you a hard time?'

Roland nodded.

'Yeah, well, fuck them,' Darren said. 'Because one day that's going to be you in those queues. Plenty of money. Nice clothes. Nice way of talking. Those girls are going to be all over you. Maybe you can say to them, "Come and meet my old mate Darren."'

He grinned at Roland, sitting up and taking a last drag of his cigarette before he flicked it over the fence.

'I'm just joking. But you got to dream, don't you?'

On the evenings that Darren, Troy and Curl did not go out, Roland sat with them until late at night in Darren's backyard. They were sometimes joined by another friend of theirs, Floyd, who only ever turned up after dark. Floyd was a crim, Darren told Roland, just like his father, who grew up in the Box Hill Boys' Home and had spent time in Pentridge. He told the story of how once, when they were children and he had been staying over at Floyd's house, Floyd's father had woken them up in the middle of the night and taken them into the garage, where the entire contents of a toy shop were spilled out on the floor.

'Take what you want now, because it won't be here tomorrow,' Floyd's father had said.

Floyd would steal anything: bikes out of front yards, shoes off patios, sunglasses and stereo systems from parked cars, packets of Juicy Fruit when the milk bar owner's back was turned. His favourite targets were veterinarian clinics, which he knocked over for animal tranquillisers. He mixed them with marijuana and sold to some guys he knew in Dandenong, some really fucked-up guys, he told Roland. Once they injected a girl with battery acid and dumped her body in the Yarra. It was because she was annoying them, the guys had told Floyd. She wouldn't stop talking when they were stoned. But his main income these days, Floyd said, came from drug dealing, which he hated.

'This supplier I've got,' he said. 'He's always ringing me up, telling me I should be moving more gear. I said, "Well, what do you want me to do?" He goes, "Why don't you go out and make some new friends, some people with money. Go to the nightclubs, meet some people there. Make friends with some university students." Mate,' Floyd said with distaste, 'it's like selling fucking Amway.'

Lately Floyd had been getting into rips, stealing marijuana plants out of people's backyards. He spent entire days driving around the suburbs, going down lanes and looking over the back fences. Mostly it was old hippies cultivating it, he said, and usually he only got a couple of plants growing in someone's garden or under lights in their shed. He mixed it with the bud he got off his supplier. Darren told Roland about a big rip Floyd once invited him along on.

'So, Floyd turned up with this van and we drove up to the hills to this place that's got this big cyclone fence around it,' he said. 'All covered in black plastic. I said to Floyd, "How did you find out about this?" And he goes, "This is one of the guys who grows for my supplier." It was some bikie or something.

Anyway, so Floyd opens up the glove box and he's got two guns in there. He hands me this gun, and I said, "What do we need guns for? We're just going to rip some plants, aren't we?" And Floyd goes, "Oh, yeah, but this guy's got a crossbow." And then he starts telling me about all these electric fences and mantraps and shit. I said, "No way, I'm not doing it." So, Floyd says, "Fair enough," and he jumps the fence and starts throwing plants over. There were that many plants, I could barely fit them all in the van. When we were driving back, I swear, we had to put our heads out of the window, it was that stinky.'

When Floyd came around to Darren's, he always seemed restless. He would get up and pace the backyard. His eyes darted, looking around when he was talking to someone.

'Jeez, Floyd, just chill out, will you,' Darren said to him.

He would rather be stealing, Darren told Roland later. He was hatching all sorts of plans.

IN THE AFTERNOONS, Todd and Pete started to ride up and down the road past Darren's house, watching the boys in the backyard as they sat together on the derelict kitchen chairs or stood around the motorcycle while Darren endlessly washed and polished it. Sometimes they went down the lane, skidding their tyres in the dirt to attract the other boys' attention, passing close enough for Roland to see the puzzled look on Todd's face. The hovering became restless and one day Todd started yelling abuse as he rode past, holding his middle finger up at them. Pete, following, let out a mangled string of swear words.

'Jesus,' Darren said. 'What's their problem?'

It became a regular occurrence. Sometimes Curl and Troy would leap out of their chairs and chase Todd and Pete down the road, but usually they chose to ignore them. Then Todd started spitting on Troy's car, a red and black Torana LX that Troy always left parked where he could see it from the backyard.

It became a game for Todd: he wove around the Torana on his bike, veering close to the sides and hawking loudly, looking over at the boys with a smirk. He would disappear out of sight, then come back down the road, splatter the windscreen as he passed the car and ride away with his middle finger held up as Troy shouted and gave chase. One Sunday afternoon, after Todd and Pete had passed several times, Troy stood up and looked out at the street.

'What's he up to?' he said.

Todd was squatting by the Torana, his BMX lying on the nature strip. Pete was standing on the footpath, watching him. When he saw Troy looking, he yelled to Todd, who jumped onto his bike and rode away, holding his survival knife flat against the handlebars. Pete followed. Troy crossed the road and walked around the car.

'You've got to be kidding me,' he said as he looked down to where Todd had been crouched. He held his hands to his head. 'Fuck!'

The others went over to look. There were deep scratches in the paintwork, long wavy lines across the side of the car and the word 'dickhead' scrawled in elongated letters underneath the passenger door. An arrow pointed upwards.

'I cannot believe this,' Troy said. 'Why?'

Todd and Pete had halted at the intersection and were watching them, a smug grin on Todd's face. 'Let's get 'em, Troy!' Curl shouted, going to the passenger door. 'Let's go!' They got into the car and Troy pulled away from the kerb with a lurch and a screech of tyres, accelerating after Todd and Pete as they took off down the hill and turned into the long street that dipped through the creeklands. When the car caught up to them, Troy swerved in front of the bikes and slammed on the brakes, forcing Todd and Pete to skid to a halt. Darren, Curl and Troy ran out and chased the boys as they started pedalling away. Darren caught up to Todd, grabbed him by the back of his T-shirt and pulled him down onto the road. Todd immediately leaped up and lunged at him with his knife.

'Jesus!' Darren said, jumping back. Troy tackled Todd from the side, grabbing his arm and pulling it back, and Darren prised his fingers off the handle of the knife. Pete came hurtling down the road, howling, and rocketed headlong towards Curl, who only just dodged him. Roland was standing outside the car, frozen, his heart pounding. Everyone had leapt into action so quickly that he was still trying to comprehend what had happened. An old man came out of one of the houses.

'You leave that boy alone!' he shouted. He took his wallet out of his back pocket and pointed it at Curl.

'What are you going to do?' Curl laughed. 'You going to give me money?'

'Leave that boy alone,' the old man repeated. His regimental tie flapped in the wind, twisting against his shirt, and strands of his thin hair fluttered. His hands were shaking.

Troy and Darren had wrestled Todd to the ground. 'Look what he did to my car,' Troy said to the man. He got up and showed him the scratches along the doors. The man bent to examine them, sliding his wallet back into his trouser pocket.

'He did it with this thing,' Troy told the man, picking the big black knife up off the road.

'Strike a light!' the man said. He looked down at Todd.

'He needs a good clip around the ears,' he told Troy. 'You should talk to his father.'

'I will,' said Troy.

They stood there with their arms folded, looking at the car.

'It's going to have to be repainted,' said Troy. 'Someone's going to have to pay for that.'

The man shook his head and went back into his house. Pete, who had fled up the street, reappeared, speeding towards them and bawling out a torrent of swear words that rose to an extended scream. He tried to run Curl down again. Curl, ready for him this time, sidestepped and pushed him, sending him sprawling onto the road. The bike careered into the gutter. Pete jumped up and charged at Curl. Curl punched him in the face and he fell down. Troy and Darren hauled Todd up by his arms and dragged him over to the car. 'Fuck off!' he howled, spittle erupting from his mouth. He kicked at them. 'Leave me alone! Leave me alone!' One of his sneakers came off.

'Look at this!' yelled Troy. 'Look what you've done!'

Todd tried to bite Darren's hand and Darren pulled it away and smacked him on the back of the head.

'Why, mate?' Troy asked him. 'What have I ever done to you?'

Roland walked over to where Pete was lying on the side of the road. He was staring upwards, and there seemed to be nothing in his eyes but animal fear. Roland had seen the same glazed expression in birds frightened by pouncing cats, which could have escaped but just lay there. He kicked Pete in the guts and Pete made a strange noise and a jerking movement as he held his belly, staring at Roland with that same mindless look.

'Hey, Roly,' Darren said to Roland with a frown. 'Go easy on the retard.'

Troy and Curl grabbed Todd's legs while Darren pinned his arms against his sides. They lifted him up and put him into the boot of the car. Todd struggled, kicking wildly and screaming, his voice cracking into high notes. Darren threw the shoe in after him and they closed the boot onto his head and leaned on it until it shut. Inside, Todd's cries were muted. He hammered at the door and the car shook. Curl picked his BMX up off the road and jammed it in the back seat, while Troy rested the knife against the kerb and smashed his foot down on it until it broke. He wrenched off the handle.

'Piece of crap,' he said, throwing the blade down the storm-water drain.

They drove back up the hill. In the rear-view mirror, Roland saw Pete get up and mount his bike. He rode away in the other direction.

'Do you know where he lives?' Troy asked Darren, nodding towards the noise coming from the trunk.

'Roly knows.'

'Well, let's see what his old man has to say about this.'

Troy parked the car outside Darren's and he and Roland walked down to Todd's house. Todd's father was outside, washing his white Ford Falcon in the driveway. A running hose slithered on the concrete, the water flowing onto the street and down the gutters.

'Just wait here,' Troy said to Roland.

Roland stood by the letterbox and watched as Troy walked down the drive and began talking to Todd's father, who threw his sponge into a bucket of soapy water and strode off into the house. He slammed the door on Troy as he followed him. Troy turned around and looked at Roland, holding up his hands in a gesture of helplessness. Masses of white bubbles slid down the windscreen of the Falcon, water still pouring from the hose.

'Did you see that?' Troy said to Roland as he came up the drive.

They walked back to the car. Darren and Curl were watching

it bounce on the suspension, frenzied noises coming from the boot.

'He's going apeshit in there,' Darren told them.

'His old man just ignored me,' Troy said. 'He just walked away. I was polite as well. I was calm as. Didn't even raise my voice. All I said was, "We've got a problem here with your son." I said, "It's both our problems now. I'm not blaming you, but it needs to get sorted out." You saw me, didn't you?' Troy said to Roland. 'I was polite, wasn't I? I didn't lose it or anything, did I?'

'No,' said Roland. 'He just walked away.'

'Yeah, exactly. He just walks away. Leaves me standing there like an idiot.'

'So what are you going to do?' Darren asked him.

'I don't know. His old man obviously doesn't care what happens to him. And the guy's fucking loaded. Look at his house. It's not like he couldn't pay or anything. Someone's got to pay for it.'

'What do you think we should do, Roly?' Darren asked Roland.

Roland thought about it. 'I don't know,' he said.

'What about the bike?' Curl said. 'That's probably worth something.'

They took Todd's BMX out of the car and looked at it.

'Nah, that's a piece of shit too,' Troy said. 'Just let him out.'

They opened the boot. Todd jumped out and stumbled onto the road, his arms flailing wildly as the boys tried to get hold of him. His clothes were soaked in sweat and his face was bright red, streaked with tears, thick trails of snot running from his nose.

'Fuck you!' he screamed at them in his hoarse, choking voice. 'Fuck you!'

'So, your old man's an arsehole, isn't he?' Troy said to him. 'He doesn't give a shit about you.'

They released him and he fell silent, out of breath. He stood looking at them surlily. Troy kicked him in the backside.

'So fuck off home,' he said.

'Give me my bike,' Todd said.

'What, so you can come and scratch up my car again? Spit on my windscreen?'

'Give me my bike!' Todd screamed, his fists clenched. He walked towards the car, his head bowed. Curl held him back, putting one hand against his chest, and Todd started to cry, wailing pitifully and pushing feebly at the hand. Troy picked up the BMX and hurled it onto the road. It made an awful sound as it hit the bitumen. Todd ran over to it, picked it up and leaped onto it.

'Fuck you!' he screamed as he rode away, holding up his finger. 'Fuck you!'

Troy looked at Darren and they both shook their heads.

'Unbelievable,' Troy said. 'What's wrong with the people around here?'

ANOTHER DINNER PARTY. The evening ablutions in the bathroom, the wafting of scents, the preparation of the wine cooler. Lily bounded from one parent to the other, fascinated as always by the rituals. Roland was in the kitchen, helping himself to a second serve of ice-cream, when Cassie appeared at the back door, tapping so quietly on the glass that he at first took the noise for birds' feet scraping on the roof tiles. When Joyce opened the door, Cassie greeted her morosely, her eyes fixed to the floor, before slipping off into Lily's room.

'You didn't ask Cassie to babysit, did you?' Joyce asked Graham as he came in, groomed and fragrant in cords and a tweed jacket.

'Of course not,' he said. 'I thought we'd agreed that we wouldn't ask her again.'

'Well, so did I.'

'Maybe she's just come around of her own accord. That's all right, isn't it?'

'I suppose so. I'm just a bit nervous about leaving them now.'

Roland went back to the lounge room and lay down on the couch. He was watching *Golden Years of Hollywood* again. The first movie was *Vertigo*. Bill Collins, in a velvet bowtie, was showing pictures from a book of stills.

'She might not have been his first choice,' he said, holding up a picture of Kim Novak lying on a bed, her brown hair loose and wild. He picked up another photo that showed her in a gown, now with blonde hair pinned back in a spiral. 'But isn't she beautiful,' he said. 'Just stunning.'

'Roland,' his mother said, coming into the room.

'Yes?'

'You'll keep an eye on the girls, won't you? Ring us at the restaurant if there are any problems. Anything at all. And try to make sure Lily doesn't get overexcited again, or whatever it was that happened last time.'

After the parents left, Cassie and Lily went into the kitchen and made hot chocolate in the microwave. They brought it into the lounge room and Cassie sat on the couch next to Roland. Lily was cross-legged on the floor, already in her nightie. She blew on her steaming mug. On the screen, Kim Novak had just jumped into the San Francisco Bay. James Stewart took off his coat and dived in after her, rescued her and took her to his car. In the next scene, she was lying naked in his bed, her clothes drying in his bathroom.

'Why did she jump into the water?' Cassie asked Roland.

'I don't know,' Roland said.

'Is he meant to be in love with her or something?'

'No. He's just following her around.'

There was a noise from the kitchen: a loud thump as someone tried to open the sliding door against the lock and the muffled sound of a man swearing outside. The door banged heavily again and rattled. Roland's heart started to race. Lily was looking at him, wide-eyed. He got up and went timidly to the kitchen. The girls followed, throwing each other quick, frightened glances. Peering through the doorway, Roland could see Reg Noble standing outside in the dark, fiddling with the handle of the door. Cassie gave an exasperated snort and went back into the living room. When Reg saw Roland, he rapped on the glass with his knuckles. Roland opened the door for him.

'Hello there, mate,' Reg said, putting his hand on Roland's shoulder and squeezing it hard. He smelled of alcohol and cigarettes. The collar of his polo shirt was turned up on one side. He stood there for what felt like a long time, gripping Roland's shoulder and gazing at him, his eyes unfocused.

'I don't suppose my daughter's around here, is she?' he asked.

'She's in the living room,' Roland said. He was eager to get away from Reg and started to move towards the lounge room door, but the heavy hand only clutched him tighter.

'We've just had a bit of a blue at home,' Reg said. He was standing so close that Roland could feel the heat off his body. His hand was damp, his brow beaded with sweat. Livid spider veins exploded across his already flushed cheeks.

'You know what that's like, don't you? You'd have bust-ups with your old man. From time to time.'

'Sometimes,' Roland said.

'Of course you do,' Reg said. Roland avoided his gaze. 'Doesn't mean he doesn't love you.'

'I know.'

Reg took his hand off Roland's shoulder and pounded him on the back.

'Good,' he said. 'Good man.'

He staggered into the living room and sat down on the couch next to Cassie.

'What are you watching there?' he asked her.

Cassie shrugged. She was sitting stiffly, her shoulders hunched and her eyes fixed on the television screen. Reg reached over and stroked her cheek. She flinched, pulling away.

'Don't!' she said sharply.

'All right,' Reg said quietly. 'Jeez. All right.'

He looked around the room and at Lily, who was watching him. He winked at her.

'Hello there,' he said.

Lily beamed, sipping on her hot chocolate. The living room was in darkness, the only light the flicker of the television across the room. Reg closed his eyes and then opened them with a start. He stretched and yawned, slapped his legs and got up.

'Who feels like some McDonald's?' he said.

Lily threw her hand up. 'Me,' she cried. 'I do.'

'How about you?' Reg asked Cassie, nudging her leg with his. 'You want to go to McDonald's? Or not.'

'Please, Cassie,' Lily pleaded. 'Please can we go?'

Cassie folded her arms, eyes still fixed on the screen. 'All right,' she finally said.

Reg staggered to his feet, hitched up his shorts and mumbled something about getting the car. He lurched out, letting the front door swing shut with a crash, and tripped, swearing, in the darkness of the patio.

'Come and help me get changed,' Lily begged Cassie, tugging on her arm.

'I'm watching this,' said Cassie. She stretched out across the couch, folded a cushion over and pressed her face into it. She was wearing pink tracksuit pants with a fuzzy white jumper, her arms drawn out of the sleeves so that they hung with a mannequin lifelessness, her hands clasped across her chest underneath the wool. Roland noticed that the small silver hoops she normally wore in her ears had been taken out. Lily pattered reluctantly down the hall.

On the television, James Stewart was in a dingy hotel room, lit by the green light of a neon sign. Kim Novak came down the hall, her hair dyed blonde.

'I don't get this,' Roland said to Cassie. 'Is he trying to make her look like the other woman?'

'It's the same woman,' Cassie said, her voice muffled by the cushion.

'But didn't she die?'

Cassie lifted her head to look at Roland. She seemed tired.

'He thought she died,' she said. 'But she just changed her hair.'

Lily pranced back in, wearing her best party dress. Plastic necklaces were looped around her neck, an iridescent sheen to the beads that was meant to make them look like pearls. Reg's car pulled into the driveway, the headlights swinging across the room. He honked the horn and Lily ran to the front door. Cassie got up with a sigh.

'I can't believe we're going to McDonald's,' Lily exclaimed as she skipped down the driveway, slowing herself to the beat of Cassie's trudging. The tall girl squinted irritably in the high beam of the idling car, lifting her hand to her eyes. Their long shadows mingled with Roland's as he followed them. 'We're just sitting at home and then, "Oh! Why don't we go to McDonald's!" And then we just go!'

Lily continued to chatter as they drove down the highway. Cassie remained silent. At the McDonald's, they stood in the queue, looking up at the menu behind the counter with its backlit photographs of the food. Reg blinked in the bright fluorescent light and rubbed his eyes with his palms. Everything was conspicuously clean. The floors, recently mopped, shone. Cassie ordered a huge meal: a cheeseburger, French fries, chicken nuggets, a thickshake and an ice-cream sundae. But when they were seated, she only picked at the fries. She opened her cheeseburger and took out the slices of pickled cucumber, and stuck them against the window.

'Are you going to eat that?' Reg asked her.

Cassie picked up the cheeseburger, took an enormous bite and chewed it with her mouth open, glaring at Reg. She stuffed the rest into her mouth and slumped back in her seat, looking out of the window where cars roared along the highway. Lily ate her meal with an air of careful diligence—one bite of her hamburger, one French fry, a sip of Coke—visibly savouring each mouthful. Roland watched Cassie nervously. Reg drank a black coffee.

A group of young men came into the restaurant, cans of Victoria Bitter in their hands. They had the hard gauntness of builders' labourers. Long, careless hair. One of them was bare-chested, although the night was cool. His arms and torso were covered in tattoos, a Chinese dragon unravelling over his shoulder. They talked loudly and swore. A middle-aged woman with diamante glasses and a bouffant came out from behind the counter and strode up to them.

'You can't drink those in here,' she told the men.

'Oh, come on,' said the men. 'Fair go. Nobody minds.'

'Youse don't mind, do you?' the shirtless man asked the diners, looking around at the tables and the booths with glazed eyes.

'Out!' the woman ordered, pointing at the door. 'And you mind your language if you're planning on coming back in here.' The men began to file sheepishly out the door. 'What would your mothers say if they heard that sort of language?' the woman scolded. The men stood outside on the tiled pathway, lighting cigarettes and swigging their beers.

Cassie, who had turned to watch the men, hiccuped and burped at the same time. She covered her mouth with her hand and looked up in embarrassment, her face flooding red and her eyes sparkling. Reg started to laugh and Cassie smiled but tried to hide it, turning away and affecting a scowl. She glanced at her reflection in the window and hiccuped again. Lily was also laughing. Reg leaned over and tickled Cassie's stomach. She pushed his hand away, but she was still smiling.

'You all right now?' Reg asked her. 'You stopped sulking?'

Cassie nodded and hiccuped. She started to eat her sundae.

Back at the Arthursons' house, they all sat back down in front of the television. *Rear Window,* the second of the double feature, was playing. James Stewart was there again, but this time he was in a wheelchair, wearing his pyjamas. Grace Kelly brought him a tray of food from the kitchen. She was wearing pearls and an elegant bodice gown.

'I wouldn't mind being in a wheelchair if I had her looking after me,' Reg said to Roland, winking.

WINTER IN GLENELLA brought grey days and nights of luminous cloud cover. Cold winds rasped through the heads of the tall trees, bending them, and rattled the weave of branches, water splattering down long after the rains had stopped. Irises bloomed among the ferns along the deep bitumen gutters in Oak Grove and Oleander Street, muddy water flashing in the potholes and trembling with the passing of cars. Wattle waved like fingers in the breeze. The inhabitants rugged up: walkers wore oilskins and hiking boots and Akubra hats on misty mornings, their breath steaming. They greeted each other like old comrades through the gloom, rubbing their hands together as they stopped to talk. Graham woke while it was still dark and went outside in his pyjamas to get the paper, sucking the air between his teeth as he walked barefoot through the frost.

Nothing, it seemed, would send Darren inside. He dug a shallow pit in the backyard, encircled it with logs, and built a fire that burned there day and night. Eucalyptus smoke wafted thick through days that never brightened, and grew melancholy; lush moss crept across the damp terracotta roofs, and central heating units churned. He and Curl and Troy huddled over the flames, making their usual relaxed conversation, their faces growing raw from the chill and the wind. Curl, apparently immune from the cold, continued to wear singlets, his massive arms never paling.

One Friday afternoon, Roland came home from school and found Troy and Curl still at Darren's house. Troy was arguing with Darren, who shook his head as he stoked the fire with a rusted iron pipe.

'Oh, come on,' said Troy. 'You're not serious, are you?'

'I am serious. I told you last week. I'm not going. You go.'

'Oh, yeah. Me and Curl. Come on, Darren. We need you.'

'No,' said Darren. 'I'm staying here. Me and Roly will do something.'

Troy turned to Roland. 'You know why he's doing this, don't you?'

'I told Roly ages ago,' said Darren. 'I said, "I'm sick of it. It's not worth it."'

He leaned over the fire and spat into the flames.

'So last week,' he told Roland. 'We even get KB'd from the Tunnel. We didn't get in anywhere. Came back here with our tails between our legs. If they don't want me in their clubs, then fuck them. I don't need them. Fucking yuppies running those places.'

'It was just that one dickhead bouncer,' said Troy.

'It was one time too many, mate,' said Darren. 'I've had enough of it.'

After some talk, and with Darren unrelenting, they decided

to stay in Glenella and go to the bar and bistro on the highway. Roland told his parents that he was going out as he wolfed down a dinner of fish fingers with boiled potatoes and four bean mix. On Friday nights, the children were allowed to eat in front of the television, and Lily was sitting cross-legged in front of the screen, blowing bubbles in her glass of milk. *The Golden Girls* was on.

'Where are you going?' his mother asked Roland.

'Down to the shops.'

'Why can't you make friends with some nice boys from school?' she complained. 'Someone who's going to do something with their life.'

Roland changed into jeans and a jumper. In the bathroom, he smeared a handful of his mother's styling mousse through his hair, brushing his fringe so that it stuck upwards. It became hard and brittle as it dried. His father went outside with him as he left.

'I had a group of mates when I was your age,' he said as they stood on the patio and looked out at the glowing windows of the neat array of houses along the street. Far off there was the sound of cars tearing along the highway. Roland was eager to go, but his father seemed to have something else to say. He was pensive for a moment and then shook his head, as though dismissing a thought. He took out his wallet and handed Roland a ten-dollar note. 'In case you want to buy a pizza or something,' he said.

Darren was waiting for him in his backyard, staring into the fire. He flicked his cigarette into the darkness as Roland approached.

'All right,' he said. 'Let's rock and roll.'

*

The Glenella Bar and Bistro was a long windowless cement-board building painted in pastels with a trellised walkway running down the side. It announced itself and its various facilities in a series of scrawled neon signs, stacked one atop the other on a concrete plinth, like a totem pole. There was a drive-thru at the front, where two men attended the line of cars that spilled dog-legged from the entrance off the highway, idling engines growling and tyres shrieking on the concrete as the drivers paid through their open windows and pulled away and other cars gently throttled into place under the fluorescent lights. Outside the door to the bistro, a bouncer in a black suit stood cracking his knuckles, coloured spotlights pulsing through the windows behind him.

Curl and Troy were already inside the public bar at the back of the building, sitting at one of the chipboard tables with a jug of beer. Next to them, three unshaven men and a woman in a trucker's cap sat at a table cluttered with empty pots. A group of Maoris in blue overalls and white T-shirts sat on bar stools at the counter that ran along the side of the wall. The room was brightly lit by perspex-covered ceiling lights that gave the place a feeling more of a cafeteria than a pub, the mass of faces rendered stark as a flash photograph.

'You see Angela there?' Curl asked Darren as they sat down, nodding at the girl behind the bar.

'Yeah,' said Darren. 'So it is. Do you want a Coke, Roly?'

He strode over to the bar. Roland saw him lean over the counter and grin at the girl. She smiled and they chatted, her hand resting on the tap.

'Floyd's girlfriend,' Troy told Roland. Curl poured beer into the plastic pots.

'It's pretty dead tonight,' he said.

Darren came back with Roland's Coke. He took one of the beers and drank it standing up as he looked around the room. They watched as a man came in carrying a cardboard box, two girls following him. His hair was slicked back in a tight, glossy ponytail and his baggy grey suit was fashionably rumpled. He stood a sign up on the bar: 'Jim Beam Special Promotion. One shot for $2.00 and one spin of the wheel. Three shots for $5.00 and three spins of the wheel.' The girls wore white Jim Beam T-shirts tucked into their jeans, the insignia tight against their chests. They were pretty girls, young and slim. Roland thought they didn't look much older than he was. The man with the ponytail went outside and came back with a large cardboard wheel and put it on the bar. He directed the girls to stand on either side of it, waving them into position.

'What do you get?' one of the Maoris called over to the girls, who smiled at him. He climbed off his stool and went over to look at the wheel, then returned to his friends.

'T-shirts and caps,' he said.

Another of the men went to the bar and bought six shots of Jim Beam. The girls stood aside as he spun the wheel. He won two caps, which the girls took out of the cardboard box, beaming as they handed them to him. He put one of them on his head, downed one of the shots, and took the other glasses back with him, squeezed together in his big hands.

Roland looked over to where Angela was standing with the bartender who had been working on the other side of the long mirror that divided the public bar from the bistro. He was standing in the doorway, holding the swinging door open with his shoulder as they talked. Through it, Roland could see into the darkened area, where men in suits and blazers were crowding the bar. The women wore brightly coloured dresses and miniskirts, shiny fabrics, their hair teased. They minced delicately across the dancefloor on their high heels. Pop music bounced into the public bar, drowned out only when someone put a song on the jukebox by the pool tables. A fat man with a horseshoe moustache was standing in front of it, leaning against the glass and looking at the song lists. He was wearing a yellow T-shirt, on the back of which green letters had been sewn by hand, slightly crooked. 'AUSTRALIA' it read. 'BEST COUNTRY IN WORLD.' Angela said something to the bartender, who nodded, and she came over to the boys' table.

'Hey, you guys,' she said, sitting down. She took out a cigarette and Darren lit it for her.

'I didn't know you smoked.'

'I didn't until I started working here,' she said. 'I started getting cravings on my days off. It's no wonder. I spend my whole shift breathing in everyone else's smoke.'

'So now you're addicted.'

'Pretty much,' Angela said. The sleeves of her white Aran jumper were pushed up and a silver charm bracelet tinkled on her wrist. Her black hair was cut in a neat bob that curved to her slender neck. When he had seen her smile at Darren earlier, Roland had noticed how small and white her teeth were.

'So how come you're working here, anyway?' Darren asked her.

Angela shrugged.

'I mean,' said Darren. 'It's not like you have to, do you?'

'Better than doing nothing,' Angela said. 'I got sick of spending all day waiting around for Floyd to come home.'

'Where is Floyd, anyway?'

'Who knows.' She reached across the table to tap her cigarette over the ashtray. The charm bracelet slid onto her hand.

She lifted her arm and shook it back down again. Darren pushed the ashtray over to her.

'Who knows where Floyd is, or what he's up to,' Angela said. 'Don't ask me. I'm the last person to know.'

'You reckon?'

Angela shrugged again and made a face. All the Maoris were now buying Jim Beam shots, lurching from the bar carrying handfuls of small glasses. Most of them were wearing Jim Beam caps and T-shirts. They were becoming drunk and rowdy, their voices raised, their eyes shining. One of them walked over to the wheel and read from the sign.

'Two dollars for one shot. Five dollars for three shots,' he said loudly to the girls, who nodded earnestly.

'So how much for the two of you?' he asked them.

His friends guffawed. Roland could see the man with the ponytail sitting at a table in the bistro with a drink in front of him, watching the dancers. The bartender, still standing in the doorway, was glaring at him.

'You ever get any problems here?' Darren asked Angela. 'Gets pretty rough sometimes, doesn't it?'

'Nothing I can't handle,' she said.

'I suppose you can always get Floyd down here, bring along one of his guns,' said Darren, grinning.

'I don't need Floyd or his guns,' Angela said. 'I can take care of myself. Besides, Floyd never comes here. You know Floyd. He's so paranoid.'

'Yeah, he doesn't like crowds, does he?'

'He won't even go into the city anymore.'

'Yeah?'

'Floyd won't go anywhere anymore. At least, not with me.'

Angela stubbed out her cigarette and went back to the bar.

She resumed her conversation with the bartender, who was now watching the Maoris.

'Jeez, Floyd's girlfriend has nice tits,' said Curl.

'She's gorgeous,' said Darren. 'She's smart, too. We used to be in English together at school. The teacher used to read her assignments out in class.'

'One time I went over to Floyd's house,' said Curl. 'And Floyd wasn't there and Angela was still in bed, so she sits there talking to me in this white T-shirt, no bra. I swear, they are perfect.'

The Maori was still standing with the girls, leaning down so close to them that they had to shuffle out of his way. His head bobbed drunkenly as he leered at them. He waved his big hand in the air and the girls flinched.

'I'm serious,' he said. He reached into the pocket of his overalls and took out a wad of banknotes. 'How much for the two of you?'

The girls giggled nervously and looked around.

'Why don't you leave them alone?' Troy shouted at him.

The man's gaze veered towards Troy, then he looked back at the girls, muttering. His friends, who had been laughing and calling out, became stony-faced. One of them, a stocky man, shorter and older than the others, walked over to the boys' table.

'Look,' he said to Troy. 'He's just joking. They know he's joking. We're just having a good time. A few drinks after work.'

'You're scaring them,' Troy said. 'Look at the size of youse. You think those girls aren't going to be scared?'

The man looked over at the girls.

'My friend wasn't scaring you, was he?' he asked them. 'You're not scared.'

The girls shook their heads, smiling.

'You see,' he said. 'They're not scared.'

'Yeah, whatever,' said Troy. He lit a cigarette.

'Listen,' said the man. 'How about a round of shots here. On me.'

'Nah, we don't want any shots,' said Troy.

'It's all right,' said the man, holding out his hands as though he was pushing something away. He went to the bar and came back with four shot glasses.

'You get four spins of that wheel over there,' he said as he put them down on the table.

'Cheers, mate,' said Darren.

'All right?' said the man, holding out his hands again. 'So no worries. All right?'

He went back to his friends. Curl went over to the wheel and spun it. He won a cap and a T-shirt. He put the T-shirt on over his singlet and stood talking to the girls, who seemed relaxed now, flicking their hair and laughing. Curl, grinning, wandered back.

'There you go, Roly,' he said, putting the cap on Roland's head.

'I just don't get why a girl like Angela goes out with someone like Floyd,' said Darren. 'Look, I've got nothing against Floyd, but he's a criminal, isn't he? Why is it always the crims have these amazing girlfriends?'

'Money,' said Curl.

'Yeah, I suppose.'

'Nah, it's because they get off on it,' said Troy. 'They pretend they don't like it, but they love it.'

'You reckon?'

'Yep. I know for a fact that Floyd knocks over places for stuff for Angela. Jewellery, perfume, whatever. She knows where it comes from. It's a turn-on.'

'I don't know about that,' said Darren. He shook his head. 'I just don't get it.'

A security guard came through the door from the bistro and talked to the bartender, both of them watching the Maoris. He was enormously fat, his epauletted shirt straining at the buttons, his belly slumping over his belt. His face glistened with sweat. He hitched up his pants and began walking over to the group on the barstools, but then hesitated, looking around. He changed direction and walked over to the boys' table.

'IDs,' he said.

'What?' said Darren. 'Are you serious?'

Curl and Troy pulled out their driver's licences and put them on the table by the beer-soaked coasters.

'I left mine at home,' said Darren. 'I didn't even think of it.'

'If you don't have ID then you have to leave,' said the security guard.

'Come on,' said Darren. 'I've been coming here for years. Besides,' he said, pointing at the Maoris. 'They're the ones causing all the trouble. Why don't you go hassle them? We weren't doing anything.'

'Either you show me some ID or you're out.'

'Ask Angela,' said Darren. 'She'll vouch for me.' He swore under his breath.

The security guard gestured to Angela, who was wiping down the counter, watching them. She came over.

'He says you'll vouch for him,' the security guard said to her.

'Yeah,' she said. 'That's fine.'

'You'll vouch for him?'

'Yes,' said Angela, irritated.

'What about this one?' the security guard asked, pointing at Roland.

'She doesn't know him,' said Darren. 'But he isn't drinking alcohol, anyway.'

'So he's underage.'

'Yeah, but he's drinking Coke, so it doesn't matter.'

The security guard straightened his back and hitched up his pants again.

'How do I know that's not a rum and Coke, or a vodka and Coke?'

'Taste it,' said Darren.

He picked up the glass and held it out to the security guard, who glanced over at the Maoris and the hardened drinkers at the next table. Roland could hear the song 'Holiday' start up in the bistro, women crying out happily as they rushed onto the dance floor. The bright lights made halos of their teased hair.

'He goes or you're all barred,' said the security guard.

'All right,' said Darren, standing up. 'Fuck you, then.'

'Hey,' said the security guard. He pointed a finger at Darren, who ignored him.

'See you later, Angela,' Darren said.

'See you.'

Troy and Curl skolled their beers and, in one casual movement, Troy put down his pot and knocked over the jug. It spilled across the table and onto the floor and fizzed, the white suds popping as the boys walked away.

'Oh, come on,' Angela shouted after them. 'I've got to clean that up.'

Outside in the cold, Darren, Curl and Troy lit cigarettes and stood glaring at the security guard through the open doorway. Angela was cleaning the table, soaking up the beer with a tea towel. Some of the Maoris turned to look at them.

'Fat fuck,' Troy said, watching the security guard as he went behind the bar and through the swinging door to the bistro.

'What do you reckon now?' Curl asked Darren. 'Drive down to the Burvale?'

'The Burvale's full of Maoris,' said Darren. 'I'm sick of fucking Maoris.'

'You think they're going to come after us?' Troy asked, looking back into the pub.

'Nah, I don't reckon.'

An icy wind blew down the walkway. There were maiden-hair ferns growing in the planter boxes along the path, their fronds lit from below by small spotlights that cast them sharply against the blackness. The bouncer outside the bistro yawned and stamped his feet, while inside they played more Madonna. Darren zipped up his jacket and stood hunched over with his arms crossed, shivering, the cigarette dangling from his lips. Cars zoomed past on the highway.

'Pool hall?' Curl suggested.

'Yeah, it'll have to be.'

Curl took off the Jim Beam T-shirt and threw it out the window as they drove along the highway towards Nunawading. It flared out in the air for a moment and then fell lifeless onto the road, disappearing as they sped along, the white lane-markers incandescent before them and the median strip sallow under the streetlights. Reg Noble's smug face looked down at them from the illuminated sign above the car yard. It loomed gigantic over the silent floodlit ranks of cars, their windows beaded with dew in the clear cold night. Troy turned off at a side street by the closed Skate Ranch and drove into a carpark behind a warehouse.

Two lit doorways opened onto the carpark. Through the first was a weights room, the clanging of dropped iron and the grunts of bodybuilders carrying into the night as they waddled about, girt by thick belts, and flexed their muscles before the mirrored walls. An AC/DC tape played on the ghetto-blaster sitting on the floor by the squat rack. The boys paused as they passed the doorway, watching as a man with spiky peroxided hair tried to bench press a barbell massed with concrete plates. Another man in a yellow fluoro singlet stood behind the bench, his hands hovering over the bar.

'Come on, come on,' he shouted as the other man strained. 'You can do it.'

The man's arms bulged and the veins on his neck popped out as he pushed the barbell off his chest. He let out a roar.

Troy turned away, unimpressed.

'Those guys might be big,' he told Roland. 'But they can't fight for shit. They're slow as. As long as they don't grab you, you're all right.'

They went through the other door into a room crowded with pool tables. Green-shaded lights hung down on chains from the warehouse rafters, islands of illumination that turned the baize a vivid jade. The players stood with their cues, beer bottles on the wood, their voices murmuring over the clicking and clattering of the balls. The crash of weights from next door sounded through the plasterboard. Troy and Curl went to the counter and came back with a tray of balls and some stubbies. Curl handed one of them to Roland.

'They don't care here,' he said.

One of the lights went on towards the back of the hall. Troy went to the table and set up the balls, while Curl, Darren and

Roland picked cues from the rack along the wall.

'You see Belinda and that over there?' Curl said to Darren, nodding at a group of girls. One of them was leaning over the baize as she lined up a shot, the cuffs of her embroidered denim jacket turned up.

'Yeah, I see them,' said Darren.

They were standing close together, pretending not to look. Curl twirled his cue ruminatively.

'I don't reckon we're going to do much better than that tonight,' he said.

'Yeah. I know.'

They joined Troy at the table.

'Belinda's over there,' Troy said.

'Yeah, we know.'

They began to play. It was Darren and Roland against Troy and Curl. Darren broke.

'Let them come over here,' he said to Troy, who kept glancing at the girls.

A man in a black leather jacket went to the jukebox and put on 'Bad to the Bone'. As the opening guitar riffs twanged, he swaggered back to his friends, who nodded their heads and thrust their chests out as they gulped down their beers. Troy mouthed the words of the song as he took his shot. The girl in the denim jacket came over.

'How are you guys?' she asked.

'Yeah, all right, Belinda,' said Darren. He was walking around the table, his eyes fixed on the balls.

'How's your night going?'

'Shithouse. Fucked.'

'Yeah,' she said. 'Us too. We were thinking of going over to the bar and bistro. You guys want to come?'

'We were just there,' said Darren. 'That fat security guard kicked us out.'

'Why?'

'Because he's a prick.'

'Anything happening there?'

'Nah, it was dead.'

He took his shot and the balls crashed around the table.

'How about we go to the drive-thru and get some beers and go back to your joint?' Troy said to Darren.

'Yeah, we could do that,' said Darren. 'I got a fire going there up back,' he said to Belinda. 'If you want to come along. Sit around the fire. Have a few drinks.'

'I'll check with the girls,' said Belinda. She went back to her friends. There was a rapid conversation, the girls glancing over, and Belinda came back.

'Yeah, all right,' she said. 'We'll meet you outside.'

Darren, Troy and Curl watched the girls leave, eyes fixed on the jostle of their buttocks in the tight Fabergé jeans they all wore. They put their pool cues down on the table and skolled their beers.

'You going to drink that?' Troy asked Roland, who had only sipped a little of his.

'Give it here,' Troy said. He skolled it.

'All right there, Troy?' Darren said.

'Yep,' said Troy. 'Let's go.'

The girls were standing in a huddle in the carpark; their voices dropped to whispers as the boys approached. They looked up at them warily.

'We need to drop Janet off on the way,' said Belinda.

'We'll follow you,' Darren said. They walked to the Torana.

'Is Janet the fat one?' Troy asked Curl, lowering his voice.

'Yep,' said Curl.

'Good,' said Troy.

'You know anything about that redhead?' Darren asked Curl.

'I think her name's Jennifer,' said Curl. 'Some friend of Belinda's. Or her cousin or something.'

'She's all right, don't you reckon?' Darren said to Curl. Curl shrugged. 'Yeah, she's not bad,' he said. They opened the doors of the Torana and stood watching the girls as they finished talking outside their car. Belinda trotted over.

'I'll come with you guys,' she said.

They followed the girls' car along the highway and then through a series of small quiet streets of brick veneer houses, their black aerials tilting at the stars. Inside a garage, a man was bent over the open bonnet of his car, a dazzling white work-light throwing stark shadows against the wall and the array of tools hung on the plasterboard. Sitting between Roland and Curl, Belinda straightened her headband and adjusted the angle of the bow. Each of her nails was painted a different neon colour.

'So how are you anyway?' she asked Curl.

'Yeah,' Curl said. 'Yeah, I'm all right.'

Ahead of them, the girls' car slowed and stopped and Janet got out. She stood talking to the other girls through an open window before crossing the road, her handbag hanging from the crook of her arm. She shone for a moment in the streaming headlights. Belinda opened the window on Curl's side and leaned out, waving.

'Bye Janet,' she said. 'I'll call you tomorrow.'

Janet waved back. They watched her disappear into the darkness of the driveway and come up to the lit portico, where she waved again before going inside. Belinda wound the window back up, pressing against Curl. The girls' car moved again and they followed its tail-lights, the exhaust fumes thick and rising in the cold.

The night was bright, the drifting clouds frayed by the moon, and the embers of the fire still glowed in the backyard. Darren wheeled the Triumph out of the shed and showed it to the girls, the chrome parts catching the moonlight and glinting silvery and mysterious in the darkness. The boys broke up some sticks and threw them on the fire as the girls stood watching, shivering and hugging themselves. Once it was blazing, they sat down on the logs.

Darren sat with Jennifer, the redhead, and Curl sat with Belinda. The other girls, Shelley and Melissa, stood looking around awkwardly and then sat down next to each other. Roland and Troy took another of the logs. Troy had gone silent, smoking steadily with his head down, his eyes fixed on the ground. Darren handed him a beer and he skolled it right away.

'Can you get us some glasses?' Belinda asked Darren, who grabbed hold of the paper bag at her feet and dragged it towards him. He peered inside.

'What's this?' he asked, taking out one of the bottles. It glowed green in the firelight.

'It's like this fake Midori,' she said. 'The other one's fake Malibu. And lemonade.'

'And you're going to drink that?'

'Yeah,' she said. 'They're really nice together. You guys should try it.'

Darren went into the house and came back clutching a number of washed Vegemite jars with peeling labels to his chest. They tinkled as he put them down.

'You going to have some of this stuff, Curl?' he asked.

'Nah,' said Curl, holding up his beer can.

'I'll have some,' said Troy.

'What about you, Roly? You want to try some of this crap?'

'Okay,' said Roland.

Belinda placed the glasses at her feet and mixed the drinks. Darren handed them around. Roland tasted the cloudy green liquid. It was sweet and strong and it warmed his stomach. Troy swallowed his down in one gulp and got another beer.

'All right,' said Darren, sitting down next to Jennifer. 'We're set.'

There was a long silence. Everyone stared at the fire.

'So, how do you guys know Belinda?' Jennifer asked Darren.

'From school,' Darren said. 'Glenella North High. A long time ago.'

'And me and Shelley,' said Melissa.

'Yeah, I know. You and Shelley and Belinda. Me and Troy and Curl. But we left after fourth form.'

'Did you go to tech then or something?' Jennifer asked.

'No way,' said Darren. 'Troy went to Box Hill Tech for about a year. But then he saw the good life me and Curl were living.'

'So, you're living the good life, are you?' she asked with a smile.

'Fucking oath we are,' said Darren. He touched Jennifer's scarf, rubbing the material between his fingers. She giggled as he pulled her closer.

'So what do you do then exactly?' she asked him.

'Whatever we want,' said Darren.

'Yeah?' she said. 'Really? You mean you're on the dole?'

'No way I'm going to live my life with some prick telling me what to do.'

'There are no jobs anywhere,' Belinda said from the other

side of the fire, where she was flirting with Curl, poking him in the stomach whenever he took a drink. He poked her back and tickled her with one hand, the other still holding the can to his mouth.

'Yeah, but it's not because of that. I'm never going to work,' Darren said.

'You have to get a job sometime,' said Belinda.

'Why?' Darren asked, leaning back on the log, his eyes flashing with sudden anger.

'I don't know. Because that's what people do. You just have to.'

'Yeah, and my old man worked every day of his life and where did that get him?' said Darren. 'Didn't get him anywhere. Put him in the ground. Gets lung cancer from the asbestos on some demolition job he did twenty years ago. Never smoked a cigarette in his life.'

He picked up his stoking pipe and vigorously raked the embers. They sparked up into the air and drifted bright in the darkness before fading to nothing. The sharp ridges of his jaw protruded in the glow, his cheeks mottled by the sudden warmth as he bent over the fire.

'So what's the point of that?' he said. 'You're meant to get up and work every day of your life just so you can maybe, if you're lucky, make it to retirement? And then what? Play lawn bowls until you die or something? Fuck that. No way. I'm not doing it. Not me.'

Troy finished his beer and stood up and went over to the slab. He tore off another tinnie and sat down next to Shelley without saying a word or even looking at her. He stared at his feet. Melissa got up, brushing down her jeans. She sat next to Roland.

'How are you?' she asked him.

'Good,' he said. He took a gulp of his drink. There was something intimate about the quivering circle of light cast by the fire, the rest of the world banished to the darkness and the cold. The alcohol had relaxed him and it made everything seem pleasant and slow-moving and strangely lucid. The air felt soft. Melissa peered at him from out of the veil of dark hair that cascaded down the sides of her face. It was curly, coarse-looking. Her cheeks were pitted with acne scars, covered by a thick layer of foundation that looked orange in the firelight. It reached to her neck, a clear line where it met the natural freckled paleness of her skin. Roland liked her smile, the way it trickled out of her eyes. She's pretty, he thought to himself. He hadn't thought so before, in that draughty pool hall, everyone's faces slightly ghoulish under those green-shaded fluorescent lights. But she was pretty when she smiled. He tried to think of something to say, but his mind had gone blank. He moved his leg, rubbing it where the heat of the fire had made the denim scalding. Melissa seemed to look at him for a long time before turning back to the others with a sudden alert expression on her face.

'So how long have you been living here?' Belinda asked Darren. She was snuggled up against Curl, her head against his chest and his big arms around her. Their legs were entwined.

'Since the start of the year.'

'So not long, then.'

'No.'

'It's nice,' she said, looking around. The trees were dark against the stars, waving in the breeze. The white limbs of the ghost gum swept over them like a nakedness.

'Yeah, its all right, but I'm thinking of moving down to Rosebud with my sister and her family,' said Darren.

'Do they have a house there?'

'Yeah. My mum gave them the money for it after my dad died. She got this big payout and she'd already sold the house in Glenella North, so they bought the place down there. They're going to build a granny flat for my mum to live in. She doesn't want to move yet, so I thought maybe I might go and live with them for a while. My brother-in-law Brendan's got a boat, which'd be pretty cool. You know, take it out now and then. Go for a swim every day, lie on the beach. Take it easy.'

'So why did your mum leave Glenella North?'

'Dunno. She's always wanted to live around here, though. Likes this area. 'Cause it's posh, I suppose.'

'I'm thinking of moving up to Queensland,' said Belinda, taking hold of Curl's arm and pulling it tighter around her.

'Bullshit,' said Darren. 'No, you're not.'

'I might.'

'What are you going to do there?'

'Might try and find work in one of the resorts.'

'Weren't you going to hairdressing school or something?'

'I dropped out of that ages ago.'

'You're never going to do that, though,' said Darren. 'You're never really going to move to Queensland.'

'We'll see.'

Darren looked at her through the smoke and the flames.

'You serious?'

'Maybe.'

She leaned back against Curl's chest and reached up to touch his face, running her fingers over his pale stubble.

Melissa turned to Roland again.

'I like your cap,' she said breathlessly. 'Jim Beam. That's cool.'

Darren and Curl laughed.

'What?' asked Melissa. 'What's funny? You guys. What's the joke?'

She turned to Roland. 'What's so funny?' she asked him.

'Curl won it,' he said. He told her about the wheel and the Jim Beam girls, relieved to finally have something to say to her.

'It's still a cool cap,' she told him. 'Can I try it on?'

'Sure,' he said.

She took the cap off his head and put it on, pressing her leg against him. Her breasts brushed his arm.

'How do I look?' she asked.

'Good,' Roland said. 'It suits you.'

'Yeah?' she said, pulling the peak down low over her eyes and grinning at him. 'Can I keep it?'

'It's yours.'

'I'm just joking.' She took it off and put it back on Roland's head, straightening it and smoothing down the sides.

Darren was playing with Jennifer's hair, curling it with his finger and then letting it go. She was lying against him with her head back.

'Ow,' she said.

Darren talked to her in a murmur, his mouth close to her ear. On the other log, Curl and Belinda began kissing. They got up and walked to the girls' car, holding hands. Troy turned abruptly to Shelley.

'You want to go to my car?' he asked her.

She nodded, stood up and followed him in the direction of the Torana. Darren also stood up.

'Come and help me with something, will you, Roly,' he said. 'You girls mind if we leave you for a moment?'

Jennifer pouted. 'Don't be long,' she said.

Roland followed Darren into the house and through the laundry to his room in the fibro lean-to. It was narrow and sparsely furnished: a rack of clothes in the corner, a chest of drawers and a bed with a bare mattress, a sleeping bag scrunched up against the wall. The small electric bar heater was turned off and the room was frigid and slightly damp. The walls were papered with pictures of girls, torn from magazines. Most were naked, straddling motorcycles or lying across the bonnets of sports cars; others were in bikinis and lingerie, posing with their hips cocked, their breasts and buttocks thrust out, throwing smouldering looks at the camera. One girl was getting out of a pool, water cascading off her bare breasts.

'If you're going to fuck Melissa, you're going to want to use one of these,' Darren said, taking a pack of condoms out of a drawer.

He handed Roland a couple.

'Otherwise your dick's going to fall off.'

They went back outside. Jennifer was standing by the door and went in with Darren, passing Roland without looking at him. He was vaguely aware of the shadows behind the fogged windows of the Torana and the girls' car, parked one behind the other in the driveway. The suspension creaked in the quiet. Melissa was a lone figure sitting by the fire, the light dancing across her face. She seemed hypnotised by the flames, and it was not until he was close that she looked up at him and smiled. She took his hand and they went into the dark lane, stopping and kissing against Darren's neighbour's fence. An automatic light switched on behind them, revealing the brickwork of a barbeque area. Roland was surprised by the way Melissa pushed her lips hard against his, the wetness of her mouth, the darting and rolling of her tongue. He could taste her lipstick and acne cream, cigarettes and the hotness of the alcohol. She smelled of shampoo and fabric softener. It was the first time he had kissed a girl, and he worried that he wasn't doing it right.

Melissa slid a hand into his jeans and took hold of his penis.

'Are you feeling horny?' she asked him, rubbing it. Her hand was very cold. They continued to kiss, and he reached underneath her jumper, feeling the silkiness of her skin, the slenderness of her waist. She flinched at his frozen touch, laughing, and pressed against him. The automatic light went off and clicked on again almost immediately with the breeze and the movement of the branches.

'Are you not into this?' Melissa asked him.

'Not really,' he said.

'That's all right. That's cool.'

They walked down to the end of the lane and along Oleander Street under the canopy of rustling trees, the streetlights winking through the swaying foliage. Vaporous clouds drifted beneath the stars and possums crawled through the branches, cracking twigs, their long rattling snarls shredding the silence. A dog barked nearby and others replied in the distance before falling quiet again. Cars dripped with dew, blinded with tarps as they sat in the driveways. The naturestrips were hoary with frost. Melissa and Roland walked with their arms around each other's waists.

'How old are you anyway?' she asked him.

'Fourteen,' he said.

'Really?' she said, screwing up her nose. 'I didn't know you were *that* young. You talk like you're much older. You talk like you could be thirty or something.'

They went down Creek Road, over the bridge, and crossed the vast whiteness of the rimy park, the frost crunching under their feet. At the children's playground, they sat on the swings, first brushing the icy condensation off the seats. It was dark, the nearest streetlight shrouded by a willow. Their breath was visible as they talked.

'Darren and that think I'm a real slut, don't they?' Melissa said, holding on to the chains of the swing and pushing it back. She lifted herself until she was standing on her toes.

'No,' Roland said. 'They don't think that at all.'

'Really? I thought they did. I thought they all thought that.'

'No, I promise. They don't.'

She sat back down on the swing, pulling up her legs and soaring forwards. Roland watched as she gained momentum, rising up and up. She stopped the swing with her feet, sliding through the muddy furrows, and looked at him. Her hands still gripped the chains.

'You seem like a really nice guy, Roly,' she said. 'You remind me of my brother when he was your age. He used to be just like you. Really sweet and polite. But now he's using heroin. I'm worried that he's going to die.'

She told him about her brother and the rest of her family. They had all been so close when she was little, she said. But then her parents separated, her father moved in with his new girlfriend and her brother went off the rails with alcohol and drugs. Everything seemed to be falling apart and she felt like she was the only one who actually cared about what was happening; everyone else was so busy doing their own thing that they barely seemed to notice. Sometimes, she said, she just lay on her bed and cried.

They talked about other things and then walked back up to Darren's house, which was in darkness. The Torana was gone and the girls' car was now parked on the street. The engine started as Roland and Melissa approached; the headlights turned on and flashed twice on high beam and the wipers swept across the windscreen. Through the streaked glass, the inside of the car seemed as though underwater. Belinda was talking to Shelley, her embroidered jacket lying over her chest like a blanket, their faces bruised with tiredness. Jennifer was fast asleep across the back seat, her legs tucked up on the upholstery. Belinda leaned back and tapped her and she sat up, sweeping her hair off her face and blinking groggily.

Melissa and Roland kissed before she got into the car. It was a long, lingering kiss, almost passionate. They held each other very tight.

'Bye,' she whispered, opening the door.

Roland waved as the car pulled out from the kerb. Melissa waved back. Belinda honked the horn and it seemed very loud in the darkness and the quiet of the frozen night.

WHEN HE FINALLY went to bed, Roland's sleep was restless and full of dreams. Fast-moving, they teemed with people and voices, faces lit by firelight. He dreamed of Melissa, of kissing her and touching her, and there was no hesitation, no uncertainty, as there had been in that icy laneway, only bodies and the pleasure of it. It was all so vivid, so familiar, that when he woke he imagined for a moment that he was not alone.

The day outside was umbrous and still, without colour. It seemed bereft of life. Roland found himself listening for the sound of the distant trains as though for proof of the world. He spent the morning staring at his schoolbooks, taking nothing in, and after lunch walked to Darren's house, where Darren, Troy and Curl were sitting by the embers of the fire. Troy watched as he came down the footpath.

'Well?' he asked. 'You get your end in?'

Seeing Roland's hesitancy, his face darkened.

'You're shitting me,' he said.

Darren was smoking a joint. He took a toke and handed it to Curl.

'Yeah, well, so what,' he said to Troy, his voice straining as he held the smoke in his lungs. 'He doesn't have to do anything he doesn't want to do.'

'Oh, come on,' said Troy. 'If that was me or Curl, you'd be the one paying us out. You would give us so much shit.'

'Well, maybe Roly can do better.'

'Oh, you reckon, do you?'

'Yeah, I do. Give him a couple of years. You know, just fucking chill out and let him take his own time. Do his own thing.'

'Jesus Christ, Darren. When did you start talking like that?'

Troy shook his head sourly, his eyes flitting menacingly from Darren to Roland. Darren returned the stare.

'Yeah, 'cause you're a real ladies man, aren't you, Troy? They're all queuing up for you, mate.'

Curl, who had been holding in a lungful of smoke, let it out in a wheeze of laughter and started coughing. He handed the joint to Troy.

'Fuck you,' said Troy, scowling at the ground. He took the joint. 'Fuck youse all.'

They started to talk about other things. Roland held his hands out to the coals and felt the warmth on them. There was a solace in the voices around him, protection against the deadness and loneliness he had been feeling all day. He waited for the conversation to return to the subject of the previous night, but it did not. He wanted to know more about Melissa and her friends, to hear stories about them: what they were like at school, about their families, other friends. He found himself imagining that someone would suggest going to find them on that drowsy afternoon, returning to the pool hall or to the streets of brick veneers where they had dropped off their friend Janet, where, he imagined, they all lived and were now all gathered together, as he and his friends were, sitting cross-legged in someone's bedroom or standing outside talking in the fresh weekend air, the pale winter sunshine, as loath to leave one another as as he was to leave his own friends. He wondered how Darren and Troy and Curl could sit there in the same way they did every day—talking carelessly, joking, yawning, making another thin joint out of the last fragments of bud and leaf dust at the bottom of the deal bag—unaffected, it seemed, by the events of the previous night. As he walked home in the crepuscular chill, the empty afternoon streets, the winter flowers vivid in the dying light, he felt sad again. He felt like crying.

DARREN REMAINED STEADFAST in his decision not to go to any more nightclubs. He now stayed by the fire, immovable, his motorcycle on the grass behind him, and would get up only to fetch a log from the rotting pile stacked against the fence in the lane, dumped there years ago when George Kyriakides hired a tree lopper to take out one of the giant eucalypts. Roland started to join him and Troy and Curl on Friday and Saturday nights, when Darren would build huge roaring fires that licked the sky and burst and crackled and lit up their faces as they talked, their shadows sent squalling across the backyard. The older boys drank beer and smoked marijuana, making bongs from plastic soft-drink bottles, lengths of garden hose and cones made of aluminium foil. They were all quiet, thoughtful, slightly maudlin drunks, wistfully recalling their school days and falling into silence when they were stoned. Floyd started to appear more frequently, although he neither drank nor did drugs. He needed, he told Roland, to stay alert at all times.

'Don't get high on your own supply,' he advised him.

There was a noticeable increase in traffic. Dark figures started to stalk the footpaths, stopping by the post box across the road until Floyd went out to them. There was a covert, almost wordless exchange of drugs and money, and when Floyd came back with the palmed banknotes, he would unfold them in the firelight. Cars crawled down the street and stopped outside the house, their engines rumbling, brake lights glowing and exhaust fumes billowing white in the cold air. Sometimes there were so many that they formed a queue along the kerb as Floyd got into each one and sat for a moment in the passenger seat before he strolled down to the next waiting car.

'Hey, Floyd,' Darren said one night. 'Are you using my place to deal out of?'

Floyd laughed.

'No, I mean, are you telling them to come here? Are you giving my address out to people?'

'Nah,' said Floyd. 'They just find me. They'll drive around all night looking for me if they have to.'

The police also made themselves known: patrol cars and divvy vans came down the road, often doubling back and slowing as they passed. Sometimes they parked in places where the fire was visible from the street and sat there watching the boys for hours. Floyd could identify a police car by its engine noise, picking them from among the other distant sounds of traffic. The big souped-up V8 engines of the police cars had a certain rumbling tone, he said, unlike any other car. While they were sitting there, the street quiet, he would look up, listening.

'Cops,' he would say.

Some minutes later the car or divvy van would come past, or an unmarked car, which could be identified from its three aerials, Floyd told Roland, pointing out the large radio antenna on the roof of one, a silhouette against the cloud cover.

One night, a police car pulled into the lane and stopped. Two policemen got out: a burly, moustached senior constable and a fresh-faced probationary, a big boy who towered over his superior, arms bulging in his tight acrylic jumper. They came down the lane, their duty belts jingling, radios crackling, the moonlight glinting off their handcuffs and the slickness of their batons. A bright light shone onto Darren's face.

'Jesus,' he said, holding his hands over his face and turning away.

The senior constable held the torch up over his shoulder, shining it downwards, the light flicking to each of the boys' faces. When it came to Roland, he was blinded and turned away, instinctively holding his hands out in the same way Darren had done. The light seemed to linger on him longer than on the others before moving on to Floyd.

'Hello, Floyd,' said the senior constable. 'I thought you were in Pentridge.'

'No,' said Floyd, shifting, annoyed.

'Well, you'll be there soon enough, won't you?'

Floyd shrugged.

'What did I get you for?' the senior constable asked. 'Was it vehicle theft?'

'No,' said Floyd contemptuously. 'I've never been arrested for vehicle theft.'

'What was it then?'

'I don't know. Look it up.'

'Was it breaking and entering?'

'It's your job to remember these things, mate. Not mine.'

'Oh, is that right, is it?'

'Yeah. That is right.'

'You think you're going to come out of Pentridge as cocky as that?'

'I don't care.'

'Well, you should care. You know what they do to young boys like you in Pentridge, don't you, Floyd?'

'Bullshit.'

'You'll find out. You'll find out very soon.'

The torch turned off.

'Right, so the rest of you can give me your names,' said the senior constable. The young policeman was stretching his neck, looking at the boys with bored disinterest. He leaned over and spat into the darkness before taking out his notebook.

'We don't have to give you our names,' said Darren.

'Is that right?' asked the senior constable, turning the torch on him. Darren flinched again in the light, turning away and swearing under his breath. 'Where did you get that idea?'

'It's the law,' said Darren. 'Besides, we're on private property. You can't talk to us without a warrant.'

'We've got a bush lawyer here,' the senior constable said to the younger policeman, who said nothing, staring at the boys coldly. Their radios hissed and babbled and clicked back into silence. 'You know what that is?' the senior constable asked Darren.

'No.'

'It's someone who knows a little bit about everything and not much about anything.'

The light moved and Roland was blinded again.

'How old are you, Sunshine?' the senior constable asked him.

'Fourteen.'

'You want to end up like your mates here, do you?'

'Don't answer him, Roly,' Darren said. 'You don't have to talk to him.'

The light shone back on Darren's face and then turned off. The senior constable muttered something to the probationary and they started walking back to the car, their feet crunching on the leaves and twigs.

'Fuck off then,' Darren said quietly.

The footsteps stopped and then came swiftly back up the lane. Even in the dark, Roland could see the fury on the senior constable's face, his mouth twisted into a snarl. They marched around the fence and into the backyard. The senior constable walked up to Darren, his shaved head glimmering in the warm pulse of the firelight.

'What was that, cunt lips?' he shouted, aiming the torch in Darren's face. 'What did you say to me?'

Darren seemed to wither. He shied away from the light.

'Nothing,' he said. 'I was talking to my friends.'

The senior constable turned off his torch and put it back in the holster in his belt. He took out his baton.

'Stand up!' he yelled.

'Hey, you can't do this,' said Troy. 'This is his property.'

The policeman turned, pointing the baton at Troy.

'You want some of this too?' he yelled. 'Because there's plenty to go round.'

He whacked the back of Darren's chair with the baton.

'You going to just sit there, or you going to stand up and take it like a man?' he growled.

Darren stood up and the senior constable thrust the baton hard into his solar plexus. Darren made an *umph* sound and bent over, gasping. The policeman walked around him and hit him hard across the back of his knees and Darren fell heavily onto the dirt.

'I hope I see you out there one day, mate,' the policeman said to Darren, pointing the baton down at him. 'I'm looking forward to it. Because when I see you out on the street, I'm going to pick you up and I'm going to take you down one of these lanes and I'm going to shove this *fucking baton* up your *fucking arse*. You are going to be shitting blood. You understand?'

He bent over and thumped Darren across the back.

'You understand?' he yelled, raising the baton up over his shoulder again.

Darren nodded, coughing.

'Yes,' he gasped.

The senior constable straightened up and put the baton back on his belt.

'Not such a smartarse now, are you?' he said.

When Floyd wasn't at Darren's, his customers waited on the footpath under the streetlight, casting surreptitious glances in the direction of the boys around the fire. They hugged themselves in the cold, their heads bowed, before sliding off into the shadows, the ember tips of their cigarettes streaking the darkness. The cars sat briefly at the kerb before moving off. They never actually approached the backyard, until one night, when a hulking boy named Liam came through the carport, flanked by a group of younger boys with the quick eyes and giddy excitability of animals escaped from a menagerie. They could be heard from a distance as they swaggered down the lane, howling like wolves as they jostled each other and kicked the fences. One boy yanked at Tilly Johnson's letterbox, trying to wrench it off its base.

'Floyd around?' Liam asked as he stepped into the aura of the fire.

'Nah,' said Darren. 'Haven't seen him tonight.'

Liam sniffed and spat and sat down on one of the logs. He had heavy features and black hair cropped close to his skull on the top; the long locks at the back lay flat against his neck. His eyes were large, almost beautiful, and impassive as a shark's. The other, smaller boys crowded around him like a troop of monkeys.

'Yeah, I don't know whether he's going to show at this stage,' Darren said. 'It's getting pretty late.'

'That's all right,' said Liam. 'We'll wait.'

He reached out and took one of the cans of Victoria Bitter from the six-pack at Darren's feet, twisting it off the plastic rings.

'You mind if I have one of these?' he asked, an afterthought, his thumb already prying the stay-tab.

'Yeah, sure,' said Darren. 'Help yourself.'

The can opened with a hiss that was loud in the silence. Liam swigged from it and put it on the ground, shaking the froth from his hand. He wore a blue nylon bomber jacket with bright orange lining, his jeans rolled up to reveal a pair of tightly laced GP army boots. A silver claw-shaped earring dangled and flashed in the firelight.

'What have youse been doing tonight?' Troy asked him.

Liam took a soft pack of Marlboro out of his pocket, shook one out and held his hand up for a lighter, which one of the younger boys produced. He cupped his hands around the cigarette and lit it.

'Poofter bashing,' he said, handing the lighter back to the boy.

'Whereabouts?'

'Down at the footy oval. The toilets behind the stadium.'

'What, here?' Darren asked. 'In Glenella?'

'Yep,' said Liam, pointing towards the shops. 'Toilets behind the stadium. Toilets behind the library. Station toilets. We got a whole lot of poofters around here. And not ordinary ones either. These ones are prison poofters, a lot of them. Some tough bastards, too. This idiot'—he reached over and clipped a grinning Polynesian boy across the back of the head—'decides to go poofter bashing on his own one day, in the station toilets. This big bikie poofter gets his baseball bat off him. Had to run, didn't you? The other ones are family men, if you can believe that. I don't know where from. Probably round here or something.'

His dark eyes settled on Roland.

'Probably your old man down there,' he said to him.

'Hey, go easy,' said Darren.

'I'm just joking,' said Liam, although he did not smile. He took a drag of his cigarette and then turned back to Roland.

'Because if it was your old man,' he said. 'You'd know about it. Because I would hurt him.'

'You ever get anything off them?' Troy asked Liam.

'Yeah, we get watches, jewellery. I got a decent leather jacket once. Got it dry-cleaned but still didn't want to put it on, you know. Who knows where it's been. Got this—'

He took his keys out, pulling at the long chain that hung in a loop from his jeans pocket, and showed them a gold wedding band attached to the keyring.

'Got this off the first poofter I ever bashed. I said, "You don't deserve this," and then, bam. Stomped his head.'

He demonstrated, lifting up his boot with its heavy lug sole and pounding it on the ground.

'So what do you do with all this stuff?' Troy asked him.

'Sell it. Pawn shop. You boys are welcome to come along if you want. Anytime. I got a boot full of baseball bats back there.'

'Yeah?' Troy said, looking around at Darren and Curl. 'Yeah, maybe.'

Liam and the boys sat with them until past midnight.

'I don't like that guy,' Darren said after they left.

'I don't know,' said Troy. 'Liam's all right.'

'See him just take a beer like that?' Darren said.

'Was a bit cheeky, wasn't it?' said Curl.

'Fucking Floyd,' Darren muttered, and lit a cigarette.

Liam began to turn up nearly every weekend, always with a group of younger boys, although the group seemed to change each time. When Floyd was there, they bought their deals and left; if he was not, they waited, never in any hurry to leave. Darren started to become irritated when they arrived.

'I don't know why you're always waiting for Floyd,' he said to Liam one night. 'You know there're other dealers around?'

'Yeah?' said Liam, opening a beer. 'Like who?'

'Like Moses, in Glenella North. You know Moses, don't you?'

'Moses isn't dealing anymore.'

'Why not?'

'Because he reckons the cops are watching him. Some kid ratted on him.'

'How does he know that?'

'Because his brother-in-law's a cop. Tipped him off.'

'Well, what about that girl who deals out of the back of that granny flat?'

Liam looked at Darren with a sneer.

'That cunt,' he said. 'Fuck off. I'm not buying from her.'

'She rip you off?' Troy asked him.

'Nah, didn't rip me off. Just don't like her.' Liam shook his head, his face twisted into an expression of disgust. 'Fucking bitch cunt.'

'Once we went over there,' said Troy. 'And she was having sex with some guy on the bed. There was probably at least four ounces spread across the table. In deal bags, but I reckon at least four, probably more. So, she's on top, fucking this guy, with her back to us. You know, really going at it. And Darren's standing by the table and I'm pointing at the gear, like, "Just take it." We could have, too. So easily. She wouldn't even have known who it was.'

'So why didn't you?' Liam asked Darren.

'You know,' said Darren. 'She's all right. She's been pretty cool with us. Given us some gear on tick and that.'

'Yeah, well. If that's how you want to live,' said Liam.

'What's that mean?'

'I mean, you got to take your opportunities, don't you?'

'Not if it means fucking someone over. You don't have to do that.'

'You don't fuck them over, they'll fuck you over. It's the law of the jungle, mate.'

'Nah,' said Darren, shaking his head. 'Nah, I don't believe that.'

IT WAS ONE of those still winter days, heavy with cloud. A Sunday. Roland, Darren and Troy walked to the Quix service station on the highway under a motionless, gunmetal sky. The shops and showrooms were shut, their wares eerie in the dim windows, the rows of bathroom sinks, lounge suites, mattresses, car tyres and kitchen benchtops as though abandoned, left in some apocalyptic rush. Inside the lighting warehouse, chandeliers of amber glass rippled with the passing boys' reflections. Traffic lights changed for no reason and pigeons nodded on the bitumen. Not a single car dipped over the rise of the road. Everything was deserted. The whole world seemed to have stopped.

'Look out,' said Troy, pointing to a group of boys in baseball caps and Nike sneakers as they came out of a side street on the other side of the highway.

They went into the Quix as the boys started to cross the

road. Darren and Troy stood on either side of the automatic doors and watched them approach through the bowsers. Troy swung at the first one who came in, hitting him in the jaw. The boy fell against one of the shelves and tipped it over, bottles of tomato sauce and jars of condiments smashing on the hard polyvinyl floor. The others turned and ran. The boy was out for a moment, lying spreadeagle among a cascade of chip packets before he leaped up and bolted out of the closing doors.

The service station fell quiet again. The radio behind the attendant, a flabby, unshaven man, seemed very loud. Roland followed Troy and Darren down the aisle and they looked out the window at the boys gathered on the footpath. Their hurt friend limped towards them across the petrol-stained concrete, his hand against his back. The boys stood about talking, peering back at the Quix, before walking to the intersection and out of sight.

'So what do you reckon?' Darren muttered to Troy.

'Probably going to try to jump us.'

'But if we stay here, you're going to get hassled by the cops,' said Darren. 'It's your call.'

Troy thought about it. 'Wait for the cops,' he said. 'They've probably got knives or something.'

They paced up and down the aisles, looking out the windows at the grey, desolate day. A small Renault drove in and an elderly man filled it at the bowsers. He wore a sky-blue suit and a trilby hat. A woman with pearly white hair sat in the passenger seat, holding her handbag on her lap. When the man came in to pay, he slipped on the pool of tomato sauce, which had been spreading across the floor by the collapsed shelf.

'What's this?' he asked the attendant, inspecting the soles of his shoes. He glanced at the fallen shelf and the mess in the aisle. The attendant said nothing.

'You going to clean this up?' Darren asked the attendant after the man had left.

'Not my job,' said the attendant, impassive. He closed the cash register and sat down again, crossing his arms. His candy-striped shirt was too small for him, revealing a white fold of belly beneath the hem. A tuft of golden chest hair sprouted through the gaps in the placket.

'Yeah, but you can't just leave it like this,' said Darren. 'Someone's going to hurt themselves.'

The attendant shifted on his chair, sniffing.

'Jesus,' said Darren.

'Hey, you called the cops?' Troy asked the attendant.

'Nope.'

Troy and Darren looked at each other.

'Why not?'

The attendant cleared his throat and looked out the window.

'What do you reckon?' Darren asked Troy. 'We can't stay in here all day. And they could go and get more guys and come back.'

Troy nodded. 'We should get some glass bottles, though,' he said.

They bought bottles of tonic water and emptied them into the grate between the bowsers. Holding them by their necks like clubs, they walked back up the empty highway, the three of them spread out across the road like gunslingers in a Western. Troy's gaze seemed even harder than usual, his jaw clenched. Darren scanned the fences. When they reached Hammond Street, at the top of the hill, they stopped and looked back towards the Quix. Darren snorted and grinned.

'Ah, well,' he said.

'Wonder what happened to them,' said Troy.

They walked down Hammond Street, past the bowls club, where old people in white flocked the lawns and sat in rows along the benches. Cars negotiated the tight spots in the packed carpark, screened by an undulating line of she-oaks. Behind, on the oval, a man was kicking a football to his son. He clapped and cheered as the boy caught the ball, the thud of the leather sounding with the slight delay of distance through the cold air. When they reached the bridge over the creek, Darren and Troy threw their bottles into the water.

'Give it here, Roly,' Darren said, taking Roland's bottle and tossing it over the rusted cyclone fence. Roland watched as it bobbed in the muddy water and floated towards the underground drain.

Only the milk bar was open down at the shops, chip packets and ice-cream wrappers and crushed soft-drink cans scattered along the graffitied lane. A stray Dalmatian sniffed about a bench and trotted down the footpath, its nose sweeping the ground. Sparrows and willy wagtails flounced about the bin. On the station lawns, a group of men stood around a pair of motorcycles, drinking out of tinnies wrapped in brown-paper bags. They were laughing uproariously at something. Cassie Noble sat cross-legged on the steps of the bank with two girls in hooded surfers' tops, smoking cigarettes.

'You girls got a couple of spare smokes there?' Darren asked them.

A girl wearing a necklace of cowrie shells handed him a packet of cigarettes. She was dark, with the sleek, starved look of a wild animal. Her wrist was lined with friendship bracelets, woven in rainbow-coloured stripes and chevron patterns.

'Cheers,' said Darren. He and Troy picked out cigarettes and lit up. One of the men on the grass nodded at Troy, who nodded back and raised his hand.

'What have you guys been doing?' Cassie asked them.

'Just got into a fight down at the Quix,' Darren said.

'Really?'

'Look at this,' said Troy. He showed the girls his bruised fist.

'Cool,' said Cassie.

'Guy went right down,' Troy told them. 'One punch.'

'Wow, that's cool,' said Cassie. She tapped her cigarette ash between her knees onto the concrete. 'That's awesome.'

The other girls were watching them in silence, their eyes grave.

'You girls enjoying your Sunday?' Darren asked them.

'It's all right,' said Cassie, making a face.

'Yeah? Sitting around taking it easy, are you?'

'Yeah,' she said. She ran her hand through her fringe. Roland could see her collarbone through the loose neck of her tracksuit top, the dipping hollow and the swell of her small shoulder. Her skin had a glow to it.

'There's Moses,' Troy said to Darren, pointing at a gangly bearded man as he came out of the station tunnel, talking to a skinhead.

'See youse later,' Darren said to the girls. 'Enjoy the rest of your afternoon.'

They wandered over to the group of men on the lawn, where Moses and the skinhead had joined them.

'How's it going?' Darren said to no one in particular.

Troy showed the men his fist.

'Just got into a fight down at the Quix,' he said. 'Dropped

a guy. One punch. The rest of them ran.'

'Who was it?' asked the skinhead.

'Kids in baseball caps and that,' said Troy. 'About six of them.'

'I hate them,' said the skinhead, spitting onto the grass.

'They're fucking everywhere, aren't they?' said Troy.

Moses was looking at the motorcycles, smoking a cigarette.

'Heard you got busted,' Darren said to him.

'Nah, not busted,' said Moses. 'Just ratted on. My brother-in-law told me I better keep my head down. So that's what I'm doing.'

He was wearing an old velour windcheater and a filthy pair of Dunlop Volleys. His hair was tied in a ponytail with a glittery pink scrunchie.

'Yeah, that Liam guy told me. You know him?'

'Yeah, I know him.'

'What do you think of him?'

Moses kicked at the tyre of the motorcycle. 'Yeah, he's all right.'

'He's buying off Floyd now.'

'Yeah?' said Moses. 'Yeah, I put some business Floyd's way.'

'Hey, it's not true all that shit Liam says about bashing fags down at the toilets behind the oval and that, is it? Robbing them and stuff. That's bullshit, isn't it?'

Moses shook his head, scratching at his wispy beard.

'Nah, it's not bullshit. Even the cops know about it. They nearly killed some guy the other night. Put him in hospital. He's on a machine and everything.'

'They know it was Liam and that?'

'Nah, but they're not really trying that hard to find out, you know. Been turning a blind eye to it up till now. There's cops go poofter bashing too, round here.'

'Hey, Darren,' said a man wearing dark wraparound sunglasses. 'Where's the Triumph?'

'Yeah,' said Darren. He rubbed his jaw, looking at the motorcycles. 'Yeah, I should've brought it down.'

Across the road, the girls got up and brushed off their jeans. Cassie waved goodbye to the others, who left in the direction of the level crossing. The men glanced at them in a lazy, appraising way, squinting in the satin light before returning to their conversations, tossing back locks of straggly, unwashed hair. Cassie crossed the road and stood hesitantly on the footpath by the grass, fiddling with the zip of her tracksuit top. Roland could see that Darren had noticed her, but Darren did not say anything and turned back to Moses, who was telling the story about the boy who ratted on him.

'I said to him,' said Moses, "You know what a rat is where I'm from? It's the lowest form of life there is." I said, "You know what some of these guys think I should do to you?" Because there were guys saying, "You got to kill him. It's the rules."'

'Yeah?' said Darren.

'Yeah, but I got a soft heart, don't I? I told him, "If I get busted and they put me inside for this, I'm going to send a guy around to your house to punch you in the head every day I'm there." I mean, that's fair enough, isn't it?'

Troy was still talking to the skinhead. The owner of the milk bar came out, the bell above the door tinkling. He stood by the rotating boards advertising Cornetto ice-creams and Four'N Twenty pies, looking up and down the empty street with his arms folded. He yawned and stretched, his neat beard tilted. The clouds cracked open and pale sunlight flooded the grass. Cassie looked up to face the warming rays, her eyes closed, her face illuminated and her hair golden in the light. The clouds moved and shadows returned. The milk bar owner went back inside again. The men chuckled, taking cans of Victoria Bitter out of the motorcycles' saddlebags. The man in the sunglasses handed one to Roland, wrapped in a wrinkled paper bag. Roland pretended to drink it, tipping back the can, although he was only wetting his mouth with the beer, the taste and smell of which had already come to remind him of slow and wistful days, such as this one was. Of fading afternoons. The chill in the dying light. He waited for Cassie to come over, but she did not.

SHE WAS WAITING for him at the station as he got off
the train the following afternoon, standing on the other side of
the gate with her schoolbag slung over her shoulder. Roland
showed the stationmaster his pass as the man reached up to
unhook the stopping-all-stations sign, his pale face smudged
with redness in the cold and the whistling wind. He nodded
and started sorting through the row of enamelled signs leaning
against the wall. Cassie was in her blazer and long winter dress,
white socks folded just below the knee.

'I saw you before, when I was waiting for the train,' she said
to Roland as they went down the ramp. 'You walked right past
me.'

'Did I? I mustn't have seen you.'

'Yeah, I know. It was like you were in a world of your own,'
Cassie said, her voice sing-song and echoing through the
dank concrete tunnel. Water was dripping from the ridges of

mortar segmenting the ceiling, forming pools in the crumbling bitumen floor. The children stepped around them. They walked up the lane beside the milk bar and through the carpark to Creek Road, Reg Noble's face watching them from the back windows.

'So are you friends with Darren Wilson now?' Cassie asked Roland.

'Yeah, we're pretty good friends.'

Cassie nodded. 'I thought you might be.'

A bus rumbled past, belching thick exhaust fumes as it went up the hill. It had been washed by the recent rains and its windows and fluted sides gleamed. A girl knocked on the glass and waved. Cassie waved back and turned to Roland, a loose tress flaring at her ear. She brushed it back.

'Hey, is it true what happened with that Todd guy? And that spastic friend of his? That they scratched up someone's car or something?'

'Yeah,' Roland said. 'Troy's car.'

'Yeah, because they were going around boasting about it to everyone.'

'Really?'

'Yeah. They're such idiots.'

'Where did you hear about that?'

'I don't know,' said Cassie. 'Just from people.'

When they came to the Nobles' house, Cassie invited Roland in. Colleen was lying across the couch in the living room, watching *Wheel of Fortune*. A half-drunk vodka and orange sat on the coffee table.

'Hi, Mum,' Cassie said as they came in.

Colleen replied in a blurred voice. On the screen, the wheel spun, music playing as the moustached host chattered. Smoke curled from the cigarette lying in the ashtray.

They got some Cokes out of the fridge and went up to Cassie's room. It was exactly as it had been last time Roland was there: immaculate, everything frilly and childish, that same powerful smell of lemon-scented washing detergent coming from the crisp, clean sheets on the freshly made bed. They sat on the carpet.

'What does Darren think of me anyway?' Cassie asked Roland.

'I don't know.'

'Hasn't he said anything about me?'

'All I can remember is that he told me you got really angry at him once.'

Cassie frowned. 'When?'

'After he told Lily off. When he told her to leave him alone.'

'Yeah, but that was ages ago. Hasn't he said anything else about me?'

'No. Not that I can remember.'

'Because I've sort of been bugging him,' said Cassie. 'I've been writing letters to him and leaving them in his letterbox. Just about stuff. About me. I sort of think, "Oh, I might write Darren a letter," and then I write one even if I don't have anything to say. I don't know why. And sometimes I go around to his house when I can't sleep. I tap on his window and wake him up and stuff. And I'm all sort of, "Hi, I can't sleep and I'm bored, what are you doing?"'

She was tracing patterns on her lap as she talked.

'I brought flowers over to him the other day. I just started picking flowers from everyone's gardens on my way home from school, and by the time I got to Darren's house I had this huge bunch of flowers, but all different flowers and bits of weeds and stuff. It was sort of a mess. So, anyway, I just walked into his backyard and handed them to him.'

Crimson spread across her cheeks as she glanced at Roland, her eyes sparkling. She buried her face in her hands and let out a single, muted shriek.

'This big messy bunch of flowers. From people's *gardens*. And his friends were all sitting there looking at me, probably thinking, "Who is this weirdo?" I was too embarrassed to say anything so I just sort of ran off. I think he thought I was completely crazy. I think that's what he thinks about me, that I'm just this weird crazy girl who's hassling him all the time. Which I am, I suppose.'

She took a sip of her Coke and uncrossed and recrossed her legs.

'I just really like him,' she said. 'I get all hyped up and overexcited. That's what my mum says all the time. She's always saying, "Cassie, you're overexcited, you need to calm down." I suppose she's right. I don't know. I go around to his place and I just talk and talk and talk. And, you know, Darren's always so cool and everything. I think I sort of freaked him out when I showed him my scars, though. Have I ever shown you my scars?'

'No.'

'Do you want to see them?'

'Okay.'

Cassie held out her arm, turning it, and showed Roland the crisscrossed rows of raised white lines along the inside.

'Cool,' said Roland.

She examined the scars, running her fingers over the pearlescent skin.

'I did them a while ago,' she said. 'I can show you the other ones, like the fresh ones, but you'll have to trust me.'

'Okay.'

She uncrossed her legs and hitched up her skirt, then gathered the material and rolled her leg over to reveal the fine red lines and pink welts down the creamy skin of her inner thighs, the freshest of them beaded with dark dry blood.

'When I was doing it on my arm, my mum said I was just doing it for attention,' said Cassie. 'So now I do it there, where no one can see it.'

She pulled her skirt back down, smoothing it over.

'I'm pretty fucked up,' she said, her eyes meeting his. She ran her finger along the carpet, picking at it.

'I don't know what Darren thinks of me now,' she said. 'What do you think?'

'I don't know,' said Roland.

'Do you think I would have scared him off or anything?'

Roland thought about it. 'I think what Darren's really good at is that he sort of understands other people. Sometimes, even if I don't say anything, he seems to know what I'm feeling anyway.'

Cassie's face lit up. 'Yes,' she said. 'That's what I think too. That's exactly what I think. Sometimes, when we're talking, I think, "Oh, he actually seems to get me." Like he really gets who I am and everything.'

She blushed furiously and remembered her Coke, gulping it down. They both stared at the floor in silence.

'Hey,' Cassie said finally. 'Do you want to do Valium and listen to some of my dad's records?'

'All right,' said Roland.

She left the room and came back with a portable record player and a pile of records, a slim box of Valium slipped into her blazer pocket. Roland saw Colleen's name on it.

'Won't your mum know?' he asked Cassie.

'She knows anyway,' said Cassie. 'My mum was the one who started giving them to me, to calm me down when I get over-excited and stuff. So now I just take them whenever.'

She sat back down on the floor and began flipping through the records.

'My dad got most of these when he was in the army in Vietnam,' she said. 'He was friends with this black American guy who used to get them from America. Whenever my dad went around to see him, he used to go, "Man, you got to dig this."'

Cassie did the accent, rosiness creeping across her cheeks again. She pulled out one of the records and showed it to Roland. It was a single by The Doors, 'Riders on the Storm'. Cassie traced her finger over the picture of Jim Morrison, who looked out at the camera from under a shock of thick hair, one hand outstretched and his fingers splayed in a gesture of supplication.

'I used to be so in love with Jim Morrison,' said Cassie. 'I actually used to write him letters as well. Like, a heap of them. And so then I went and asked this teacher at school about him. She's pretty cool. She's lived in America and everything. So I asked her if she knew how I could get Jim Morrison's address. And she said, "Oh, didn't you know, he's dead." And no joke, but I actually burst into tears right there. I'm *such* a dork.'

She put the album back in the pile and continued shuffling through them.

'Anyway, so apparently he died years ago. Before I was even born. He's buried in this cemetery in France, and all these people have written signs in the cemetery that say things like, "Jim is here" and "This way to Jim", with arrows showing the way to his grave, and people sit around and play his music and stuff. I'm going to go there one day. I've got it all planned out.'

She took out another album: Marvin Gaye's *What's Going On.*

'This one's my favourite when I'm on Valium,' she said to Roland, showing it to him. She took the blister pack out of the Valium box and pushed out six yellow tablets. She handed two to Roland and took four for herself.

'I've built up a tolerance,' she told him. 'Two used to be heaps for me, but now I just feel normal unless I take at least four.'

They swallowed them with the metallic dregs of their Cokes. Cassie turned off the lights and put the record on. There was laughter and voices, the wail of a saxophone and the throb of a bass guitar, a voice that was almost tearful. Lying on the carpet with the music playing, the two of them fell asleep like children.

ROLAND SAW DARREN and Cassie together for the first time a few weeks after that. He was walking home from the station up the lane towards Darren's house when he spied them coming the other way through the fringe of overhanging branches. They were walking slowly, their arms around one another, too absorbed to notice him as he approached. When they did see him, they dropped their arms.

'How are you, Roly?' Darren said, grinning uncomfortably. Cassie's head was bowed, her face scarlet.

There was a light drizzle, the sky like gauze. The falling droplets seemed to float, to circle about them and drift in the breeze, and when the sun came out and streamed through the barren branches, each tiny drop illuminated, it was as though they were standing together in a shower of lights, a feeling of the whole world waking up from some slow, spectral dream. Cassie did not lift her head or look at Roland as he talked haltingly to

Darren, and they parted quickly and Roland continued home.

An hour or so later, his mother knocked on his door.

'Your friend's here to see you,' she told him.

Darren was standing in the kitchen, seeming out of place in his Lee jeans and flannel shirt and long heroic hair. Joyce was baking bread, flour sprinkled across the kitchen bench. Her arms were dusted white to the elbows. A large earthenware bowl sat on the ducted heating vent with a tea towel over it and the sour, yeasty smell of the rising dough filled the room. Darren was grinning nervously at Lily, who sat at the kitchen table, scowling at him.

'I'm going to get my own motorbike,' she was telling him. 'And it's going to be bigger and faster and better than yours and you're going to wish you had a motorbike like mine.'

'Yeah?' said Darren.

'Yeah. And I'm never going to let you ride it. Not ever. No matter how much you ask me.'

'Hey, Roly,' said Darren, looking up and smiling broadly at him. 'I was just thinking of going down to the fish-and-chip shop. You had your tea yet?'

'No,' said Roland.

'You want to go and get something? On me.'

Roland looked at his mother.

'Yes, that's fine, Roland,' she told him. 'I haven't even thought about what I'm going to do for dinner.'

Darren seemed unusually talkative as they walked down to the shops, while Roland was quiet, barely responding to his friend's earnest remarks. At the fish-and-chip shop they ordered hamburgers. The owner's usually sullen teenage daughter smiled at Darren, showing the braces on her teeth. He winked at her.

'How are ya?' he asked, and she blushed.

It was a Friday night, which was fish-and-chip night for many of the families in Glenella. Men stopped off at the shop on their way home from work and sat along the bench reading newspapers as they waited in their suits, briefcases and umbrellas at their feet. The owner stood at the counter, calling them by name as he shook salt onto the orders and wrapped them. He bade everyone a good weekend. 'You too,' said the men as they exited into the chill. Mothers came in with rabbles of kids, some already dressed in pyjamas and belted dressing-gowns, their pinched faces turning rosy and eager in the heat and pleasant smells of the shop. Roland and Darren took their hamburgers and sat on a bench outside the station, underneath the gently shifting wattles and banksias as they turned to ink in the dying light.

'Yeah, I'm sorry I didn't tell you about me and Cassie,' Darren said as he unwrapped his hamburger. 'It's just that she didn't want anyone to know. She doesn't want her old man finding out or something. Apparently, he doesn't like her going out with guys. Doesn't even like her hanging around with them.'

Roland nodded. 'I know,' he said.

'I mean, I know she's only fourteen and everything, but she's mature for her age,' said Darren. 'I forget how young she is, you know? Sometimes I feel like she's older than I am, the things she says. And, I mean, she knows what she's doing. It's not like I'm the first guy she's been with or anything.'

He opened his Coke with a hiss.

'I've never met anyone like her before,' he said, growing enthusiastic and struggling for the words. 'She's not like she seems at all. She's amazing.'

Roland nodded.

'Don't you think?' Darren asked.

'Yes,' said Roland. 'Yes, I think the same thing.'

They ate in silence. The streetlights had flickered on, the evening wrapped in blue light, the sky a pewter cavern above them. The rain had stopped, but there was slickness on the road. A train arrived at the station and rattled off, the figures in the windows bent over newspapers and books. Passengers came up from the tunnel. Women's heels clicked along the footpath and into the gloaming and were gone.

'What's weird, though,' Darren said, 'is did you know that Cassie's already on the Pill? Her mum gets it for her. She goes to the doctor and says it's for her, but then she gives it to Cassie.' He scrutinised Roland's face, his brow creased. 'I thought that was sort of weird. What do you think? Do you think that's weird?'

When Roland got home, he sat at his desk, surprised at how little he could feel, surprised that his bones and muscles could still carry such a dead weight when that was all he had become now. He was empty, numb to everything. That she was not interested in him anyway was something he had been telling himself for some time now, but there had always been hope and it was the dashing of this hope, his pleasantly drifting imaginings shattered by the reality, the shock of seeing them together—that was what had so shaken him. He wondered if he had stopped feeling altogether now. Maybe he would not care about everything so much after this, he thought, and this would mean that he would no longer be so easily hurt. Maybe this is what happened to people to make them no longer children. And he wondered if it would be this that would finally make him strong.

HE SAW THEM again the following day, a Saturday, as he came out of the station tunnel. They were sitting on the steps of the bank, lost in their nuzzling, their legs plaited in contrasts of faded denim. Darren's hand revealed the whiteness and large russet moles of Cassie's back as he stroked underneath her jumper. She wiped an eyelash from his cheek, holding it out for him to blow and he blew it and leaned into her neck, whispered his wish to her. She hugged him, her face so rapturous, so nakedly aglow, that it hurt Roland to see it. He felt suddenly weary and started walking in the other direction, but Darren saw him and called out his name. As he crossed the road, he saw Cassie murmuring into Darren's ear.

'It's all right,' he heard Darren say. 'Roly's my friend. He's not going to tell anyone.'

She glanced up at Roland, still murmuring, her hand

shielding her mouth. The wind rattled the half-crushed cans by the steps.

'Because I'll ask him not to,' Darren said to Cassie. 'I trust him.'

He kissed her on the forehead. She clung to him, her head against his chest.

It was just past twelve-thirty and the shops were shutting. The butcher was standing outside his door, his blue-striped apron still on, while inside the shop his apprentice cleared the trays of meat and tripe from the window. He was talking to Bill Worthy from Worthy's supermarket, who was in a short-sleeved shirt, a pair of thick-rimmed glasses poking out of the pocket. They both greeted the hairdresser as she emerged from the carpeted stairwell of the salon above the newsagent's, the walls decorated with framed headshots of women. Her own hair was immaculately coiffed, copper-coloured; she threw an armful of towels into the boot of her Datsun coupe. Bill Worthy started walking back to the supermarket, where the liquor section was still open, a bored-looking girl at the register.

'You're all dressed up,' Darren said to Roland, who was wearing his sports uniform of a striped blazer over a white jumper and the school tracksuit pants.

'I had soccer,' he said.

'I didn't know you liked soccer.'

'It's school sport. It's compulsory.'

'Yeah?' said Darren. 'So, we were thinking of maybe doing something. You up for it?'

'Doing what?'

'Dunno. That's what we were trying to decide.'

Cassie seemed to have relaxed and was sitting in her poised manner, one leg crossed over the other, a packet of menthols sitting beside her on the step. The jumper she was wearing was too big for her, a man's ribbed turtleneck, her hands folded like cats' paws within the rolled-up cuffs. Roland caught a whiff of musty wool, of naphthalene and Old Spice. She met his gaze with her own unwavering but uncertain stare. There seemed to be a question, a beseeching in it.

'How about we ring up Troy and get him to bring the Torana over,' Darren suggested. 'Go up to the pool hall or something.'

Cassie shook her head.

'Why not?'

'I don't like Troy. He's mean.'

Darren laughed. 'That's true. He is mean.'

He looked down the empty street. 'I've got some mull on me. We could smoke that.'

'Okay,' said Cassie. She picked at a loose thread sprouting from one of her white bobby socks, her head against her knee.

'So, you want to go back up to my place?'

'No, I still want to go somewhere.'

'Where?'

'Just somewhere.'

'We could go up to the lake.'

'All right,' said Cassie. 'I haven't been to the lake since I was a kid.'

'And you're such an old woman now, aren't you?' said Darren, grabbing hold of her. He squeezed her and she squealed. They kissed.

They walked past the library and the tennis club, where a rangy man was hitting balls to a line of children, bright chartreuse brimming from the wicker washing basket that sat beside him on the en-tout-cas. A game was being played on the football oval, shouting boys buffeting each other as they chased the skewing ball. A crowd of scarved girlfriends and family members stood at the sidelines, urging on the teams with voices that rasped like squabbling crows across the churned field, mud from the cleated boots scattered about the grass like sheep's dung. The sun burst through the winter day, gilding the trees and the neatly trimmed shrubs and turning the terracotta roofs to flame. Wattles festooned everything in a sea of yellow and silver. Insects had come out of nowhere: false births in the winter warmth, the briefest of lives. Darren and Cassie walked slowly in front of Roland, arms around each other. Occasionally one of them, or both together, would turn to look and smile at him, Cassie's gracile figure swaying insouciantly within the looseness of her clothes.

At the lake, they found a spot on the scrubby banks and lay down on the grass. Roland and Cassie watched as Darren tore a piece of bud into fragments and then kneaded a cigarette between his fingers, the tobacco spilling into his palm. He carefully repacked the cigarette with the mix, lit it and handed it to Cassie. She inhaled deeply, holding her breath with her cheeks blown out, then held the joint out to Roland, who shook his head.

'Why not?' she asked in a hoarse voice, blowing out a long plume of smoke.

'Roly doesn't smoke it,' Darren said, taking the joint. He inhaled and held it for a moment. 'He does his own thing. He looks at what other people are doing and he thinks about it, but in the end he always makes up his own mind.'

'No, I know,' Cassie said to Roland. 'I wasn't making fun of you. I mean, it's true.'

She was blushing, a deep rhubarb blotting her face and throat.

'It's, like, everyone's always carrying on and Roland sits there in the middle of it all just watching. Taking it all in.'

Her eyes skimmed across Roland's. Darren lay down on the grass, his head on Cassie's lap, the joint in his mouth. She stroked his hair. On the lake, the wind ruffled the water; it flashed like a scattering of coins.

'Are you sleepy?' she asked him.

'Yeah,' he said. 'A little bit. Someone woke me up at three in the morning,' he told Roland, tickling Cassie. She squealed and fought him off.

'But I couldn't get out till then because my parents were still up.'

'I know.'

'I didn't get any sleep either and I feel fine.'

'Well, you're a freak, aren't you.'

'What's the latest you've ever stayed up?' Cassie asked Roland.

'About that. About three.'

'I bet that's because you were studying.'

'Yeah,' he admitted. 'I was doing an assignment.'

'That doesn't count, though,' she said. Darren handed her the joint and she took a drag on it and coughed, burying her mouth in the crook of her arm. She gave it back to Darren. 'What's the latest you've been up because you wanted to be up. Like for fun?'

'I don't know. Two o'clock maybe.' A bolt, the shock of memory, as he thought of Melissa, that frozen night not so long ago. He must have thought of it every day since, of the things unrealised.

'I knew it would be because he was studying,' Cassie told Darren.

'You two have known each other for forever, haven't you?' Darren said.

'Yeah, sort of,' said Cassie.

'That's sort of nice,' said Darren. 'I wish I'd known someone that long. Well, Floyd, I suppose. But me and Floyd aren't really that close anymore.' He puffed on the joint, watching Cassie as she leaned over to pick the white and yellow daisies that grew in patches across the grass. 'You can meet up some-time, you know, in ten years or something, and you can say to each other, "Remember back then? Mucking around and everything?" And you'll go, "Remember that Darren guy? He was a weird one, wasn't he? Wonder what ever happened to him."' He smiled, his eyes crinkling.

'The problem with me, though, is that I can never remember anything,' said Cassie. She was making a daisy chain, split-ting the stalks with her fingernails and weaving the flowers through them, her fingers stained with green juices. 'I can't even remember what I did last week. My friend Sharon is always saying to me, "Do you remember when we did this and this?" or whatever, and I can never remember any of it. It just disappears out of my brain or something.'

'So, you telling me you're going to forget all about me one day?' Darren asked her, tickling her ribs. 'Love 'em and leave 'em. That's what you do, is it?'

Cassie squirmed and pushed his hand away. 'No, I wasn't saying that. I was just saying, I wish I didn't always forget every-thing all the time. I remember stuff I did when I was a kid, just nothing from now, from recently. It bothers me sometimes.' She spliced the ends of the daisy chain together and placed it on Darren's head, smoothing down his hair.

'Now you look pretty,' she said.

'You're the pretty one,' Darren said, taking hold of her arms and pulling her down to kiss him.

'Look at this girl,' he said to Roland. 'Have you ever seen such a beautiful girl as this? Such a sweet thing as this?'

Cassie giggled as they kissed again, sprawling together onto the grass. She blushed and cast another embarrassed glance at Roland.

COMING HOME ONE afternoon, he saw Troy, Curl, Floyd and Moses on the lawn outside the station. Troy was sitting on the back of one of the benches, his feet on the seat. He was watching a boy from Roland's school as he walked along the footpath. It was an older boy, a prefect, his uniform immaculate: crested tie, white jumper trimmed with the school colours, a neat, short-back-and-sides haircut. He had a ski tan, his face a deep bronze.

'Hey, faggot!' Troy yelled out to him. 'Hey, pretty boy!' He made kissing noises as the prefect passed along the footpath. The boy turned and sneered at Troy.

'Go fuck yourself, loser.'

Troy spat on the ground and got off the bench. 'Yeah?' he said. 'Come on, then. Let's go.'

The prefect shook his head and walked off grimacing, leaving Troy standing in front of the bench with his arms outstretched.

Curl nodded his head at Roland as he approached them.

'Here's Roly,' he said.

Roland put his bag down on the grass. Moses was sitting at the end of the bench with a little girl's pink bicycle leaning against his knees. There was a flower-adorned basket attached to its front, and a rainbow of plastic streamers flowing from the handlebars. He seemed to be on the verge of falling asleep and kept sinking forward, his eyes closing and his mouth gaping; then his head would jerk back and his eyes would open for a second before they started to close again.

'Whose bike is that?' Roland asked them.

'Dunno,' said Curl. 'Moses rode it here. Hey,' he said to Moses, elbowing him in the ribs. 'Whose bike is that?'

'It's my niece's,' said Moses.

'Yeah?' said Curl. 'That hers too?' he asked, tugging on the glittery pink scrunchie tying Moses's greasy-looking ponytail.

'Yeah, probably,' said Moses, his eyes closing again.

Curl grinned at Roland and mimed injecting himself in the arm.

'Darren's got his little girlfriend with him,' Troy told Roland. 'Didn't seem to want us around.'

'She's jailbait,' said Floyd, who had been watching the passing foot traffic, his cap pulled down low over his face. He was smoking a cigarette, holding his palm over it.

Curl and Troy laughed.

'No, I mean it,' said Floyd. 'How old is she?'

'Dunno,' said Troy. 'Do you know?' he asked Roland.

'She turned fourteen last month,' Roland said.

'Yeah, well, there you go,' said Floyd. 'She's fourteen. Darren's nineteen. That's enough to put him inside for a couple of years. My dad once told me that if I ever end up in Pentridge, or any of youse, then there'll be guys there to look after us. Except for that. Underage girls. If any of us get put inside for that, then we're on our own. That's the rules.'

'Probably why they're keeping it a secret,' said Curl. 'Although Darren says it's because of her old man. Says she reckons he'd go ballistic.'

'That's that Reg Noble Auto guy, isn't it?' Floyd said. 'With the big house on Creek Road. Wears that gold chain.'

'Yeah, Roly knows them.'

'Yeah?' Floyd said, looking at Roland with interest from under the peak of his cap. 'He ever take that chain off, you reckon?'

'I don't know.'

'I don't reckon he does. I've seen him walking around in his underdacks and he's still got that chain on.'

Curl turned to look at Floyd.

'When have you seen him walking around in his underdacks?'

'From the lane behind their house. You can see into the whole place, practically, at night. They've got those big back windows. I've seen him lying there in the bedroom, watching TV there. Putting away those UDLs. The wife and daughter watching TV downstairs. They've got two TVs going at the same time. One time, I've seen him come down, he gets a UDL out of the fridge and he stands there and, I'm not joking, he eats a whole block of cheese. With his hands. Bits of cheese falling all over his gut, all over the floor. Skols his UDL, gets another one and goes back upstairs again.'

'And, what, so you're standing there in the lane watching them?'

'Yeah.'

'What were you doing there?'

'You know,' said Floyd, 'Just passing through.'

He finished his cigarette and flicked it onto the road.

'Well, I'm going,' he said. 'You want a lift home, Roly?'

'All right,' said Roland.

They walked to Floyd's car, parked outside the shops. It was a brand-new Range Rover, painted racing green.

'Nice car,' said Roland.

'Yeah, I know,' said Floyd, unlocking the door. 'And it's completely legit too. I got a discount for it because I paid in cash. You know, they pocket the cash, fiddle the books, don't pay tax on it. It's a scam.'

He shook his head as he put the car in gear.

'They're all in on it.'

He honked the horn as they drove past Troy, Curl and Moses, who now looked as though he was fast asleep, his head drooping against his chest. At the intersection, they turned onto Creek Road.

'Have you seen the new shopping centre up at Forest Hill?' Floyd asked Roland.

'No.'

'Yeah, they just finished building it. I'm thinking of going up there and checking it out. You want to come along?'

'Okay,' Roland said.

'Yeah, it's not bad. They got a space lift, like the one in the city. Big food court. Heaps of cinemas.'

They continued to the end of Creek Road and turned onto Canterbury. The shopping centre was on their right, a long, tiered building of glass and painted concrete rising from the dipping road where smaller shops had once clustered around a broad paved path. They parked close to the main entrance, Reg Noble leering at them from the back windows in the dim multi-storey carpark. Floyd opened up a toolbox in the boot of the Range Rover and took out a set of screwdrivers, a torch and a small crowbar, which he put in Roland's schoolbag. He led him to a grille in the wall by the automatic doors.

'Just stand there and look respectable,' he told Roland, his eyes darting. He watched a man pushing a snaking row of shopping trolleys along the concrete. 'Here,' he said, rummaging around in the schoolbag. He took out a mathematics textbook, which he handed to Roland. 'Pretend you're reading this.'

Roland looked at equations while Floyd unscrewed the grille and took it out of the wall, his head whipping back as he scanned the carpark. A woman came out through the doors, pushing a shopping trolley with a child sitting in it, two more in tow, all contentedly sucking on milkshakes from the Wendy's upstairs. When the woman saw Floyd, she looked away.

'Quick, quick,' Floyd said to Roland, indicating the open vent.

Roland crawled into the duct. Floyd, close behind him, pulled the grille back into the wall. He switched on the torch and the light reflected blindingly off the sheet steel.

'Are you sure this is safe?' Roland asked him as the metal buckled and popped underneath them.

'Yeah, yeah. It's fine. We're going to the storage cages in the basement. It was my dad's idea. One of his mates showed him the plans when they were building this place. Said he'd do it himself if he wasn't so old and fat.'

They continued through the long passages of the ventilation system, Floyd telling Roland which way to turn as they reached the intersections. Eventually they came to a vent in the side of the duct.

'All right,' said Floyd, shining the torch on the grille. 'I've been down this one. Just keep going along and pick another one. It's the luck of the draw which cage you get.'

They continued to the third vent along. Following Floyd's instructions, Roland pushed out the grille and it clattered to the floor below. Inside, it was dark. Cyclone fencing jutted out from the wall.

They climbed down and Floyd shone the torch around the cage. Large plastic bags full of popcorn, nearly as tall as Roland, were stacked against the fencing. Plastic flagons sat near the gate, next to a life-size cardboard cut-out of Paul Hogan, 'Crocodile Dundee II' emblazoned across the bottom.

'Aw, shit,' Floyd said. 'This is the cage for the cinemas.'

He went to the gate and rattled it. There was a thick padlocked chain wrapped around the poles. He inspected the lock.

'I knew I should have brought some bolt cutters,' he said, shining the torch into the corridor that ran between the rows of cages. 'We could have cut this lock and got out of here and into one of the other ones, easy.'

The beam of light moved around to the next cage, where T-shirts wrapped in cellophane were stacked against the wire. Sunglasses in Perspex boxes lined a trestle table at the back. Their mirrored lenses glittered.

'And that's the surf shop cage right there,' Floyd said, exasperated. 'Right next to us. I could have moved any of that stuff.'

He pressed his face against the wire as he shone the torch around the cage.

'The place I really want to get into is this shop that sells all this American stuff. They've got genuine NBA caps, Harley-Davidson belt buckles, Zippo lighters, stuff like that. I could move any of that so quickly. And the sports shop. Get some

Nikes, Air Maxes or whatever, some of those Fila tracksuit tops. Kids pay top dollar for that stuff. Oh, well,' he said, turning off the torch and leaning over to pick up one of the plastic flagons by the gate. 'I'll just have to come back with some bolt cutters. Do the job properly.'

He opened the bottle and sniffed it.

'Might do it tonight,' he said, hefting up the bottle and looking at the dark syrup sloshing around inside.

'This is what they make Coke out of,' he told Roland. 'All they do is water it down heaps and that's your cup of Coke you pay like two dollars fifty for when you go and see a movie.'

He put the bottle on the floor and screwed the cap back on.

'It's a scam,' he said. 'It's all just a big fucking scam.'

They left the way they came, climbing up the sides of the cage and back into the vent. Floyd dragged one of the big bags of popcorn behind him, barely able to squeeze it into the duct. They came out into the daylight. More women passed with their shopping trolleys, children trailing behind them, watching with open mouths as the two boys emerged from the wall. Floyd screwed the grille back in and carried the bag of popcorn to the Range Rover.

They drove to Darren's house, where he was sitting by the fire with Cassie, his leather jacket draped over her and her head resting against his shoulder. Next door, Tilly Johnson's husband was trimming the topiary balls that flanked the slate path running through his front lawn. The shears hissed and clicked.

'You want some popcorn?' Floyd asked Cassie and Darren, dragging the bag across the grass.

Cassie sat up and yawned, raking her hair back.

'I'll have some,' she said.

Floyd pulled up his jeans leg, under which a butterfly knife stuck out of a rolled-up football sock. He drew it out and flipped over one of the perforated handles, twirling it over his knuckles and revealing a sweeping false-edged blade.

Darren watched quizzically as Floyd cut into the bag. 'That's a very big bag of popcorn,' he said to Floyd. 'Where did you get that from?'

'You know,' said Floyd, winking at Roland. 'Around.'

NOW, WHENEVER ROLAND went to Darren's, Cassie was there, and the couple would kiss and cuddle and whisper love to each another as though they were entirely alone. They had private jokes, they babbled like infants; their pinching and tickling turned to long moaning pash sessions on the logs. Roland spent a lot of his time attending to the fire, raking it and breaking up branches, his eyes averted. One afternoon, as he came up the lane, Darren called to him out of the open window of his bedroom. He was wearing only his jeans, lean as a cat, his bare torso the same pallor as the ghost gum that sprawled over the house. Steel-blue veins twisted like cables down his arms. Cassie was in his room, lying on the ticking, hair mussed and drowsiness in her eyes. Her school dress and blazer were flung over the back of the chair, shoes and socks scattered across the carpet. She drew the sleeping bag to her shoulders as Roland came in, the smell of sex as apparent in the room as her nakedness under the quilted nylon. Darren sat down on the bed and stroked her leg as he talked, Cassie and Roland too embarrassed to look at each other.

He started to spend time with Troy and Curl and sometimes Floyd, who told him that he had gone legit for the moment. He had gone back to the storage cages at the Forest Hill shopping centre and was surprised by a security guard, who he hit over the head with his bolt cutters. The man was old and nearly died. He identified Floyd from a collection of police photographs while lying in his hospital bed. Floyd was arrested, gave a 'no comment' interview, and was let out on bail. With his prior convictions and the fact that he was already on a good behaviour bond, Floyd was pretty sure he would finally be going to jail.

'So what?' he said to the others, shrugging.

On Friday and Saturday nights, they hung around the Glenella North shops, where they ran into other groups of teenagers wandering about as aimlessly as they were. They sat with them along the concrete supermarket ramp, hunched over and shivering as they talked. Girls hugged their knees, their teeth chattering. Curl usually invited one of them to sit on his lap and she would invariably take up his offer, throwing her arm casually around his neck, a cigarette hanging from her fingers as she met his flirtations with a furtive, half-supressed smile. Sometimes they collected stray supermarket trolleys and the girls sat in them and shrieked as the boys raced them around the carpark.

Once, they saw Liam and his mates: he was standing like a sentinel outside the video shop in his bomber jacket and GP army boots, the hems of his jeans folded up over the bootstraps. He hardly looked at Troy and Curl as they tried to make conversation and they fell silent, standing there uneasily as they listened to the beeping and *wah-wahing* of the arcade machine inside the shop.

'See you around,' they said to Liam as they left.

Liam took his cigarette out of his mouth and nodded to them.

If they couldn't find someone to hang around with, they usually ended up at Curl's house, drinking with his father, who spent his nights working at a bench in his garage under the ice glow of an under-hood light bar that he had taped to an old biscuit tin for stability, surrounded by old radios and televisions and tape players that he kept stacked on galvanised shelving racks that reached to the ceiling. Locals brought them to him to repair, Curl told Roland, or he would buy them from people who collected them on indestructible rubbish day and fix them up and sell them in the *Trading Post*. Curl's father would lurch to his feet when the boys arrived, his weary figure suddenly energised as he looked up from his wires and circuit boards, and he would stagger off to the fridge that sat humming on a rubber car mat in the corner of the garage. The boys pulled out folding garden chairs and arranged them around the electric heater. Curl's father talked about the war.

'Sometimes I don't leave the house for weeks,' he told Roland, his eyes welling. They were haunted eyes, so pale and blue and soft they seemed to be melting before you. He had a droopy moustache, fading tattoos of women and birds on his arms. 'For months even. I get these panic attacks. I'll be out on the street, at the shops, then suddenly I've got to get out of there, got to run off and hide somewhere. Can't breathe. My heart's thumping. I feel like I'm dead, right there. Like I'm going to die for sure.'

Curl sniffed loudly, tears streaming down his face as he listened.

'Can't go to Richmond, can't go to Springvale, not even Box Hill anymore,' said Curl's father. 'Can't go into the city. I see them on the street, I hear them talking their language, and that's it. Sets me off. Heart starts up, everything goes blurry. I'm too scared to go out and get the paper in the morning sometimes. Had to cut down all the trees in the backyard, because I was always seeing Viet Cong behind them.'

When Troy and Roland left, Curl and his father would still be drinking, holding each other and weeping. Troy told Roland they would keep drinking and crying until dawn.

He saw Melissa again, at a party thrown by a girl called Katie, who had gone to school with Darren and Troy and Curl. That night, Roland met Troy and Curl at the Glenella shops, where they were sitting in the Torana smoking a joint. They talked and listened to the radio for a while and then drove up to the highway and picked up a slab at the drive-thru before continuing on to the Nunawading McDonald's, where they bought hamburgers and thickshakes and French fries. They smoked another joint in the carpark.

The house was already packed with people when they arrived, figures spilling out onto the front lawn and sitting on the doorstep, cigarette embers flitting like insects in the darkness. The streets were lined with teenagers' battered second-hand cars, the odd immaculate sedan of someone's parents. When they found a park, Curl and Troy broke a couple of cans off the slab and drank them sitting on the bonnet of the Torana. They could hear the distant party: the chorus of voices, laughter, shouting, the song 'Venus' blasting through the sleepy streets.

'All right,' said Curl, sliding down onto the road. He was wearing his paisley shirt, the top two buttons undone, showing off a leather shark-tooth necklace. His golden hair was stiff with gel at the sides.

In the house, they pushed through the crowd to the bathroom. Troy crammed the slab into the ice-filled bathtub and broke off two more cans. He and Curl skolled them standing in the bathroom before wrenching off two more. They lit cigarettes.

'We better go and say hello to Katie,' said Curl.

Katie was a small girl wearing bubblegum jeans and a pink denim jacket, the cuffs folded and the sleeves pushed up to the elbows. Her wrists jangled with masses of thin silver bangles.

'Hi, guys,' she said, dwarfed by the group of boys standing around her. 'Where's Darren?'

'He might come along later,' said Curl.

'Hey,' she said, lowering her voice. 'Did you tell Floyd?'

'Yeah, yeah,' said Curl. 'He's coming. He'll be here.'

'Good,' she said. 'Because everyone's been asking me, "Is there anyone here I can score off?"' She rolled her eyes.

Roland saw Melissa as she arrived with another girl, both carrying handbags and six-packs of wine cooler. She was in a turquoise miniskirt and a white blouse, her curly hair tied with a lace bow. Large hoop earrings, dark make-up around her eyes. Roland's heart started to pound. He passed her in the hall and stopped, catching her eye.

'Hi,' he said.

'Hi,' she replied, distracted, and then looked at him again with a flash of recognition. 'Oh, hi!' she said, smiling. 'How are you?' She squeezed his arm and kept going down the hall. Roland went outside with Troy and Curl and found Floyd, who was at the side of the house, standing in the dark by the hot water service. People bought deals off him as the boys talked.

At one point, a queue formed along the brick pathway.

'I thought you'd gone legit,' Roland said to him.

'I have,' said Floyd. He kept looking around, craning his neck to peer down the drive and stomping his feet in the cold. 'This is just on the side. No one's going to bust me here.'

A boy approached them, pulling a crumpled twenty-dollar note out of his pocket with a handful of coins. He stood there counting them, his mouth moving silently.

'No. Fuck off,' said Floyd, waving him away. 'I don't want your spare change.'

The boy ducked his head and left.

'Come back with some more notes,' Floyd shouted after him.

'Hey, Floyd,' Curl said to him. 'Can you give us a gram to give to Katie?'

'What?' said Floyd. 'Give it to you?'

'Yeah, come on. It's her party and everything.'

'So?'

'Come on. It'd be a nice thing to do.'

After some grumbling, Floyd took a deal bag out of the backpack and handed it to Curl. They went back into the house to find Katie.

'Thanks, guys,' she said as Curl slipped her the bag, winking at her. She wriggled her fingers at them.

'Can I have one of your beers?' Roland asked Troy. Troy seemed surprised. 'Yeah, sure,' he said. 'Go ahead.'

He forced down a beer in the bathroom and then took another one and went looking for Melissa. She was in the kitchen, standing around the bench with a group of girls. They looked up as Roland approached and one of the girls said something. There was a flutter of stifled laughter.

'So, how have you been?' he asked her.

'I've been okay,' she said, raising her eyebrows with an odd half-smile. 'Are you here with Darren and Curl?'

'Troy and Curl,' Roland said. 'Darren's got a girlfriend now.'

'Does he?' she said, eyebrows still lifted.

'I didn't know you were going to be here.'

'Well,' she said with a high quavering laugh. 'Here I am.' She turned back to the others. Roland stood there listening to their conversation and drinking his beer, but they ignored him and Melissa didn't look at him again. He went into the lounge room, where Troy and Curl were sitting on the couch with some girls. One of the girls was showing Curl how to wolf-whistle, sticking her thumb and index finger in her mouth and letting out a piercing note. Curl put his hands over his ears, his face screwed up. Other people turned to look. Curl tried to do it, but couldn't. The girl showed him again, whistling even louder than before. Troy got up.

'You want another beer, Curl?' he asked. 'Roly?'

Roland nodded.

He was on his third beer when he saw Melissa going through the sliding door into the backyard. He followed her. Outside, the partygoers were standing around the lawn. Voices and laughter swelled. A group of girls perched on the edge of the garden table, one of them lying across the laps of the others. She was giggling hysterically. Smoke rose in a haze above the crowd, haloed by the outdoor lights, the familiar smell of marijuana drifting and disappearing in the frigid air. Melissa was smoking a cigarette, holding a bottle of wine cooler and looking out at the rose-coloured sky. When she saw Roland approaching, she smiled at him and walked back into the house. He watched her go.

There were sudden angry shouts from down by the back

fence. Two boys were swinging wildly at each other, feet tearing the grass. A girl shrieked as she tried to hold one of them back. They grabbed at each other's shirts and pulled each other across the lawn, heads rocking as the short sharp blows of fists and elbows connected. A big man came running out of the house, yelling, and grabbed them both in headlocks. The boys tried to break free, buffeting the man about. He tightened his arms around their necks.

'This is Katie's house!' he shouted at them.

He started pushing one of them, a lanky, denim-clad boy, across the backyard.

'Get out of here!' he yelled. 'Get out!'

The boy stumbled backwards, arms flailing. He had only just regained his balance when the man pushed him again. The other partygoers moved out of the way: girls held their drinks to their chests and boys looked suddenly alert, raising their heads and putting their arms around their girlfriends. The boy tripped and fell on the slab under the Hills Hoist and the man scooped him up and threw him hard against the garage wall. He escaped down the drive, slipping about on the concrete. The man turned and marched over to the other boy, who was sitting, dazed, on the grass. The girl who had tried to break up the fight was crouched next to him. She screeched at the man as he approached, throwing her arms protectively around the boy. The man backed off and stood there with his arms folded, grinning sheepishly.

Roland went back inside the house. Curl was lying on the couch with his head on one of the girls' laps, his eyes closed as she ran her fingers through his hair. Troy and the other girls were squeezed together up the other end.

'What happened out there?' Troy asked Roland.

'There was a fight,' he said.

The girls were watching the comings and goings, faces bright with expectation. Troy was looking at the floor. Someone put 'Locomotion' on the stereo. Two girls who had been standing by the door started dancing, swinging their hips and elbows, cigarettes in one hand, drinks in the other. They threw their heads back, laughing. A man groaned. 'Turn it off,' he said as he walked past. Curl sat up and started kissing the girl who had been stroking his hair.

Roland spent the rest of the night sitting outside with Troy and he got drunk for the first time in his life. After they ran out of beer, they passed around a bottle of Napoleon brandy. Someone put a thrash metal album on and the night grew frenzied with the accelerated drums, the wild, rising riffs and shouted vocals. Two boys sat back-to-back on an esky, whipping their long hair about in time to the music. The police arrived and told Katie to turn it off. Everything went quiet, voices dropping to a murmur. The lights were switched on. People started to leave. Roland got up and walked around the emptying house.

'Do you know where Melissa is?' he asked Katie, slurring his words.

'I think she's gone,' said Katie.

Roland asked Troy for a cigarette, smoked it and threw up in the garden, everything spinning around him. Troy stood watching him.

'Oh well,' he said. 'At least now you know your limits.'

HOLIDAYS ARRIVED AGAIN but they were short, two weeks between the terms. Roland spent them studying for exams that were now only months away, the hard knot that formed in his stomach over the course of every school year growing tighter and tighter as they approached. One dismal, thundery day, so dark that the chooks next door failed to cluck and roosted fluffed and sleepy on the floor of the veranda, there was a knock on his window. Darren and Cassie were standing outside, grinning at him. They were soaked by the rain, their wet hair stuck to their necks in tangled stringy locks. Their faces were exalted, pale with cold. When he opened the door, they sprawled into the kitchen, dripping and giggling uncontrollably. Roland was alone in the house. His parents had taken Lily to one of the free holiday concerts at the Forest Hill shopping centre: the flyer had promised a talking dog, yo-yo tricks and an appearance from one of the stars of *Young Talent Time*.

The three of them went into his room.

Cassie, shivering—she touched her icy fingers to Roland's cheek to show him how cold she was—wanted dry clothes. Going through Roland's wardrobe, she picked out his school tracksuit pants and an old V-neck jumper and took them into the bathroom. Darren seemed fascinated by Roland's books, taking them off the shelves and staring at the covers. Cassie came back in, drying her hair with a towel, her pupils huge.

'I kept looking at myself in the mirror,' she said. 'But it was too weird, so I had to try not to look.'

'Yeah, you shouldn't look at your reflection,' Darren said. 'You'll freak out.'

'We're on acid,' he told Roland.

Cassie sat down at Roland's desk and pushed the keys of his typewriter, watching closely as the typebars clacked against the platen.

'How much longer are we going to be in here for?' she asked Darren. She swivelled around in the chair. 'We've been in here forever.'

'You want to go?'

'Yes! I've got to get out of here. I hate being inside. It's like being in prison or something.'

'What about Roly?'

'But Roland's coming with us, isn't he?' Cassie said, turning to look at Roland. 'He's one of the group. Me, you, Roland.' She looked around the room, one finger against her cheek. 'Me, you, Roland, me,' she said. 'We're missing someone. Who's the other one?'

'There's no one else,' said Darren, laughing. 'It's just you and me and Roly. Wait,' he said, looking around. 'Was there someone else?'

'I feel like there's someone else,' said Cassie.

The rain had stopped by the time they spilled out onto the street, the sun a ripple of silk behind the cloud cover. Cassie and Darren were blissful as they walked along, holding hands, Cassie remarking on things as they passed and telling Roland how beautiful it all was, describing the movement around them, the spiralling trees, the shifting colours, the blooms of purple that burst from the grass: how everything looked like a wonderful painting, how the whole world was breathing and alive. They caught a train into the city, sitting together on the row of seats close to the doors. The carriage was full of football fans in scarves and beanies. Across from them, two old women were wearing hats swathed in red-and-white crepe paper. They were passing a roll of mints between them.

'Can you see this?' Cassie asked Darren. She was staring out the window, her forehead resting against the glass, one knee up on the torn vinyl seat. It was one of the old blue Harris carriages and some of the upper windows were open, the cold air whistling in and making the loose doors rattle. Mud and wet leaves streaked the rubber floor.

'Yeah,' said Darren, chuckling. 'I sure can.'

'Can Roland see it?' she whispered to him.

'No,' he said. 'He can't see it.'

'Poor Roland,' said Cassie. 'Poor, poor Roland.'

They got off at Flinders Street and went to look at the floral clock opposite the gallery and then walked through the blocks of lawns and trees that seemed to ramble endlessly up from St Kilda Road, past bandstands and fountains, trellises roped with stark wisteria and the ivy-mantled walls of Government House. The white tower soared above them, its flag fluttering, and Cassie and Darren both pointed at it, exclaiming.

Darren disappeared, running towards the ice-cream vans, and Roland and Cassie clambered down some stairs into a walled garden where lily pads quivered on the surface of a long tiled pond. Cassie stepped forward, trying to walk on them. Roland grabbed her just before she plunged in.

It started to drizzle and the clouds darkened and then it began to pour. Roland and Cassie ran up the hill and took shelter under a rotunda that overlooked the river, ripples bursting across the water as the traffic slowed on the bridge. Drops slid down the limbs of the leafless trees, gathering at budding points and dripping, and liquid curtains spilled from the eaves. Cassie sat in silence on the stone floor, her knees clasped to her chest. Her white breasts swelled over the neck of the scratchy brown jumper. She looked out at the greyness, the stark lines of trees, the seething river. Raindrops jewelled her face like tears. Roland sat down next to her and she turned to him, looking at him with her enormous black eyes.

'You don't have to worry about me anymore, Roland,' she told him. 'I'm okay. I really am. Everything's good now.'

She glanced up at something behind him and started to laugh as Darren's bedraggled figure squelched through the rain towards them, clutching ice-creams.

ROLAND WAS READING at the kitchen table one Saturday afternoon when he saw Reg Noble lumbering up the driveway. His father, working in the backyard, called out in greeting as he took off his gloves and slapped them down on the brimming pile of weeds in the wheelbarrow, but Reg veered off towards the side of the house. He came into the kitchen through the sliding door and sat down heavily in the chair opposite Roland. He was drunk, his breathing laboured, his face florid. Roland shifted nervously under his gaze.

'What's your mate doing with my daughter?' he said.

'I don't know,' Roland said.

He looked over to the doorway, where his father was taking off his gumboots. The smell of damp soil and onion weeds filled the room. Reg took a deep breath that whistled through his nose hairs, still staring at Roland with glazed eyes, then leaned over the table and hit him backhanded across the face.

The sudden sharp crack rent the lull of the morning; there was a sickening knock of knuckle on bone. It felt like something had exploded inside Roland's head. Everything turned bright, like a camera flash in his eyes. A single shrill note rang in his ears, drowning out everything but the thud of his own heartbeat. Pain throbbed through his skull. As the white light faded into strobing patches and turned red, he could see Reg getting to his feet. He was swaying, gesturing drunkenly as he talked to his father.

'His mate,' he said, pointing at Roland. 'Getting off with my daughter. I know all about it. I'll kill him. Don't think I won't, Graham.'

The two men went outside, Reg gesticulating wildly as Roland's father tried to calm him down. After a long exchange, Reg lurched off.

When his father came back inside, he was furious. 'Did you know about this?' he asked Roland.

'No.'

'You better not have. I'll tell you what. If Reg finds out that you have anything to do with this...'

He shook his head and strode back outside, thumping the sliding door shut.

Roland took his book and went to his room, trying not to cry. His head pounded and he felt dizzy and nauseous. His face was beginning to swell where he had been struck. He lay down on the bed and buried his face in the pillow, trying to control the sobs that spasmed through him.

He heard his mother come home and talk to his father in the kitchen. She came into his room.

'Show me,' she said.

He turned his face to show her the gathering bruise on the left side. Reg's wedding ring had left a welt across his cheekbone.

'Right,' she said, her mouth tense. She marched back into the kitchen.

'That's it,' Roland heard her tell his father. 'I do not want to have anything to do with that man anymore. Ever.'

'Now, come on, Joyce. Put yourself in his position. I'd be out of my mind if that was my daughter. Imagine if Lily was fourteen and there was some nineteen-year-old boy preying on her.'

'But what's any of this got to do with Roland?' his mother yelled. 'It's got absolutely nothing to do with him. Why doesn't he go and slap this Darren Wilson boy around, if he's so upset about it? Or Cassie? I mean, don't think she's so innocent in all this, Graham. They never are.'

Roland could hear her moving about the kitchen as she talked. Chairs scraped, dishes clinked. A tap was turned on.

'I've had enough. I don't want Reg coming around here ever again. I don't want to see either of them.'

'Oh, come on,' his father said. 'Let's not go over the top.'

'I've always thought he was a pig of a man. I've never liked him.'

'Well, what about Colleen? You like Colleen, don't you?'

'Colleen will defend Reg to the ends of the earth. And she's as vulgar as he is, sometimes. She's ignorant.'

'So what do you want me to do?' Roland heard his father ask, anger rising in his voice. 'You want me to go over there and say what? "Joyce doesn't want to see you anymore because she thinks you're vulgar and ignorant. So you're not welcome at our house now." Is that what you want me to say?'

'Yes!'

'You're serious?'

'Why do you think I'm saying this?' his mother shouted. 'Do

you think it's because I like the sound of my own voice?'

'Well, all right then. I'll go and tell them.'

He left, slamming the door. Roland heard his mother continuing to bustle about the kitchen. After a while he got up and went in. She was wiping down the bench, her face tight.

'How are you feeling, pet?' she asked him.

'I'm all right.'

'Would you like me to make you something? How about some ice-cream?'

'Yes, please.'

She went to the freezer and took out the ice-cream and a bag of frozen peas, which she gave to Roland to put over the bruise.

'I don't want you seeing Darren Wilson and his friends anymore,' she said as she served up the ice-cream at the bench. 'You've got all those nice boys at school to make friends with. We're paying an absolute fortune to send you to that school and then you go and spend all your time with these local yobbos. And look at the trouble they've already got you into.'

'But I hate school,' said Roland with a vehemence that surprised him. 'I hate it so much.'

'Well, I don't think you're making the effort to like it.'

'You don't understand. No one likes me there. They're awful to me. They're all horrible.'

'They wouldn't be if they knew you. You just have to give them a chance. Why don't you invite some boy home one afternoon? Someone you like.'

'You just don't understand.'

'What don't I understand?'

'They're not nice boys. They're not like that at all. And they're all rich and we're not rich. They'd laugh if they came out here. They'd laugh at this house.'

'Oh, rubbish,' said his mother.

She brought the ice-cream over and sat down opposite him.

'We're making a lot of sacrifices to send you to that school. You might not realise it, but we're scrimping and saving so we can afford your fees. All I want you to do is to stop being so negative about it all the time and at least try to like it. Will you do that for me? Just make a little bit of an effort?'

Roland jabbed his spoon into the ice-cream and squished it. He *did* realise and he *was* trying. He *was* making an effort. He studied all the time. It was all he ever did and he hated it. He hated studying, he hated school, he hated everything. He hated his life. His face was numb from the frozen peas.

'Roland? Are you there?'

'Okay, I'll try.'

'Good. That's all we want you to do.'

She went back to the sink.

'Shit,' she said, looking out the window.

His father was coming up the driveway, talking to Reg, who was listening to him with his head down, nodding seriously. Colleen walked behind them in a pair of bright flower-print leggings, her high heels clattering on the concrete. Roland watched as his mother went out the sliding door and Reg approached her with his hands raised as though in surrender. The theatrically sorrowful look on his face became an indulgent smile as he hugged her, rocking her gently as if comforting a petulant child. His mother accepted the embrace stiffly, her arms at her sides. Colleen trotted over and joined the hug.

189

They stood there talking. Reg laughed and joked, his arm around Roland's mother's waist. He managed to coax a wan smile out of her. His father, evidently satisfied that peace had been made, ushered Reg and Colleen inside. Roland retreated to his room.

IN AUGUST THE weather changed and the first of the plum blossoms appeared, lighting the depths of winter. Pink sprays lined Carlington Street and Creek Road like still, soft fireworks, pulsing under the streetlights at night. The pittosporums flowered and the mournful trees became bright and alive, a hail of creamy petals falling across the lawns and driveways. There were a few days of warmth, the nights almost sultry, before it became cold again.

Roland obeyed his mother and stopped going around to Darren's house or meeting up with Troy and Curl at the Glenella North shops . He did not see Cassie anymore either. She had stopped visiting the Arthursons when she started going out with Darren, and while she no longer ignored Roland when she saw him on the train, he had avoided her since the day Reg came to his house. He simply did not know what to say to her.

One afternoon, when he was at the station, he was approached by two girls from Cassie's school. They had spotted him from the ramp and strode purposefully up to him, the hems of their school dresses dancing about their knees.

'Haven't I seen you talking to Cassie Noble?' one of them, a tall, wiry redhead, asked him imperiously. The lapels of her blazer were braided and lined with enamelled badges, school colours embroidered about the gold crest on her pocket. Her face was spattered with orange freckles.

'Probably,' he said.

'Cassie's the biggest slut at our school,' she told him. 'And we know that for a fact.'

The other girl was short and pudgy, a red birthmark across her face that looked like the map of a country. When Roland glanced at her, she looked away.

'And she lies,' the redhead continued. She was looking at him triumphantly, her eyes blazing. 'You wouldn't believe the lies she tells people.'

She watched his reaction with scornful elation, her lips pursed primly, before she continued along the platform with her nose in the air, the other girl in tow.

Roland also avoided Reg and Colleen when they came around on Sundays, although he always eavesdropped on their conversations with his parents. In winter, they sat in the kitchen, where it was the usual UDLs and glasses of wine and packets of chips and endless cigarettes, smoke wafting through the house. Voices rose to crescendos of hilarity as the afternoon wore on, Colleen's voice trumpeting above them all. One afternoon, she announced that Cassie had run away from home. Darren had disappeared as well, she said. Tilly Johnson had told her that she hadn't seen the motorcycle in the yard for days, so he had obviously taken her god-knows-where on it. Colleen wanted to call the police, but Reg had told her that he'd handle it himself.

'And I'll tell you what,' Colleen said gleefully. 'That boy is going to have hell to pay when Reg catches up with him. Reg will sort him out, don't you worry about that. He will be *wishing* we called the police.'

They were not gone for long. The following week, Roland heard Cassie's voice in his sister's room. Drawers slid open; something thumped. The girls shrieked with laughter as they ran up and down the hall, the house shuddering with their footsteps. Irritated by the noise, Roland went and knocked on Lily's door. More giggling. He opened it to find them sitting on the floor with Lily's Ken doll, his mother's sewing kit open on the carpet next to them. The doll was naked, wearing a wig fashioned out of what looked like doormat bristles. Ball-headed quilting pins were stuck into its eyes and groin.

'What are you doing?' he asked them.

'We're making a voodoo doll,' Lily said excitedly. 'We're making a voodoo doll of Darren Wilson.'

Cassie shushed her.

'Don't tell him,' she said, throwing Roland a scornful look.

Roland went back to his room and the girls continued their raucous game. The front door slammed, their voices fading as they walked down the drive. There was silence but for the contented clucking of Maurice's chickens as they foraged and scraped the dirt. After about half an hour, the girls returned and there was more boisterousness and slamming doors. Roland threw down his pen and rubbed his eyes, exhausted, and looked out the window. It was sunny outside: a breezy day of agate skies and cirrus clouds, seething branches, scattered light. He arranged his notes, picked up some of the dirty mugs from his desk and went to make himself another cup of tea.

The girls were in the kitchen, filling balloons with water and placing them in a plastic bag by the sink. A carton of eggs sat on the bench. Cassie shushed Lily again as Roland came in.

'Don't say anything,' he heard her whisper.

They took the bag and the eggs and went out through the sliding door. Roland, sensing that something was afoot and loath to return to the dullness of his desk, put on his shoes and followed them at a distance as they crossed the road and jaunted down Carlington Street. They stopped outside Darren Wilson's house, where Cassie opened the egg carton and started hurling the eggs into the backyard, her arm flying back, her hair wild. She pivoted on her long bare legs, an ungainly gracefulness to her throw, like a newborn foal finding its gait. Lily heaved balloons from her shoulder. Roland ran up to see Darren standing beside the house, watching the attack gloomily. Cassie had walked through the carport and was deliberately throwing eggs at the Triumph's engine from only a few feet away. They splattered on the chromed metal, spreading thickly along the elegant lines of the cylinder. There was something meaningful about the action: one egg after another, her brow furrowed with intent. She smeared the last egg across the seat and looked pointedly at Darren before strutting off. Lily ran after her, the remaining balloons left wobbling on the footpath. Darren went to the garden tap and started uncoiling the hose.

'What did they do that for?' Roland asked.

'Just leave it, Roly,' Darren said, without turning around. 'Trust me. You don't want to get involved.'

TEACHERS AT SCHOOL always said that if you couldn't find time to study then it was because you were not making time for it, because you were procrastinating, for which there was no excuse: you had to have a schedule and a routine; you had to create good habits now, otherwise when the final year came it would all be too late. It might be years away, they told the boys, but it would arrive very quickly and they did not want to be caught unprepared. Roland had listened carefully to these instructions and he took them seriously. He had vowed that he would not be one of those boys who were like animals caught in headlights, run down by time. He would not fritter the moments away.

It was the only thing that was certain in his life, the only thing the adults had told him with definiteness. Success in the final year, the HSC, was paramount; it was what all the years were leading towards, and without it you would go nowhere in life. There would be no future. It would be misery, drudgery, a type of living death. Just get through the exams, they told him, and the rest of life would be an idyll, a glorious midday romp. For Roland, they meant an end to the bullying, to the constant taunts and sniping; they promised the possibility of a future where he might no longer be an outcast among his peers. If he could do well, there would be university. All its grandeur, the civility and gravity of learning. Clever girls, kind girls who would understand him and see something beneath his shyness. A new world would be opened up, one that would welcome him, all things better if he could just wear this grind, this purgatory before the judgement.

Despite the changes in his life over the past year, Roland had not slackened, and he tried to make up for the lost time spent with his friends by studying all the more furiously, by imposing a ban on television and reading that was not for school, by cutting down his mealtimes and working late into the night. If there was a test, he would get up before dawn and bend bleary-eyed over his books as the sun rose. But it was only now, bereft of his friends, stripped of the temptation of wandering down to Darren's house or joining Troy and Curl somewhere, that everything seemed to fall apart. As August became September and the exams loomed ever closer, he found he couldn't study at all. There was too much turmoil in his head, too much restless-ness. Too much of a living, breathing world out there.

He started to procrastinate, to avoid going home in the after-noons to face that blank desk, those bloodless books. Instead of taking the train home after school, he went in the other direc-tion, into the city, although even its charms seemed to have shifted as everything had shifted and changed over the year. No longer the enchantment of the coin and stamp shops, the pawn shops, no longer a fascination with things, but rather a seeking out of this quick world and its real and present life, the places of tumult and hustle, other teens likewise city-bound, their uniforms absolved by the carelessness of torn stockings, undone T-bars, loosened ties and flapping shirt tails. The glorious rebellion of them, their refusal, their sneering intransigence, which seemed to the studious boy like some contempt of fate. Groups with bags flung down in the shadowed alcoves of the station, going into McDonald's, Brashs—where excitable girls listened to music through stereo headphones among the racks of tapes—the clothing shops and sports shops, rap pumping out of the speakers, boys hunched over smoking in nearby lane-ways, readying themselves to steal. Roland wandered among them with the longing of an exile.

There was a wondrousness of confusion here, of finding his way around, often half-lost, having to wend his way through the lanes and arcades in search of familiar landmarks. He was only just learning the names of the main streets: Flinders Street, Collins Street, Bourke, Elizabeth. Swanston Street was shrouded in exhaust fumes, grit kicked up by the trams and the cold, acrid winds. The shop windows were grimy: cafes with chromed jukeboxes at each booth, strip joints and adult cinemas and bookshops with their ember-red Xs in the window. 'Girls! Girls! Girls!' flashed above descending stairwells in a scrawl of neon. Derelicts sprawled on the footpaths among blankets and overcoats, plastic bags full of fruit and cling-wrapped rolls. Outside Young and Jackson's, a grey-suited drunk in a stained homburg sat under the architrave, shouting at the pedestrians as they crossed the road. 'Fuck you, you fucks!' ran the awful rasp of his voice, echoing across the street. 'Fuck you, you fucking fucks!'

On Flinders Street, there was a pinball parlour down a flight of stairs that seemed to descend into nothing but darkness. It thronged with teens, a crowd Roland discreetly joined. He made himself look busy, perusing the beeping arcade machines, the lurid flashing pinnies, his hand in his pocket as though he were jingling coins there. An unsmiling man in black, a long ponytail glimmering down his neck, changed notes in a caged booth and attended the counter, watching the teens hatefully as they bashed buttons and wrenched at joysticks and thrust their hips against the pinball machines in hope of influencing the ball. Faces ticked with concentration. When they lost, they swore and kicked the machines. Once, a girl approached Roland while he was trying to look occupied. She wore the uniform of one of the private girls' schools, her bobbed hair dyed a chemical auburn, a rash of lumpy acne across her face.

'I'm just waiting for my friends,' he lied, craning his neck to look up the stairs.

'I haven't seen you here before,' she said.

'No,' he said. 'I usually go to other places.'

'Like where?' she asked. She was drinking Coke from a cardboard cup, rattling the ice around.

'Me and my friends usually go to the pub or the pool hall. We hardly ever come into the city.'

'Really?' she asked, her eyes widening. 'What pub?'

'The Glenella Bar and Bistro.'

'I haven't heard of that one before. Is it any good?'

'It's all right.'

'Do you have fake ID?'

'No,' he said. 'I just go in. If we get chucked out, we go to this pool hall. You can get beers there and they don't even check your ID.'

'Really?' she said. 'That's awesome. I wish I knew some-where like that.'

Roland shrugged, looking around the room. The girl slurped at the last of the Coke and melting ice.

'Do you ever go to nightclubs?' she asked him.

'No,' he said. 'My mates do sometimes, but it's too hard to get in.'

'Do you mean underage nightclubs or proper nightclubs?'

'Proper nightclubs.'

'Yeah,' she said. 'Underage nightclubs are pretty shit. I've been to one or two but, yeah, they're sort of shit. I went to a blue-light disco once and that was the worst. That was really shit. I've got this friend who's really beautiful, and she always gets into proper clubs, even though she's only fifteen.'

Roland nodded, still looking around the room. He was surprised by his own disinterest.

'She's so beautiful,' the girl said. 'She could be a model or something. We're really good friends. She's probably my best friend.'

'It sounds like they're just letting her in because of her looks.'

'I know!' The comment induced such enthusiasm in the girl that she came close to shouting. 'She doesn't have fake ID or anything. I can't believe they just let her in. I tried to get into Hard n' Fast at Chasers once. I borrowed my sister's ID, but the bouncer asked me what my date of birth was and I just went blank. I couldn't remember what year my sister was born. When I turn eighteen, I'm going to go out to clubs every night.'

Roland watched as a swarthy, heavy-browed man in a choco-late suit came down the stairs, patently out of place among the teens and the frenetic jangling of the pinnies. He brushed off his lapels with big, calloused hands as he looked around the room, before making a beeline for a boy who sat on a stool in front of one of the upright arcade machines, a mane of black hair flaring at his shoulders. The man grabbed the boy by the arm and shook him violently, yelling at him in a foreign language. For a moment, everyone stopped to watch, boys still pounding the buttons of their machines. The boy jerked himself loose and bolted up the stairs, his stool crashing to the floor. The man followed. On the street, he started shouting again. The players sniggered, catching each other's gazes before turning back to their machines, which they hammered and shoved with renewed vigour. The girl finished with her drink and put it down on the floor by the window. 'I know a few guys from your school,' she said to Roland. She named them, asking about them.

'They're idiots,' Roland said. 'They're morons.'

'Yeah,' she said. 'I thought they probably were. Once they wagged and came to my school. They were hanging around the fence at lunchtime and talking to us and everything and they all took their shirts off. I think they were meant to be showing off their muscles and stuff. There were these girls who were really into it. They were screaming like the guys were rock stars or something. Some people are so stupid.'

'Do you like your school?'

'Yeah! It's the best school. I love it! I've got so many friends there. I'm really popular. I'm friends with just about everyone.'

Roland peered up the stairs.

'I don't know what's happened to my mates,' he said. 'I better go and look for them.'

He was more drawn to the slender sullen creatures with the rattily hemmed dresses, the thin silver necklaces, frayed friendship bracelets lined along slim arms and streaked, home-dyed hair, who stared so evenly at you as you passed, eyes flashing, who made his heart race, although he knew he would never have the courage to approach one of them: they seemed as though they might hiss, or kick like skittish horses. Anyway, they were always with tough older boys who threw apish arms around their shoulders and gave other boys hostile, proprietary looks. Sometimes, he stood close by such girls as they draped themselves about the benches on the station platforms, rolling their eyes at everything. He listened to their vapid chatter, their exaggerations and screeching play fights, somehow all so alluring.

The thrill was perhaps most of all in the imagining, in the wandering, the walking and walking, following the slightest hint of happening. It was the joy of discovery, the sense of nascence that dazzled through it all, that invested even the smallest things with meaning. He often thought about Cassie during these afternoons among the swarm and liveliness of other teens, especially when catching a flourish of blonde hair, the flutter of a blue gingham dress, always with the shock of recognition, but it was never her. It had been heartscalding for Roland when she had been so scornful to him on the day she egged Darren's motorcycle. She had never been so contemptuous towards him before, and he felt it now like a lingering pain, a near-forgotten ache that would return with full rendering force at the recollection. What had he done wrong? he wondered. She was only ever interested in Darren anyway, and kind to him only because he was Darren's friend. And now that seemed to have gone wrong, she had no use for him anymore. Such thoughts were a brief check to the excitement, the rap of something hollow and dull, and he found he could only thwart them with movement, more movement and more new things.

At home in Glenella, the restlessness did not leave him and, though he sat himself in front of his books and notes and tried every day, there was often no point. And so he continued to walk, tramping the familiar streets, his mind sifting, dreaming, trying to make sense of all those things he had witnessed and anticipating things to come. One day, during the last bitter suspirations of winter, he watched a storm gather from the pedestrian bridge over the highway, the far-off towers of the city enfolded in gloomy clouds and vanished, the suburb cut off, become forlorn, like an island in a turbulent sea. Winds ripped through the embowering trees with a sound that was something like rage, something like the very cry of desperation he himself had never been able to voice. The air was ozonous, electric; it was like breathing crystal, so clear that he felt it might shatter. There was a boom of thunder that seemed to shake the world and then the rain began to pour, furious striations that boiled on the road and rose again like mist. He felt a strange exhilaration, as though he had become incorporeal, as though he were floating, luminous, as though he were made of light. And with that awe came a realisation that those awakenings he had only just sensed the year before had happened, were happening now, that the possibilities he had anticipated had already arrived, come as quickly and abundantly as the first tentative buds of spring.

He saw Darren twice during this period, both times on his interminable treks around Glenella. The first time it was only a glimpse, Darren turning into the weed-choked entrance to the lane that ran behind the houses on Creek Road. He was walking slowly, his head bowed, hands thrust into his pockets, a weariness about him that made his figure seem almost wretched. Roland did not call out, but watched Darren disappear behind a thatch of honeysuckle, something unapproachable about his friend.

The second time, Darren was standing outside the Nobles' house, looking up at the big front windows as he smoked a cigarette. Again, he appeared morose, lost in thought, and hardly seemed to register Roland's presence.

'Are you looking for Cassie?' Roland asked him.

'Cassie?' Darren said. 'No, not Cassie.'

He took a heavy drag on his cigarette, eyes still scanning the looming façade of the house.

'Fuck it,' he mumbled, turning away. 'It's got nothing to do with me anyway.'

Roland was coming up Creek Road on a Friday night when the Torana slowed and stopped alongside him. The rear door opened, a waft of aftershave. Darren, Troy and Curl were in their nightclub clothes, faces still pink from a recent scrubbing.

'It's been a bad night,' Darren told him after he got into the car. 'As usual. As fucking usual.'

They turned into Carlington Street and parked in the carport, the headlights sweeping across the motorcycle on the concrete, prickling the chrome. Troy took a slab out of the boot and carried it over to the logs and the glowing fire. It was a bright night with a full moon, milky shapes, swathes of shadow, the pale grass disappearing into the darkness of the lane. The air was scented with jasmine, winter's chill dispersed by a warm, gusty breeze.

'Are you still pissed off?' Curl asked Darren.

'Of course I am,' said Darren, going towards the lane. 'I'm really pissed off.'

He came back with a fallen branch, which he broke up and threw on the fire, stoking it vigorously until the flames rose. With a sigh, he sat down on a log and ran a hand over his face. Troy threw him a beer.

'We were meant to be meeting some girls tonight,' Darren told Roland. 'Some really nice girls we used to know. Down at this nightclub in Ringwood. I mean, fucking Ringwood. How do we get KB'd from a nightclub in Ringwood?' He shook his head. 'I don't know.'

'That bouncer was a fuckwit,' said Troy. 'He was looking for a fight or something.'

'He KBs us,' Darren told Roland. 'So I say to him, "Okay, well, can you at least just let me go and tell these girls I'm not coming in?" I said, "I'll be in and out. Five minutes." You know what the guy does? He pushes me. Right out onto the road. Fell right on my arse. If there'd been a car coming I would've been killed. And in fucking Ringwood. If they're not letting us into some shit club in Ringwood, who are they letting in? That's what I want to know.'

They hadn't been sitting there long when they heard voices and footsteps coming up the lane. Dark figures came through the carport. Liam sat down on one of the logs, his boys gathering around him. He took his Marlboros from the pocket of his bomber-jacket and tapped out a cigarette.

'Floyd's not here,' Darren said to him. 'He's not coming tonight.'

Liam shrugged and lit the cigarette, his curved earring glinting in the light from the flame. He reached out to take a beer from the slab. With a sudden, violent movement, Darren stood up and kicked the cans out of reach.

'Didn't you hear what I just said? Floyd's not coming, so you can all fuck off home. If you want to find Floyd, then go and look for him.'

He glared down at Liam, who stayed motionless on the log. There was silence but for the crackling of the fire, the rustle of leaves in the wind. Darren stood rigid and intent, eyes flashing, his hands squeezed into fists. The crag of his jawbone stood out clenched and pallid in the firelight. Finally, Liam got up.

'All right,' he said calmly, avoiding Darren's stare. He brushed down his jacket and took a drag on his cigarette, blowing the smoke out of the corner of his mouth. 'See you later, boys,' he said to Roland and Troy and Curl before disappearing into the darkness. The others scuttled after him.

Darren sat back down on the log and lit a cigarette, his hands shaking.

'Oh, well,' said Curl. 'I suppose someone was going to have to do that sooner or later.'

The following morning, Roland was surprised to see the Torana pull into the drive. Fortunately, he was the only one to see the car arrive; his mother was out shopping and his father was gardening in the backyard, Lily carolling as she skipped about the grass. He had been lingering over his breakfast at the kitchen table, reading the newspaper, an open mathematics textbook pushed to one side. He went out to meet Troy.

'Darren's been bashed,' Troy said.

He told him the rest as they drove to Darren's house. Liam and his mates had gone back there last night, after Darren had gone to bed. They had kicked in the back door, pulled Darren out of his sleeping bag and put it over his head before beating him with baseball bats. Some stuff had been stolen from the house as well: an ashtray, a prized crystal vase, a collection of souvenir spoons, and other trinkets from the glass cabinet in the living room. When Darren's mother had come out of her bedroom, awoken by the noise, the boys had fled.

'He's all right, though,' said Troy. 'I think they must've just wanted to scare him.'

Darren was sitting in the backyard with Curl, his face swollen with waxy bruises, the colour of wine stains. He showed Roland his other injuries: more angry bruises around his ribs and chest and back. He moved stiffly, touching his ribs with a sharp, hissing inhalation.

'I think they broke something here,' he said in a hoarse voice. 'It really hurts.'

'What we ought to do now is get some baseball bats and that and go and jump him,' said Troy. 'Maybe get some more guys together. Find out where he lives. Teach him a fucking lesson.'

Curl nodded.

'What goes around comes around,' he said.

'You got to do it,' Troy said to Darren. 'You can't let him get away with it.'

Darren squinted at them. One eye was closed up, its hue like a gaudy eyeshadow. His feet were bare on the grass. The sun was out, spilling across the backyard. Roland looked around for the motorcycle, but it was not there.

'It's still in the shed,' Darren told him. 'Lucky I put it there last night. I must've known. I must've had a feeling about it.'

He sat up, feeling his ribs again. 'Nah,' he said to Troy and Curl. 'That Liam guy's a psycho. If we go and bash him, he's just going to come back after us again.'

'He could still come back,' said Troy. 'If someone like Liam thinks you're too scared to come after him, he's going to think he's got one over on you. You don't want to be having to look over your shoulder all the time.'

'I don't think he's coming back. He's made his point.'

'What I reckon,' said Troy, 'is we go after him and we bash him so bad he's not even going to think about coming back. Put him in hospital or something. Really scare the shit out of him.'

'No,' said Darren, wincing and hissing softly again as he reached for his cigarettes. 'Just, let's leave it, all right? Forget about it.'

WHEN ROLAND WENT to see Darren later that week, he found him agitated, pacing back and forth across his backyard. He was chain-smoking, his cigarette pack held half-crushed in his hand. The fire was out for the first time that winter, nothing more than a shallow pit of ashes from which powdery scrolls rose in the breeze, so fine that it appeared to be smouldering. The Triumph sat in its usual spot on the grass in the sun, the overgrown lawn stippled with strawflowers and dandelions, the cumquat tree by the fence alight with masses of tiny orange globes. Roland noticed that the motorcycle did not have its usual immaculate lustre, a grubby film blemishing the head-light and the chrome.

'How are you feeling?' he asked Darren.

'I'm not good, Roly,' Darren said. His eyes were bloodshot, dirty hair fallen over his face. His bruises were starting to fade into mottled purple patches, thick about his eye. He looked exhausted. 'I'm really not good.'

He tossed his cigarette butt into the dead fire and lit another one. 'I'm just so fucking angry.'

'What about?'

'Nah, it's not that it's about anything. I'm just feeling angry all the time. I can't sleep. Every time I fall asleep, I just—' He demonstrated, jerking his head forward, his eyes opening wide. 'And sort of not able to breathe. Like I'm suffocating or something. The doctor said I had anxiety. So, he gives me these antidepressants and yeah, so maybe I don't have anxiety anymore, but I can't sleep at all now. And I'm so fucking angry. I'm out of my mind with it. Troy comes around the other day and he's talking about stuff and I say, "Troy, I'm going to have to stop you there, because if you don't shut up I'm going to punch you." I said, "Just go home. You don't want to be around me right now." I've smoked about an ounce of bud this week just trying to calm myself down.'

He was making twitchy movements as he talked, occasionally looking up at Roland, those huge pupils filling his pale irises.

'What this thing with Liam was,' he said with sudden vigour, 'is it was a fucking wake-up call. I've really got to get my shit together, Roly. No more of this fucking around with people like Liam. I don't want to have anything to do with people like that anymore. Or Floyd, even. Fuck him. What's he ever done for me anyway, except get me into shit like this all the time? And no more wasting my time going to nightclubs. Forget that. No more fucking around with young girls either. I'm telling you Roly, you ever see something that looks too good to be true, it probably is. It looks good on the surface, it seems like the sweetest thing you can imagine, but underneath it's the most fucked-up mess you've ever seen. You've got no idea. There's been a lot of shit going on. And I don't mean this stuff with Liam. I mean other stuff. There's been some really bad things going on around here that you don't even know about. You don't want to either. Trust me on that.'

He rubbed his eyes with his palms and blinked.

'But something's got to be done about it. Someone's got to sort things out. And if it's got to be me then it's got to be me. And I'll do it, too. I will.'

He continued pacing up and down the lawn, dragging on his cigarette until it burned down to the filter. There was a flash of flame and a brief chemical smell before he flicked it away, swearing. Roland noticed that his hands were shaking.

'Other people might be fine doing nothing about it, just standing by and pretending it's not going on, but that's not me. Something's got to change. If it doesn't change, then I'm going to make it change. I should have done it already. I should have put a stop to it the minute I found out about it.'

Darren paused by the Triumph and wiped down the petrol tank with the sleeve of his shirt. He lit another cigarette, took a deep drag on it, and watched the smoke as it curled and unravelled in the sunshine. With a sigh, he looked mournfully back down at the motorcycle.

'You know when you saw me out here with my bike last summer? Did you think I was working on it, like fixing it up or something?'

Roland nodded.

'Yeah, well, I wasn't. All I was doing was cleaning it. Truth is, Roly, I don't know the first thing about bikes. I don't even ride it anywhere except around the block here sometimes. I'm too afraid I'm going to prang it or drop it.' He shook his head, wiping his sleeve over the handlebars. 'I don't even know why I bought it now. When my dad died, my mum got this big payout and she gave me ten grand to do whatever I wanted with it. So I decided I'd get a bike. I thought they were cool and I'd always wanted one, so I thought, "Why not?" You know, I thought whenever I wanted to get out of here, I could just get on the bike and go. Just take off. But there's nowhere to go really, is there?'

He took a heavy breath and ran a hand through his hair and over the thick stubble on his cheeks and chin, kneading his face.

'When me and Cassie went down to Rosebud last month, she thought we'd be going on the bike. But we took the bus. I left the bike in the shed. She was really disappointed, you know? But I said, "We don't need it, babe." Because we weren't planning on coming back. We were going there for good. To live there. I know it sounds crazy, Roly, but I thought I was in love with that girl.'

He took another cigarette out of the pack and lit it off the glowing butt before he flicked the butt away. The shadows had grown long, vinegar flies circling in the hazy light that streamed through the trees. Birds twittered and skirmished in a flurry of activity, the exuberance of the last hours of the day. Down the street, two of Todd McKeon's sisters were playing badminton on their front lawn, voices raised, their thin figures lunging at the arcing shuttlecock. Another struggled about the footpath on a pair of rollerskates, the wheels clacking and hissing as she grasped at fences and iron gates. Above her, a Plunkett mallee frothed with masses of white flowers, petals like the dainty limbs of sea anemones. There were only two weeks left until the exams, and Roland had been forcing the study, slogging away joylessly, and he was weary. He rubbed his eyes, realising that they were sore, that they had grown unused to it. Darren shook his head.

'But it turns out I didn't even know her,' he said. 'I didn't know anything.'

TILLY JOHNSON CAME down the drive, shoes clacking briskly on the concrete. Her two fat dachshunds were dragged along behind her, eyes popping and little legs whirring as they struggled to keep pace. She tied them to the patio railing and bustled into the kitchen, where Roland and his father were playing draughts at the table. His mother was at the sink, washing up the breakfast dishes. There was an intense, whispered conversation between the two women—some meaningful nods from Tilly—and Roland was sent out of the room. His father closed the hall door, which was almost never shut, behind him.

'Of course, everyone knew,' he heard Tilly say jubilantly as the door closed, her hushed voice released to its usual timbre. 'Everyone knew something *odd* was going on in that family.'

Roland sat at his desk and began going through the notes for his chemistry exam. Outside, the dachshunds were whining, sending Jack's cockatoo into a coughing fit. The bird spluttered and swore, hacking up a gob of phlegm. The dogs began to yap excitedly. He heard Tilly speaking to them as she came out of the house and untied their leashes. She clopped back up the driveway. Sometime later, his father came into his room.

'We're going to go for a drive,' he said. 'Just you and me. Your mother needs to have a talk with Lily, so we're going to give them some space. Get yourself a jacket and whatever else you need.'

'Why?' Roland asked. 'Where are we going?'

His father, half out of the door, scowled. 'Just do it, will you.'

Roland put on a jacket and joined his father in the kitchen. He was looking out of the window onto the road, his arms folded.

'Your mother's gone to pick up Lily,' he told Roland. 'We'll head off when she gets back.'

'What was Tilly saying? What was that all about?'

His father shifted, his expression grim.

'That doesn't need to concern you at the moment.'

The heaviness of his father's mood was palpable. The abandoned draughts board still sat on the table, the game frozen in the moment of Tilly's arrival. Outside, a dove cooed, shuffling in the branches of the pittosporum. When the car arrived there was a sudden burst of noise and life again as Lily, who had been at a slumber party, got out and ran to the door. She was in her tutu, a plastic tiara lopsided on her head.

'Look what I've got! Look what I've got!' she cried out to Roland, hefting up a shopping bag bulging with chips and lollies and a two-litre bottle of creaming soda. 'Look what I've got and you can't have none!' she sang as she skipped down the hall and into her room.

His father went outside and talked to his mother by the car. She looked weary, her face pinched, as though she had been crying. They embraced and he kissed her on the forehead, holding her hands in his as they talked. Roland hesitated in the doorway. He had been confused earlier, but now he was struck with the dreadful sense of something being terribly wrong.

In the car, they turned down the highway and drove through Nunawading. Reg Noble Auto was busy on the Saturday morning, a few young families wandering about the cars as Reg Noble's giant face smirked down at them from the sign atop the pylon. Roland saw a man open the door of a green sedan and put his head in, his wife pushing a stroller behind him. A little girl ran about the concrete in a pleated dress, her tiny white shoes a blur. They continued to Ringwood, where the violet hills appeared on the horizon, the light from the radio tower blinking through heavy clouds. Distant rain streaked the sky. His father pulled into a carpark and took out the *Melway*.

'Anywhere you want to go that you can think of?' he asked Roland. 'We've got a while, so I don't mind a long drive. In fact, I think I would prefer it.'

The car vibrated, the engine churning. Outside, the sky was darkening.

'We could go to the beach,' Roland suggested, though he didn't know why.

His father looked at him, frowning. Roland thought he was going to yell at him again, but he did not.

'All right,' he said, releasing the handbrake. 'The beach it is.'

They headed south, rain splattering the windshield as they drove through the repeating scenery of the suburbs. A race-course appeared on their right, the curve of white fences glowing through the downpour, the empty seats of the grandstand like the pleats of a bellows. Power lines passed overhead and then they were in the country. Roland watched the farmhouses glide by, smoke drifting from their chimneys, sheep and cattle grazing between the conifer windbreaks and the distant lines of poplars. Soon they could see the dark water of the bay.

They stopped in a town that was not much more than a pub and a few shops, and Roland went into the toilet block to pee. When he came out, he saw his father wandering down to the treeless foreshore past a graffitied barbeque shelter. Seagulls scavenged in bins overflowing with rubbish, cinnabar feet scraping the hotplates. Their calls were lost in the wind. He followed his father down the footpath, past the row of dark houses facing the sea.

It was high tide and the clusters of mangroves were nearly drowned in the high turbid water that smashed at the sea wall, flowing frothy and filthy over the footpath and the fenceless front lawns. Through the mist of light rain, Roland could see the blurred shape of an island crowned by the shifting patterns of a flock of swifts as they wove black against the rolling clouds and the white incandescence of the sky. His father went sombrely before him, his hair torn about by the wind, his face speckled with drizzle, not seeming to notice the water as it spilled over his shoes. He stopped and looked out at the island for what seemed like ages. Roland watched the drops gather on his jacket.

'If your father doesn't see something,' his father said, seeming to speak as much to himself as to Roland. 'Then you can't blame yourself…if even he doesn't know what to do.'

He stayed looking across the bay in silence as the rain grew heavier and then they walked back to the street.

The car crawled through sheets of rain down the Bass

Highway, buffeted by the wind, the paddocks a grey waste-land on either side. They crossed the bridge to Phillip Island and drove around the town until they found the cinema among a maze of wretched tourist shops and ice-cream parlours, an empty pancake restaurant, gumball machines and mechanical children's rides lined up on the footpaths outside the amusement arcades. They were just in time for the next screening of *The Karate Kid II*, a film Roland had already seen a few years before, alone in the cinema apart from some teenage couples who sat in the back seats and spent the movie kissing and murmuring, now and again throwing a handful of popcorn at the screen. His father left towards the end of the film.

'You stay here,' he told Roland. 'I just need to call your mother.'

Roland found him in the lobby as he came out with the other teenagers. The couples had their arms around each other, hands in the other's pockets, one embarrassed girl combing her fringe down over her face as she walked with her boyfriend to the double doors. His father was chatting to the cinema owner and seemed to be in a very different mood, grinning as he talked, his hands on his hips.

'Well, you certainly picked a good day for it,' the cinema owner was saying.

His father put his hand on Roland's shoulder. 'How are you going there?' he asked him, smiling at him. 'Not a bad film, was it?'

'It was all right,' said Roland.

'Yes,' said his father. 'I didn't think it was so bad. For something entertaining. Sometimes that's all you want, isn't it?' he said to the cinema owner. 'Just to sit back and get lost in the story.'

'It's what they like,' said the cinema owner. 'Have to give the people what they want. Otherwise, you're out of a business.'

'No harm in that. No harm in that at all.'

On the drive home, they stopped off for fish and chips in the town over the bridge.

'Well, I spoke to your mother,' his father told Roland as he unwrapped the butcher's paper on one of the graffiti-scored benches along the foreshore. 'And she had a good talk with Lily and it turns out she's fine. She's perfectly all right. It seems we were worried over nothing.'

Roland nodded, uncomprehending, but did not speak. The smell of the food wafted strong and sharp with vinegar in the chill and the brine of the sea air.

'Look,' said his father. 'We made the mistake of listening to some particularly nasty gossip and it's really not something I should repeat to you. Let's just say it had us very worried about Lily. We thought that something might have, well, could potentially have happened to her. Something I don't even want to think about now. Because what was said was malicious and hurtful and potentially very destructive. I'm actually very angry about it. And I'll tell you what, I'll be giving Tilly Johnson a piece of my mind when I see her next. Believe you me.'

He wolfed down a battered scallop, taking a handkerchief out of his pocket and wiping his mouth and beard.

'It gave me and your mum both a terrible fright, and we did overreact but we shouldn't have. We should have got our facts straight first. You do that when you're a parent. The idea that anything bad could have happened to your children is unthinkable. Which is why these rumours can be so damaging, I suppose. But you should never listen to gossip. Trust your own eyes and ears.'

They watched the water and the boats as they ate. Roland threw the occasional chip to the squabbling crowd of seagulls that had gathered at their feet. A small trawler with a streaked azure hull came in, its rigging quivering with the movement and the wind. The engines slowed and it drifted towards the pier. A man jumped off with a shout as he wound the towrope around a scarred and rust-stained bollard.

'Maybe we should get ourselves a boat,' his father said thoughtfully. 'Not a big boat like these ones. A little tinnie with an outboard motor, something like that. We could take it out around here, around the bay. Do some fishing in it. What do you reckon? Do you think you'd enjoy that?'

'I don't think I'd have the time,' said Roland. 'There's a lot of work to do in the final years. They say the HSC's going to be six or seven hours a night.'

'That's still a few years off.'

'Yes, but you have to start working for it now. Not that I am, really. Things aren't going very well at the moment at all. I'm just finding it all very difficult.' He breathed out. It was a relief to say it, almost like a confession.

'Well, don't stress about it,' said his father. 'That never gets you anywhere. And your exams don't actually count for anything yet, do they?'

'They count for what classes you get into next year. If you want to get into the top classes you have to do well.'

'But you're already in all the top classes this year, aren't you?'

Roland hesitated. 'No,' he said. 'I'm not.'

'You're not? I thought you were.'

'No.' He was embarrassed now. 'Sometimes I just can't keep up.'

'But I was sure you told me that you'd got into all the top classes.'

'I got into the top maths class, but that's only because I work so hard at it. There are other boys in the class who don't work at all. They're just good at it. I'm not one of the smart ones. I just work hard.'

'Well, that's all right, that's good, though. Nothing wrong with getting yourself up there with a bit of hard work.'

'It's just, I think, it's the other things,' said Roland. 'There's so much other stuff going on that I can't concentrate.'

'What sort of things?'

'Just stuff. Just all the things that happen.'

'It sounds to me like the real problem is that you're worrying about it too much. Look, you're giving it a go and that's all you can do. No one can ask more than that from you.'

They continued to scoop up handfuls of chips, Roland already satiated, heavy with the oiliness of it, lips tingling with salt, but munching through all the same. Another trawler was coming down the channel, streaming through the choppy waves.

'Have you thought about what you might like to do at the end of it all?' his father asked him.

'Not really,' Roland said.

'Well, I'd say it's worth starting to think about that now. You have to choose something you love, but make sure it's something that rewards you financially as well. That was my mistake. Teachers are very poorly paid these days. It's not that we're not comfortable, we're very comfortable and should count ourselves lucky, but everything is becoming about money and you don't want to be left behind, because it's a tough old world out there if you don't have the money to live in it. Academic achievement is all very well, but it isn't everything. You have to have a bit of drive and a way with people as well. You need to know how to be entrepreneurial these days.'

'But the HSC is the most important thing, isn't it?' asked Roland, a moment of panic at the thought that he might have it wrong, that all the slogging might be for nothing. 'Isn't that what everyone says?'

'Oh, it is. I'm not saying it isn't. It's your ticket to success, for sure. You do well in the HSC and the world is your oyster. Absolutely, that's true. But I'm certain you'll do very well. I've never had any doubt about that.'

'It's still a lot of work,' said Roland weakly. 'It's very difficult.'

His father flung the last scabby fragments of chips to the seagulls and slapped Roland's leg.

'It will all be over sooner than you know it and then you'll get a chance to live your life. Enjoy it a bit.'

They wrapped up the butcher's paper and put it in the bin, pausing to take a last look at the water before they drove home.

AS ROLAND CAME up the lane on his way home from school, he saw Curl standing on the veranda of Darren's house, talking to Darren's mother as she leaned against the doorway, a silhouette behind the wire of the open screen door. He looked around for Darren, but the backyard was deserted, empty beer cans and cigarette butts littering the ashes of the fire pit. The motorcycle was nowhere to be seen. Curl came down the steps to meet him.

'You hear what happened?' he asked Roland.

'No.'

'Darren's in Larundel.'

'What's Larundel?'

'The psychiatric hospital,' said Curl. 'Cops put him there.'

'But why?'

'He had a punch-up with that Reg Noble guy. They took him down the cop shop and he was acting weird, apparently. Didn't know what to do with him, so they took him to Larundel. That's what his mum says, anyway. The doctors say he has to stay there for a while.'

Curl shrugged, folded his enormous arms and tossed back his mane of golden hair. Darren's mother had gone back inside the house.

'I don't know,' he said. 'I don't get it. Me and Troy are going to drive over and see him tomorrow morning, if you want to come.'

'I can't,' said Roland. 'I've got school tomorrow.'

'So wag,' said Curl. 'Darren'll want to see you. He's been there since Saturday and no one's gone to see him except for his mum.' He punched Roland lightly on the arm. 'Come on, Roly. He'd do it for you.'

The following day, Roland left for school as usual, but went to the library instead of the station. He got changed out of his uniform in the toilets and then waited at a desk by the window, watching the peak-hour traffic as it sat growling on either side of the level crossing. It was the first time he had ever wagged school and he felt nervous and elated at the same time, thinking of all the boys trooping into assembly without him, the class-rooms, the regimented hours. It seemed impossible that he was not there, that by such a small act of will the entire day could be so easily claimed as his own. Peak hour passed and every-thing became quiet outside, the streets empty in the glare of the morning sun. Old people appeared, bent women in overcoats trailing their vinyl trolleys after them as they made their slow, determined way down the footpaths. At around ten o'clock, he saw Curl pulling up to the kerb in his mother's Kingswood.

'Where's Troy?' Roland asked him as he got into the car.

'He didn't want to come,' said Curl, reversing onto the road and gunning the Kingswood up the hill. 'Bad memories and that. You know Troy's been in Larundel as well, don't you?'

'No,' said Roland.

'Darren never told you? Yeah, I suppose we don't talk about it much. Especially around Troy.'

They were waiting to turn onto the highway. Roland had the *Melway* open on his lap. He held it up for Curl to examine.

'Why was Troy there?'

'Because of his old man. He bashed Troy really badly this one time. It was sort of our fault because we'd trashed the house while his old man and his girlfriend were away one weekend. Troy threw this big party and we all went a bit crazy, I suppose. His dad comes home Sunday morning and starts laying into him. I mean, really smacking him around. Chucked him down on the paving so he was all grazed up. Bleeding everywhere. Split lip. He was bad. So, Troy gets away from his old man and does the bolt, runs off down the street. We piss off too and go looking for him. Find him at the supermarket. He's sitting on the floor, all messed up, crying and bleeding and shit. Opening up packs of Tim Tams and scoffing them down. And we were saying, "Come on, Troy, we've got to go. They're going to call the cops." But he wouldn't listen to us. Just sat there crying, eating Tim Tams. And yeah, cops took him to Larundel, same as they did to Darren. It sort of fucked him up too. I mean, you wouldn't know it these days, but Troy used to be a really funny guy, before all that happened. He sort of got angry after that. He's angry all the time, now.'

'What about Floyd?'

Curl made a dismissive gesture.

'Floyd doesn't care about anyone except himself.'

It was a long drive, through the endless spill of the suburbs to the north. Stopped at the pedestrian crossing near the university, they watched as a couple passed in front of them, a boy with an anarchy symbol painted on the back of his leather jacket and a girl in army pants, her head shaved at the sides, a long strawberry forelock falling over her eyes. Identical canvas backpacks hung from their shoulders, the buckles loose, covered in stickers that read 'No Fees'. Curl turned to Roland, grinning and shaking his head.

The hospital was a sprawling collection of old redbrick buildings and lawns veined with covered walkways and paved paths, here and there a shrub or climbing ivy. They parked by the locked ward, a large, porticoed building that was conspicuous in the absence of activity around it. A fat man in a white uniform let them in, jingling his keys as he took the boys to another set of doors. He followed them inside and disappeared down a corridor where men in pyjamas and bathrobes ambled about with the shuffle and drowsy expressions of sleepwalkers.

They found Darren in the courtyard, sitting in the sun underneath a spreading pepper tree that almost touched the walls on either side. He was smoking a cigarette, a mug of coffee by his feet on the bitumen path. When he saw them, he nodded a weary greeting, watching with red-rimmed eyes as they approached.

'Here we are,' Curl said. He sat next to Darren and took out his cigarettes. 'Just like old times.'

'Yeah, yeah,' said Darren.

A boy sitting on the flagstones with a group of visitors had been watching Roland and Curl since they came into the court-yard. His stare was intense, his eyes stretched open like those of a startled character in a comic strip.

'Hey, Darren,' he called out. 'Are those your friends from Glenella?'

'Yeah,' said Darren.

The boy nodded, still staring. His hair was stringy, his face gaunt and pitted. He wore a nylon tracksuit, zipped up to the collar. A woman held on to his arm, as she talked to him.

'How are you feeling?' Roland asked Darren.

'Yeah,' he said. 'Yeah, I'm all right, Roly. It's not so bad here. They've given me some drug that's sort of chilled me out. I'm sleeping fine, you know. Sleeping a lot actually. And I'm not anxious or whatever it was. Only problem is, I don't feel like doing anything.'

He indicated the brand-new pyjamas he was wearing and his terry towelling robe.

'I can't even be bothered getting dressed in the morning. Just come out here, smoke ciggies, drink coffee. You know, try to get my brain going. I'm spending all day just sitting here staring at my feet.'

'But why are you in here in the first place?' Curl asked him, looking around at the other patients with their unwashed hair and hive-blotched faces, spots of blood where they had scratched at them. They sat sleepily about the courtyard, bent over their coffee mugs and hazing the air with cigarette smoke. A plump boy in a Monash University windcheater was weeping and talking to himself in the plaintive voice of a child. 'I don't get it. I mean, seriously, look at these people.'

'Marijuana psychosis,' said Darren. 'That's what the doctors say. I don't know, though. I swear, it was those antidepressants that made me feel crazy. The mull was just to calm myself down, try to get some sleep.'

'It wasn't the mull,' said Curl.

'Yeah, well, it was something. All I remember is, I went around to Cassie's house to have a quiet word with her old man. I don't know, I must have grabbed him or something. I say to him, "Listen, you and me are going to have a little talk." Next thing I know, we're down on the grass, wrestling and throwing punches and that. I'm shouting at him. All the neighbours have come out and they're standing on the footpath watching us. Then the police rock up. You remember that cop from the lane at my joint? The real arsehole?'

Curl and Roland both nodded.

'So it's him, right. So I run, which I shouldn't have. I wasn't doing anything wrong, I just wanted to talk to the guy. Anyway, they grab me and get me down on the grass, handcuff me, start dragging me to the divvy van. And I say to them, "He's the one you should be arresting." I said, "Ask him about his daughter. Ask him about Cassie. Ask him about what he's been doing to her."'

He looked at them grimly, tapping ash from his cigarette.

'Said it right in front of all those neighbours standing there gawking at me. Right in front of everyone. Serves him right, the prick.'

'Wait,' said Curl. 'So, what did you mean?'

Darren shrugged. 'You know, he's been molesting her or whatever. Sleeping with her. She told me when we were staying at my sister's in Rosebud. I suppose I just couldn't handle it. Told her I didn't want anything to do with her anymore.'

'Jesus,' said Curl. 'And they put you in here for saying that?'

'Nah, it's not because of that. I sort of lost it when I was in the divvy van. I started crying and I couldn't stop. I don't know why. Kept crying when I was in the lockup. They were all worried about me. Kept coming in and asking if I wanted some

McDonald's. But I just kept crying. In the end, they brought in this doctor. I told her how I couldn't sleep, about the anxiety and everything. How there were some guys who were out to get me. Liam and that. And she asked me if I'd been smoking marijuana and I said, "Yeah, a shitload." And she tells me I've got this marijuana psychosis and she wants to put me in hospital for a while to see what happens. So I said, "Fine." Why not? If the doctors can actually help me here, not just give me fucking antidepressants that make everything worse.'

'Hey, Darren,' the boy with the visitors called out again, still staring at them with his weird gaping eyes. 'Are those your friends from Glenella who want to kill me?'

'They don't want to kill you,' Darren yelled back. 'No one wants to kill you, mate.'

He turned back to Roland and Curl, shaking his head.

'I know I'm not crazy like some of these people in here,' he said. 'But I really did feel like I was going crazy for a while there.' He screwed his cigarette out on the bricks and bent over to rub off the black mark with his thumb. 'I just didn't know what was going on. I didn't know what to do.'

Curl and Roland left at lunchtime and said almost nothing to each other during the trip back along the meander of the eight-lane highway, through a landscape of nameless suburbs without boundary, replications of Roland's own familiar place of adjoining streets and cul-de-sacs and strips of shops, other lives multiplied innumerably here in the rows of houses that stretched to all horizons in a bland desert of brick and terracotta.

Reg was molesting Cassie, Roland kept thinking to himself, but he could barely fathom the idea. He wondered what he could do to stop it, imagining a confrontation with Reg, picturing himself ambushing him, grabbing him as Darren had done, striking him with his fists until he begged for mercy. But Reg's figure appeared to him as gigantic and invulnerable as the winking, grinning face on the sign above the highway, and he could only see himself as small and weak and young, his punches glancing off Reg's bulk as though he were trying to pound stone. It was like trying to fight off a monster in a dream, when all your limbs turn useless.

They were heading down a long residential street lined with paperbarks, when Curl turned into the gravel carpark of a cream-brick church set back from the road behind a row of fidgeting palm trees, an engorged version of the houses around it. The carpark was mostly empty, a few hatchbacks and sedans parked in the midday sun.

'Watch this,' Curl said to Roland. He put the car in neutral and planted his foot on the accelerator. The engine roared deafeningly. As the noise reached a crescendo, he put the car in gear and they lurched sideways, Curl frantically turning the steering wheel as the big Kingswood began to spin. They circled around and around, the engine screaming, a thick cloud of dust kicked up behind them. A bearded man in his shirtsleeves, the white shirt tight over a bulging gut, ran out of the church and across the lawn towards them. He was yelling, his arms thrown up, his stomach lurching from side to side and his tie flapping over his shoulder. Curl straightened the steering wheel and they pitched forward, skidding, and again began the dizzying spirals on the gravel, the back wheels churning, stones pinging against the parked cars. The man shook his fists as he ran after them through the dust cloud that had engulfed the carpark. Curl whooped as the car turned again and again in the gravel, and the quiet afternoon transformed into all this sudden noise and chaos made Roland laugh until it hurt.

ROLAND SOMETIMES FELT as though he was living behind a wall of glass, or existed within an amniotic sac surrounded by clear fluid, so that he could see the world but, when he reached out, when he tried to grasp, he could not touch it. Or that he was like some pellucid ghost that apprehends the world of the living but is itself barely seen, that passes through without the power to disturb. Always at a distance from the moment, always finding things more real in memory and in dreams; when it came to a need to act or even just to speak, to express an opinion, that moment somehow did not come. It seemed to him that he thought about things more than other people, that he spent an inordinate amount of time doing nothing but ponder and daydream. He observed, but never quite felt part of what was going on around him.

Suddenly, however, in this week before the exams started, something clicked on in Roland's mind. He went about with a feeling that he was seeing for the first time: the dullness gone, the fog of incomprehension lifted, filtered into an intense clarity. Thoughts emerged as though of their own making, and they came together and crystallised and became urgent. He knew what to do. He had a plan. And it was no longer daydreaming—this was not something he would wait for, merely hope for. It had to be done now. He felt an irrepressible energy. It coursed through him like electricity.

He visited the newsagent's after school, loitering in the aisle where the books were—mostly romance novels and spy thrillers—and read through a book he had seen there before, called *Sydney on Five Dollars a Day*. He did not even notice the disapproving gaze of the owner's wife, a bulldoggish woman who smelled of cigarettes and sat chewing mints all day.

'We're not running a library here,' she told him, her mouth working away, loud squelching of the mints. He ignored her.

His next stop was, in fact, the library, where he asked if they had the Sydney papers. They didn't, so he looked through the Melbourne ones, scanning the Situations Vacant. They needed bakers, bricklayers, butchers, cleaners, office workers, owner-drivers, plasterers, salespeople. Some required experience, but not all.

At the little V/Line office at the station, he asked about tickets to Sydney. The stationmaster took out a laminated sheet and pointed out the ones Roland wanted: single economy concession. Thirty-five dollars each. Roland glanced over the other ticket options: economy return, first-class single, first-class return, first-class sleeper.

'What's a sleeper?' he asked.

'Little private room with a bunk bed,' the stationmaster said. 'You get your own little bathroom. They bring you the paper in the morning, cup of tea.' He scratched his chest through the neck of his green shirt. 'I'd love to do that one day. Go up with the wife. I reckon I'd sleep like a baby in one of those things.'

'You've never done it?'

'On what they pay me? You got to be kidding. As long as I'm paying off my mortgage, I can't afford to do anything.'

'Don't they give you a discount?'

'A discount?' The stationmaster let out a hoot of laughter. 'From these bastards? Not bloody likely.'

Finally, he went to the bank and took out all the money in his account. He had eighty-seven dollars, plus the ten-dollar note his father had given him on the night he had gone to the bar and bistro. He thought it should be enough until he found work in Sydney, and he was expecting Cassie would have some money as well.

He found himself more than adequately prepared for the exams when they came, and they were not the snarling, unforgiving trials that he had been promised. He completed them perfunctorily, long before the clock made its slow hollow strokes towards the finishing time. But even as he found a desk in the draughty school gymnasium, as he laid out his pens and read over the papers, his mind was on other things. He was going through the minutiae of his plan, which increasingly seemed like the answer to everything, not only a means to save Cassie, but a solution to his own life as well. Finally, there would be a meaning there, a reason for it. As he thought about it, there was a feeling of freedom: an immense, impossible, soaring freedom—something like that feeling he had on the day he wagged school to visit Darren at Larundel. And this would not be momentary, not just a single day, but boundless, a whole new life.

But when he finally talked to Cassie, things did not happen as he had envisaged. In her room, unnaturally neat as usual, that chemical lemon scent coming from the newly-washed sheets, an open *Cosmopolitan* on the doona—'How can he please YOU in bed?' the cover screamed—he told her his plan. Cassie began to cry, Roland dumb for a moment as he watched the tears flow so loosely and easily down her cheeks that it seemed they did not come from Cassie at all, that there was some other force at play, something deep and powerful, like a tide.

He tried to explain it, but had difficulty with the words, realising now that it was all vague pictures in his head, like scenes from films: he and Cassie wandering around Sydney, discovering it together, sitting in cafes, restaurants, living together in a room somewhere, some rickety terrace or stained boarding house, windows open to the light and the cool harbour breeze. He had imagined himself getting up early every morning and working hard all day, envisaging a relentless physical labour that would make him strong and gruff and decisive and he would come home exhausted and battered and with callused hands, a man, his face sunburnt and money in his pockets, with which he would be generous. Everything would go to Cassie; he would ask for nothing. It all seemed to dissolve as he tried to say it.

She did not want to go to Sydney with him, Cassie told Roland. She was not brave enough to leave, to go and live somewhere else. She was not as brave as him. She had already tried that with Darren anyway, and look how that turned out.

'Besides,' she said. 'What about you? What about school? What about all the work you've been doing?'

'But that doesn't matter anymore,' said Roland, breathless. 'None of that matters anymore.'

'But what would your parents say?' said Cassie. 'They'd think I'd made you go. They'd never forgive me.'

All she wanted, she told him, was to be an ordinary girl, to go to school every day and hang out with her friends and do her homework and get excited about deb balls and formals.

'I just want to be like everyone else,' she said, the tears streaming down her face. 'Just a fourteen-year-old girl. That's all I ever wanted.'

'Then you have to get away from him,' said Roland.

'Who?'

'Your dad.'

'But I can't,' Cassie sobbed. 'I just can't.'

'But why? Don't you hate him? Don't you want to get as far away as you can from him?'

She took a shuddering breath, wiping her hot, flushed face with the heels of her hands.

'You don't understand. He's my dad.'

'But that's why this is so wrong. Can't you see that?'

She shook her head, the tears beginning again. 'Please, Roland. You really can't understand. There's nothing I can do. There's just nothing I can do.'

It had a feeling of unreality about it, as though it were somehow staged and scripted, as though he had stumbled into a scene from someone else's life. Cassie was sitting cross-legged on her bed, propped up against the pillows. She was wearing a bulky, oversized jumper that came down to her knees, and she seemed delicate and small within it. Outside, the wind was in the trees, a lonely sound. The television blared down-stairs, deep voices and car engines rattling the glass. Gunshots. Through the window, he could see the distant sprawl of the city lights, spread out like a constellation. The abrupt jut and blazing spires of the skyscrapers. That illusion of their closeness through the dark indeterminateness of the night.

'Did you know that I used to wish I was part of your family?' Cassie said, blowing her nose into one of the scrunched-up tissues she had taken from her pockets. 'I used to wish for it so much. Not that I wanted anything bad to happen to my parents, just that they would have to go overseas or something and your parents would offer to take me in and I'd come and live with you, with you and Lily. You always seemed so happy all the time. You were the complete opposite to my family.'

She dabbed at her eyes.

'I wanted to be with you all the time. I sort of used to pretend I was part of your family, even if it was just for a couple of hours while I was over there. But I know now that I'm never going to be like that. I'm never going to be normal. If you understood what I was really like, Roland, seriously, you wouldn't even want to know me.'

A sob heaved through her. She picked up a pillow, hugging it to her chest. The tears had stopped as quickly as they had started. She dabbed at her face with the tissues and her eyes met his, wet and sparkling and intent.

'I'm really, seriously fucked up,' she said. 'My family is so fucked up. I've always been so scared that someone is going to find out what I'm actually like. I've always tried to hide it. I thought that no one would ever love me if they really knew me. Then when I told Darren.' She shrugged. 'It's true. He thought I was disgusting. He thought I was repulsive.'

'He didn't think that,' said Roland. 'I think you just freaked him out a bit, when you told him.'

'No,' said Cassie, shaking her head, sniffing. 'He wouldn't even touch me after that. He wouldn't even look at me.'

They continued to talk, sitting on Cassie's bed, with barely a pause but for a moment when the bawling television was finally switched off and Reg and Colleen went upstairs, boards creaking under their footsteps in the silence of the house. When Roland had come in earlier, it had made him sick to see Reg there on the couch, the fleshiness of his figure now seeming to allude to unthinkable things, and he had gone up to Cassie's room full of rage and revulsion, his fists clenched so tightly that his knuckles turned white. All he had wanted to do was to get her out of this place, away from Reg. He had thought that the strength of his feelings—that he cared more for her than for his own life—would be enough, but now he saw that it was not enough, and as they talked, moving on to other subjects, there was an awful feeling of drifting, of moving away from that moment when things were real: a sense that, once left, it was a place that might never be returned to. They did not mention Sydney again, or Reg, or even Darren, but it was, Roland felt, perhaps the first time he and Cassie had ever really talked, unthwarted by the awkwardness that always seemed to overcome them when they were alone together.

And how much there was to be talked of, how much seemed to have happened in their short lives, how many certainties and ideas they had. They talked about their childhoods, as a time now passed, with fond reminiscences and as though it were all such a long time ago. But most of it was talk of the future, abundant with possibility: full, in their young minds, with nothing but hope, almost too radiant to speak of. Things would be better. It would be a life more heroic than now.

Whatever they did, they both agreed, it had to be something that brought good to the world, something with meaning. Neither wanted the workaday lives of the adults around them;

neither wanted the sterile comfort of the suburbs. Cassie told Roland that she wanted to become a writer.

'I sort of already am,' she said.

She took a pile of yellow Spirax notebooks out of the drawer of her bedside table.

'This is my book,' she said, opening one of them. She showed him a page, where there were lines of neat handwriting in purple ink. 'This is what I've been doing.'

'What's it about?'

'It's about me,' said Cassie, flicking through the pages. 'It's about my life.'

'Can I read it?'

'No. Not yet.'

'Why not?'

'Because it's not finished. It's a long way from being finished. Although, sometimes I think, well, what else is there left for me to do, you know what I mean? I worry that one day I'll sort of not have anything left to experience anymore, because I've already done everything. So I suppose then I'll just work on my book. Write it all down.'

'Is it like a diary or something?'

'Sort of, I suppose.' She continued leafing through it, pausing to read passages. 'It's about the things I've been doing, the things I've been thinking about. And what I've been feeling and that sort of thing. Sometimes I feel like I've got so much to say but I can't actually say it, not to a real person. It's like I need to say it so much that I feel as if I'm going to burst into flames or something.' She closed the notebook and put it down on the doona. 'Do you ever feel like that?'

'No,' Roland said. 'Not really. But I think I know what you mean.'

'This friend of mine once brought this book to school about the supernatural and mysteries and stuff, like the *Marie Celeste* and the Bermuda Triangle and things like that, and there was this part where they were talking about this woman in Germany who was at a nightclub, and she just burst into flames, right in front of everyone. But not like she caught on fire. They said the flames came out of her, like, from within her. And when my friend was telling us about it, I thought, I can totally understand how that could happen. That's exactly how I feel sometimes, when I'm just talking to people and being nice and polite and everything. I just want to stand up and scream and scream. Anyway, I'm not friends with that girl anymore.'

She looked up at him, that unwavering stare of hers, eyes still red from the tears.

'I'm like you now,' she told Roland. 'I don't have any friends at school anymore.'

'Why not?'

'I told my friend Sharon some stuff. I wouldn't normally have told her, even though we were supposedly best friends and everything, but this was after me and Darren broke up and I was so upset. I just needed someone to talk to. So I told Sharon and she went off straight away and told Elise, the girl who hates me, and so of course Elise told absolutely everyone. So they're all awful to me now.'

Roland nodded. 'Once I talked to this girl from your school,' he said. 'She came up to me and said some really nasty things about you.'

'What did she say?'

'I don't want to tell you. It was pretty bad.'

'No, tell me. They say it to my face, so it's not like I probably haven't heard it.'

'She said you were a slut and a liar and stuff.'

Cassie nodded, looking down at the floor, silent for a moment.

'They all think I'm lying about it. That's what everyone always says. When I first told my mum about my dad, she slapped me in the face. I didn't even understand what was happening. I was just telling her. I was only eleven. But she kept hitting me over and over again and screaming at me and telling me to admit that I was making it up. So I told her that I made it up, even though that wasn't true. That was the thing that was a lie. And now everyone says I'm lying. It's why I'm writing this, I suppose,' she said, gathering the notebooks together and placing them on her lap. 'To tell the truth about everything.'

She met his eyes again.

'After what happened with Darren and then with Sharon and everyone, I promised myself I'd never tell anyone ever again, I'd just write it in my book. But I'm telling you because I trust you.'

'You have to tell someone,' said Roland. 'You can't keep it all bottled up.'

'I think you're the only person left that I do trust,' she said.

Roland left at first light. It was cloudy and grey outside, shadowed foliage whispering in the freshness of a morning breeze still sweet with the night's jasmine, a fine drizzle specking and furbishing the world. Cassie walked with him to the footpath, her face pale and worn as she hugged herself in the morning cold. She waved him goodbye before returning, a nimble dash on socked feet, to the dark and sleeping house. In the east, the first rays were striking out, the clouds thinning. The sky, as pale and as clear as glass, promised a glorious new spring day.

AT LARUNDEL, ROLAND and Curl walked along the covered walkway that stretched between the open wards and skirted the dipping lawn. The identical redbrick buildings rose on their right, their faces gridded with box windows and half-timbered gables, the white lattices stark against the velvety claret of the old bricks. Trees swayed between them; a rhododendron blazed with flowers. Tranquillised patients dozed as they sat at the entrances, or stared out blankly, their hair blowing about in the wind. They found Darren hunched over on a bench under a spindly she-oak. He was smoking mechanically, looking even more dishevelled than the last time they had seen him. His face had grown swollen, hives blooming around his mouth and cheeks, his stubble turned to a wispy beard.

'You've got the life out here, don't you?' Curl said, punching him on the arm.

Darren smiled weakly. 'Yeah, I suppose,' he said.

'What have you been doing?'

Darren took a drag of his cigarette, the smoke peeling away in the sunlight. 'Just this,' he said heavily. 'Just nothing.'

They watched the other patients as they wandered about in their pyjamas and bathrobes, coffee mugs cradled against their chests. One caught Roland's eye and looked away, like a bashful child. A man with a long beard walked onto the grass, a bedsheet draped over his shoulders. He began to make a speech to no one in particular, waving his hands about. Some visitors coming out of the ward—a corpulent family in shorts and T-shirts—stopped to listen to him with the leisurely interest of tourists.

'Why don't we go for a walk?' Curl suggested to Darren. 'You can show us around the place.'

'No, I'm fine here.'

'Come on. It will do you some good.'

Darren stood up wearily, his bathrobe falling open. He wrapped it back around himself, holding it closed with his folded arms, and started shuffling down one of the paths.

'Don't go too far, Darren,' said a woman sitting among the patients by the ward entrance.

'I'm not going to,' said Darren in a thick voice. 'I don't even want to go anywhere.'

'Oh, yeah?' said the woman, shading her eyes with her hand. She was slender and dark-haired. 'No, go and have a wander. Just don't run off on me.'

Darren nodded.

'Who's that?' Curl asked Darren, glancing back at the woman.

'Gina,' said Darren. 'She's one of the nurses or whatever.'

'Yeah?' said Curl. 'She tuck you in at night?'

Darren shrugged.

'You wouldn't mind, ay?'

Darren looked at Curl, unsmiling, and stopped to light another cigarette. He had difficulty in the wind, his fingers slipping clumsily on the striker wheel, and it seemed as though he would have stood there interminably had Curl not taken the lighter from him. He shielded it with his hands as Darren stooped over it. They walked back in silence and Darren sat down on the bench again, barely seeming to notice when they bade him farewell.

'Yeah, that's the drugs doing that to him,' Curl said to Roland as they drove home. 'Same thing happened to Troy when he was there.'

Roland nodded and looked back out the window. They passed the university, where a crowd of students in black denim waited outside the bus stop.

'We've been talking to some guys around the place,' said Curl. 'And they reckon we've got to get Liam back for what he did to Darren. Everyone says he's got to pay for it. Moses and that, they're all saying it. And this guy Fat Gerald, who's a proper full-on bikie. He was really angry when he heard about it. He came up to me and Troy and asked us what we were going to do.'

'Really?'

'Yep. There's a lot of people not happy about it. They've all said they're right behind us if we want to get Liam back. So, we're going to jump him. It's all organised. It's going to happen this Friday night.'

They were stopped at the lights. Curl looked hesitantly at Roland, drumming his fingers against the steering wheel.

'You don't have to come if you don't want to. It's probably going to get pretty rough.'

'I want to come,' said Roland, surprising himself.

'Yeah?' said Curl, grinning. 'Good on you, Roly. I knew you would. Darren'd appreciate it too. I mean, look what that place has turned him into. It's not right, is it? It's fucked up. And that's Liam's fault. That's what everyone reckons. They all know that Darren was fine before he got bashed. He shouldn't be in a fucking mental hospital. Liam's got to take responsibility for that.'

That Friday night, Roland met Curl and Troy at the carpark behind the shops, where the Torana was parked in darkness by the glowing servo. Curl and Troy were inside, drinking from a bottle of Jim Beam. Troy had a sports bag at his feet. Roland slid into the back seat.

'So what we're going to do is we're all going to get together at Fat Gerald's house,' Troy told Roland, passing him the bottle. 'And Shane, you know him? He's the skinhead guy. What he's going to do is, he's going to hang around with Liam and that and pretend he's all friends with them and everything. He's going to say he's set up a deal with Moses, but he's actually going to ring us and let us know where they want to meet up, and that's where we're going to jump them. All right?'

Roland nodded and took a swig of the Jim Beam. Troy opened the glove box and switched on the map light.

'I thought maybe a taste now,' he said to Curl. 'Just to get in the mood and everything. Do the rest when it's all on.'

'Yeah, yeah. I'm up for that.'

Troy took a deal bag out of his pocket, flicked it with his finger and poured some white powder onto the *Melway*. He cut it up into neat lines with his driver's licence, then rolled a two-dollar note into a slim cylinder and handed it to Roland.

'You go first, Roly,' he said.

'What is it?' Roland asked.

'Crank. You snort it. You know how they do cocaine in the movies? Like that.'

'No, I'm all right,' said Roland.

'You should do it,' said Curl. 'It's your first fight. You don't want to freeze up or something.'

'He's right,' said Troy. 'No offence, Roly, but you're probably going to need it. With this stuff, you're not scared of anything. You're fucking unstoppable. Seriously. You'll see.'

Listening to their instructions, Roland bent over the *Melway*, the rolled-up note to his nostril, and inhaled the powder. There was a numbness and a bitter lemon taste in the back of his throat and then, with a single heartbeat, it surged through him. An acute pleasure filled his head and flowed through his limbs, like the warmth of a hot bath. He watched Troy and Curl do their lines and each turn to him, their eyes lit, pupils swollen, and they smiled at each other, recognition that they all felt it, felt the same. As they drove, Roland leaned back in the seat and watched the streetlights pass overhead. Everything was sharp and bright and clear; the movement of the car was exhilarating. He felt fantastic.

'I've never done crank before, but I've done speed a few times,' Curl told Roland. 'Some of those birds in the nightclubs, they're practically addicted to the stuff. They work in shops and that sort of thing, so they make decent money and then they blow it all on speed on the weekends. Speed and clubbing. Once I did a couple of grams with this girl and we were fucking for hours. Going at it nonstop.' He smacked his fist repeatedly into his palm. 'I was so fucking hard, I swear. Problem was, I couldn't come. And so, after we're at it for about five hours or something, she goes, "Can we stop? This is making me sore." And anyway, so she's sucking me off, sucking me off. Still couldn't come.'

'Bullshit you fucked her for five hours,' said Troy.

'No, I did. No joke. It was all night, mate. We only stopped to do some more lines and then we kept going. Had this massive hard-on the whole time, but I couldn't do anything about it. So yeah,' he said, grinning back at Roland. 'Pros and cons. What you gonna do?'

Fat Gerald's house was a frayed weatherboard in Glenella North, the sort of area where Rottweilers snarled at passers-by from behind cyclone fences and half-stripped car hulls lay rusting in the front yards like the carcasses of vanquished beasts. When they arrived, two men were taping pieces of cardboard over the sides of a van parked in the driveway, covering the blue lettering. 'AAA Custom Signage,' it read, and below that, in italics, 'We Specialise in Neon!'

Inside, five or six men were slouched around the lounge room, longnecks in their hands and boots up on the coffee table. A motor-racing video was playing on the television, all droning cars and earnest commentary and dry, desolate land-scapes. The men nodded at the boys as they passed through into the kitchen, where Troy introduced Roland to Fat Gerald, a man who was not so much fat as rotund. A horseshoe moustache and thick sideburns straddled his meaty face, ruddiness mottling his cheeks. He gripped Roland's hand in a tight fist, his stubby arm flexing.

'This Liam bloke,' he told Roland. 'He's crossed a line. You got a problem with someone, you sort it out with him, but you don't take a whole lot of guys and break into his house. Bash him in his own house. While his mother's asleep. That is not on. That's a dog act. He's got to be taught a lesson, simple as that.'

'That's right,' said Moses, who was leaning against the benchtop, randomly pushing buttons on the microwave.

'There's rules,' Fat Gerald told Roland, who nodded. The fluorescent light was lurid, glaring off the linoleum.

'Hey,' Fat Gerald said, hitching up his jeans. 'You want to see my aquariums?'

Roland followed him into the garage, Moses trailing behind them with a longneck in his hand. There was a musty, vegetable smell about the place, a chorus of bubbling in the darkness. Small motors hummed. Fat Gerald flicked a switch and lights strobed on above the aquariums lining the walls, fish flashing as they darted and turned. Roland crouched down to peer into one large tank where rainbow fish and red platies milled about a submerged forest of gently swaying cabomba, lacy fronds fanning out in the slow eddying of the water. A school of neon tetras moved in a jittery arrow past the buttresses of a mangrove root and guppies wiggled close to the surface, mosaic tails fluttering and shimmering in the light. In the next aquarium, the war-painted face of a cichlid regarded him gravely. Its scales had the cool iridescence of pearl. He moved from tank to tank. His mind was pulsing, diamond sharp, dazzled by it all.

'You see this one?' Fat Gerald said to Roland, showing him a tank containing a single gawping lionfish, its delicate fins undulating as it gulped at the water. 'That's the most poisonous fish in the world.'

'Really?'

'Yep,' said Fat Gerald. 'Pretty but deadly. Like my ex-wife,' he said to Moses, who chortled, tapping one of the tanks.

'Don't do that,' said Fat Gerald. 'That's like an earthquake for them.'

'Sorry,' said Moses, pulling his finger away.

'I've told you that before,' said Fat Gerald.

'Yeah?' said Moses. 'I don't remember that.'

'Well, I did.'

'We used to have a chuff and all sit around here stoned,' Moses told Roland. 'Looking at the little fishies. Didn't we, Gerald?'

'We did.'

'You can stare at them for hours and hours. How come we don't do that anymore?'

'Well, you started using smack, didn't you?' said Gerald gruffly, picking up a little net next to one of the tanks and scooping something out. 'I'm not going to give you a lecture about it, but I think you're stupid. I've known people who've got into that stuff and let me tell you, there isn't a whole lot left of them.'

'Yeah,' said Moses. 'But that doesn't mean I don't chuff anymore. I chuff all the time.'

'They're amazing,' said Roland, looking at a tank of clownfish and bright yellow angelfish, his mind jumping. Anemones bristled on the rocks, their waving tentacles tipped with light. There was a whole world in there. A perfect, perfect world. Watched over, kept from harm, safe from chance and uncertainty. At that moment, he could not think of anything more appealing than to spend each day tending to these tanks, looking after these delicate, flitting lives. 'If I were you,' he told Fat Gerald. 'I'd never leave here. I'd be in here all the time.'

Fat Gerald beamed, looking proudly at the tanks. 'Yeah,' he said. 'They're all right, aren't they?'

Shane rang at about nine o'clock and they all gathered around in silence while Moses talked to him.

'Yeah, yeah,' said Moses. 'How long you think it will take you to get there...so, say fifteen minutes? Okay. Liam want to talk to me? Okay.'

He hung up.

'Yeah, it's all sorted,' he said. 'I'm meant to be meeting them outside the school.'

They rose, catching each other's eyes with smiles that were almost nervous. Beers were quickly downed. New ones opened. Roland saw Curl standing in the doorway, tilting his head in the direction of the bathroom. Troy was in there, cutting up the rest of the crank on the benchtop, and this time Roland did it gladly. It was true what Troy had said. Heart pounding and mind leaping, he felt invincible, he feared nothing at all.

The van was waiting for them outside, chugging, its headlights penetrating the darkness of the street. The men sat inside with weapons beside them on the ridged floor: baseball bats, axe handles, star pickets, lengths of piping. They got in and Troy placed an aluminium bat in Roland's hand. The engine growled as the van made its way through the streets and the floor underneath them shuddered. It smelled, inside, of petrol and beer and cigarettes and sweat.

'Hey, Roly,' Troy said, opening the sports bag he had been carrying around all night. 'Look what Floyd loaned me.' He took out a gun, a snub-nosed revolver. Its dark patina sheened under the sweep of the overhead streetlights. Everyone in the van was suddenly paying attention to him.

'It's beautiful,' said Roland.

'Yeah,' said Troy. 'It is, isn't it?'

He held it up, pointed it towards the back of the van and looked down the sights, closing one eye.

'*Pow*,' he said, lifting the muzzle. He turned to the others. 'I'll fucking do it too, if I have to.'

'Probably not going to be any need for that,' muttered an older, moustached man. 'Let's not go too far.'

'I'm not saying I'm going to. I'm saying, if I have to, I'll do it.'

'Yeah, well, that's fair enough,' said the man. 'But don't go crazy with that thing.'

'I won't,' said Troy, eyes blazing. He turned back to Roland.

'You want to hold it?' he asked him. 'Course you do.' He flipped the gun over and handed it to Roland, the grip pointed towards him. 'Don't worry,' he said. 'Safety's on.'

'Yeah, but even if the safety's on, don't point it at anyone,' said the man.

Roland took the gun. It was cold to the touch and heavy in his hand, a lump of inert metal. He was almost surprised to realise that it had no agency of its own, as though he somehow expected it to ping and vibrate and move about like arcade machines when no one was playing them. He imagined firing it, the sudden response of the mechanism, the hard strike of the hammer, and he knew that the gun would buck in his hand and jar his arm if he did. It was a tool, he suddenly understood, insentient and useless unless in the hands of the knowing, like a spanner or a wrench, of which it had the same solid weightiness. And like those things, he also knew, it belonged to the world of men.

They parked on the road outside the locked gates of the high school, a long cyclone fence on either side. Spotlights lit the rectangular buildings, much of them lost in shadow, and Roland could see the expanse of the oval in the moonlight.

It was a warm gusty night, the sky curdling in dirty lavender clouds, a suffused glow where the moon was. The black limbs of the trees tossed about, the wind tearing through the foliage.

'Here we go,' someone said.

Through the windscreen, they could see dark figures swaggering down the footpath. Roland made out Liam and Shane, looming out of the shadows in their bomber jackets and army boots. Seven or eight boys followed, faces jaundiced as they passed under a streetlight. The moustached man had positioned himself by the door and as the group came alongside, he pulled it open. After that, everything seemed to happen very quickly and abruptly and all at once, yet, when Roland later recalled it, the memories were so vivid that it was as though it had all happened in slow motion.

Through the open door, he saw Shane turn to Liam and grab him by the throat, punching him again and again in the head. They were short, rapid punches, like someone pounding on a door, Shane's mouth open as though he were shouting. The men poured out of the van with harsh yells, weapons raised, and they set upon the boys, who tried to flee down the footpath or onto the road, one of them immediately turning and scrambling up the cyclone fence. Roland was surprised by their swiftness, that they seemed to instantly know what was happening. Fat Gerald tore around the side of the van, wielding the longneck he had been drinking from, and charged at one of the stragglers. Roland saw the look of fear in the boy's eyes, his long hair sweeping about as he turned to run, the wide swing of Gerald's arm and the bottle breaking into pieces on the boy's head. Fine droplets hung for a moment in the air and disappeared into nothing as the boy slumped, a dead weight, onto the footpath.

The rush of adrenalin seemed to almost deafen Roland, as though all the sounds, the yelling and hitting, the scrape of feet, the jingle of the cyclone fence as bodies were pushed against it, came from very far away. Amid the chaos, he could only think to do what the others were doing, and run after the scattering gang. He chased one shadowy figure as it hurtled down the footpath, recognising, as he caught up, the Polynesian boy Liam had jokingly chastised on the first night he appeared at Darren's. The boy turned as he heard Roland behind him, a flash of terrified eyes before he tripped and sprawled onto the footpath. He let out a single cry, a high, startlingly feminine shriek, and raised his hands in front of his face as Roland raised the bat to strike. But Roland could not do it. Though the drug ripped through him with the wild spit of a magnesium sparkler, though the cool shank of the bat felt like a part of him, an extension of his own force, the violence was not there.

'Stay out of Glenella!' he shouted at the trembling boy.

'I will, I will,' cried the boy. 'I promise.'

He leaped to his feet and ran into the darkness. Roland turned around and was surprised to see that it was all over. The others were gathered around Liam, who was lying on the footpath, his eyes half-shut and his arms around his head. His face was swollen beyond recognition, his upper lip split. Blood flowed from his mouth and nose in a broad cascade. Someone had torn out his earring, his earlobe a gaping cleft. Troy was bent over the fallen figure, yelling and gesturing maniacally with a baseball bat. The others watched, saying nothing. A piece of cardboard had come off the side of the van. 'We Specialise in Neon!' it boasted once again.

'Don't think you didn't have this coming to you, Liam,' Troy shouted. 'You brought this all on yourself, mate. You got no one to blame but yourself.' His voice sounded strange on its own in the silence and he seemed to struggle to keep his fury aroused, as though he were kindling it with the vigour of his movements. 'You think you can bash our friend? You think we're just going to let you get away with it? Ay?'

He kicked Liam in the gut. Liam groaned and curled up.

'You think you can go around doing whatever you want? You think you're a tough guy? Not so tough now, are you, Liam? Where are your boys now, you faggot?'

Troy threw the bat at him and it bounced and clattered on the footpath. He took the gun out of his belt and crouched down, showing it to Liam.

'You see this?' he asked, smacking Liam across the ear with his other hand.

'Open your eyes! Open your fucking eyes!' he shouted, his voice cracking. Liam opened his eyes. They were unfocused and seemed, Roland thought, childlike. The eyes of a frightened, helpless child.

'You see this?' Troy pointed the revolver at Liam's head. 'You see this gun? You come back at any of us and I swear, I'll shoot you in the fucking head. You understand?' He pushed the muzzle against Liam's cheek.

'Come on, Troy,' said Fat Gerald. 'We've got to go.'

Troy stayed there for a moment and then stood, putting the gun in his belt. They piled back into the van.

'Hey,' Fat Gerald said to Troy, leaning over the back of the driver's seat. 'Give us that gun for a moment.'

Troy gave it to him and Fat Gerald opened the window, put the gun out and fired a rapid succession of shots into the air. The deafening booms shattered the quiet of the sultry night, echoing off the pebbledash buildings and dark netball courts.

From the trees came a sudden chorus of birdsong. Liam, who was beginning to rise from the footpath, immediately dropped down again. Fat Gerald put the van in gear and they roared off with a shriek of tyres, the men inside whooping.

When they got back to the house, there was an impromptu party. Fat Gerald's girlfriend had come home from the bar and bistro with a group of friends and the men strutted and boasted and flocked to the laughing women with their stretch miniskirts and peroxide hair. Curl sat by the telephone in the kitchen, ringing girls up, a little leather-bound address book on the bench.

'You did good out there, brother,' said Fat Gerald, grasping Roland's hand and pulling him into a rough embrace. He thumped him on the back. 'Well done.'

After a few beers, which he barely felt, the crank still surging through him, Roland found himself talking to a girl his own age, the younger sister of one of the girls Curl had invited. Her parents were out and her sister was meant to be babysitting her, the girl explained, so she had brought her along.

'Apparently, there was some fight,' she said to Roland. 'My sister told me that this guy got bashed and so they went looking for the gang that did it.'

'Yeah, I know,' said Roland. 'I was there.'

'Really?' the girl said. She was a thin girl with braces on her teeth, which she tried to hide by putting her hand over her mouth when she smiled. Roland could make out the small mounds of her breasts through the thick knit of her jumper. 'So you were in the fight?'

'Yeah.'

'You don't really seem like the type.'

'I'm not,' he admitted. 'But this was for my friend. I'd

do anything for my friends.'

'Yeah?' she said, smiling, revealing her braces again before she remembered and quickly covered her mouth, pretending she was wiping it. 'Yeah, that's pretty cool.'

They had not been talking for long when Roland took her by the hand and led her, giggling, down the hall to one of the bedrooms. He put his arm around her and he kissed her. The girl returned the kiss, though softly. She had to be careful, she murmured to him, because of the braces. It was much like the first time with Melissa, wet and wordless, the smell of shampoo, the taste of alcohol. The girl gripped his shoulders as his hands explored her and this time his desire was unmixed. He sat down on the bed and drew her to him and she fell into his lap with a laugh, becoming quickly serious as their eyes met and they kissed again. They stayed there, kissing, until the party finished and it was time for the girl to go home.

AFTER THAT THINGS seemed to go back to normal in Glenella, apart from one incident involving Colleen and Darren's mother at the Glenella shops. According to Tilly Johnson, Colleen had started screaming at Darren's mother as she came out of Worthy's supermarket, although no one had been able to make out what she was saying. When Darren's mother tried to hurry away, Colleen chased her and grabbed one of her shopping bags; the bag broke and groceries spilled out onto the footpath. Darren's mother left them there as she fled. Colleen's rage had been terrifying, according to Marjorie White, who had been there at the supermarket doing her weekly shopping and had told Tilly all about it. The whole thing had been ghastly, just too awful to imagine. People coming out of the shop had stood there frozen and watched the scene in absolute horror, Colleen, as Marjorie White said herself, acting like a complete madwoman. Clawing at the

Wilson woman with those nasty long fingernails of hers. Tilly Johnson was sure Colleen was terribly embarrassed about it now, although she had always said herself that she suspected Colleen could be a real gutter fighter if she wanted to. One thing was for certain, which was that Colleen had given the woman a real scare, Tilly told Joyce. Someone had reported that she now did her shopping at the Forest Hill Safeway. There were further rumours that Colleen had gone to George Kyriakides and demanded that he evict Darren and his mother from the house on Carlington Street, but Graham said that even if she had, he couldn't imagine George Kyriakides getting involved in some local dispute.

Tilly Johnson now said that she had never believed what she referred to as Darren Wilson's *accusations*. She said that she now thought they were the most terrible lies.

'That boy was just trying to save his own skin,' she told Joyce over a cup of tea. 'They should lock him up and throw away the key as far as I'm concerned.'

Everyone else in Glenella thought much the same, she said, and it seemed to Roland that his parents did also. Reg and Colleen still came over on Sundays to sit outside with Graham and Joyce on the sunny days of the warming spring, and then the summer, although Cassie never came again. Roland did notice that Reg was more sedate, no longer so drunk and raucous. Colleen, on the other hand, seemed to drink and talk even more than before, her face flushed with alcohol by the early afternoon. She was quick to anger and often seemed to misconstrue things his parents said, so that they were always assuring her that they didn't at all mean whatever it was she had imagined. No one ever mentioned anything about Darren Wilson or the incident on the front lawn, but Roland felt that there was now an uneasiness that had not been there before, something always slithering under the surface of things.

And while she did not come on Sundays, Cassie did come to see him from time to time, tapping on his bedroom window, appearing like a wan spectre in the midst of thoughts that often were of her. She would already be wiping away tears as she came into his room and threw herself, sobbing, onto his bed. As they talked it seemed to Roland that they were endlessly retracing the conversation of that long night at her house, as though she needed to resay those things over and over again, and he came to realise that what she wanted, or needed, was neither a reply from him nor the suggestion of a solution to her troubles, but just someone to hear them, to listen as she plucked at unfinished thoughts. She often asked him about Darren, though she seemed to have little interest in his current situation. When he told her about Larundel, about Darren's mother's plans to move him directly to his sister's house in Rosebud after he was released, Cassie only nodded distractedly. What she wanted to know was whether Roland thought Darren had been happy when he was with her. If he had really loved her. She made him repeat every word Darren had said on the evening Roland had eaten hamburgers with him on the station lawn, and she questioned him on every detail. What did Roland think he meant by that? Why?

'Do you believe in God?' she asked him one day as she lay stretched out on his bed, her face turned to the ceiling and her feet restless in white socks.

'I don't know,' he said. 'We have sermons in assembly and stuff at school, but I never really listen to it.'

'I don't have any reason to believe in God,' said Cassie. 'I'm the last person who should believe in God, but sometimes I think it's such a nice idea. Just that you're never alone, that there's always someone who cares for you.'

He wanted to take her in his arms, kiss her, tell her that he would always care for her, that she needn't be alone and wouldn't be alone if she would only give the word. But he said nothing. He knew he could only continue to dream, and he did dream of her, dreams sustained by the brief joy that shuddered through him when she squeezed his hand while they talked, when she told him that he was a good friend, when she embraced him before she left. As school ended and the holidays arrived, he often found himself sitting in his room, hoping she would come, even if all he could ask for was the sound of her voice, her hot face against his chest, the smell of tears and shampoo she left on his pillow.

In December, a real estate agent's sign appeared outside the Nobles' house on Creek Road.

LAVISH FAMILY RESIDENCE IN TRANQUIL GLENELLA.
THE GOOD LIFE AWAITS!

THEY DROVE DOWN to Rosebud to see Darren early in the new year, greeted, as they arrived, by Darren's sister, Angie, and brother-in-law, Brendan, who waved the Torana into a space on the sandy driveway between two sedans and a boat on a trailer. Angie held a fat sunhatted baby in her arms, two grubby children peeking out from behind her legs as the boys came up the drive. The day was hot and the Torana's vinyl seats had been scalding, the seatbelt buckle searing Roland's bare legs. Darren appeared in the doorway in the same tight jeans and singlet he had worn in Glenella. His gaunt figure had filled out, the angular lines of his cheeks were softened. His hair had lightened to a dirty blond.

'Thought youse were never going to make it,' he said. 'How are you, Roly?'

'All right,' Roland replied.

The house was cool and dark inside. Striped canvas awnings

hung low over the windows, the Venetian blinds drawn. It smelled of Pine-O-Clean and talcum powder and nappies. Brendan handed out beers in foam rubber holders and they went into the backyard, a rough stretch of lawn cut into a thicket of tea-trees. Everyone took out their cigarettes and lit up. The two sunburnt children picked plastic racquets off the grass and started a game of totem tennis, shrieking and laughing as they lunged at the circling ball.

'Nice day for it,' said Brendan, looking up at the sky.

They all looked up, nodding in agreement.

After they finished their drinks, the boys walked to the beach along the shady dirt roads, overgrown with coastal grasses and scrub, and past the strip of shops facing the foreshore. Darren took the others to the pier and introduced them to two old men who were fishing off the end. The boys looked into the buckets full of bait and at the fish in the esky, wrapped in wet hessian. Their dead eyes stared. One of the men, Len, was eating a sandwich wrapped in wax paper and drinking milky tea from a thermos lid.

'You boys want one of my sandwiches?' he asked them, holding out an open lunchbox. 'My wife always makes too many for me. Doesn't want me to go hungry.'

There were deep creases in his leathery face. His hair was as white as cotton wool, poking from underneath his khaki legionnaire's hat, and his eyes were the same colour as the sunlit shallows.

'Nah, she's right, Len,' Darren said. 'Angie and Brendan are having a barbeque this arvo. You and Pat should come along.'

Pat, the other man, glanced up and then looked back at the water. Seagulls were squawking all around them, flying overhead in flocks and alighting on the railing. They shifted about impatiently, feet clattering, and called.

'Yeah, maybe,' Len mumbled, blowing on his tea.

'They never will,' said Darren as they walked back down the pier. 'They never leave that spot. They get there every day before the sun comes up and stay until teatime. Sometimes even come back and do some night fishing. Can't get enough of it, those guys. I've been going out in the mornings with them. Have to get up pretty early, but it's worth it. Come home with a nice flathead or a couple of whiting. Get Angie to fry it up. You know, makes you feel like you've done something, bringing a bit of fresh fish home. Sitting down and having a beer with it at the end of the day.'

'So you like it down here?' Roland asked.

Darren seemed surprised: as though, Roland thought, no one had ever asked him before.

'Yeah, I do, Roly,' he said. 'I love it.'

They sat on the sand by a row of old bathing boxes, a lacework of cracks across the grubby, salt-stubbled whitewash. Spindly eucalypts twisted, wind-harried, against the cobalt sky and threw capricious feathers of shade that tipped the hard tussocks and the churned ripples of sand. The boys leaned back into the shadows, eyes twitching as they settled and flicked off their faces. Curl took off his singlet and inspected his tanned pectorals, his shark-tooth necklace dangling. Towels strewed the crescent of the beach; there were sunbathers, people waist-deep in the water, kids running about with zinc cream smeared across their noses and cheeks. A man sitting under an umbrella held a transistor radio up to his ear, the cricket commentary crackling.

'Any talent down here?' Curl asked Darren, watching his muscles as he flexed them.

'Yeah, there's a few decent birds around the place,' Darren said. 'I'm only just getting to know the locals.' He nodded at the people on the beach. 'Most of this lot will be gone in a few weeks and everyone says it gets pretty quiet after that. Especially in winter.'

'So what are you going to do then?'

'There's plenty to do. I'm really getting into this fishing. I want to learn how to operate Brendan's boat as well. Take it out and go after something a bit bigger. Len reckons you can get some good-sized snapper out on a boat. And I'm thinking about selling the bike. Maybe buy a jet ski.'

'Don't sell the bike,' said Troy. 'It's a classic.'

'Yeah, but it's not much good to me down here. It's still locked up in my mum's back shed.'

'So, bring it down.'

'Nah, it'll rust here. And I wouldn't have any use for it anyway. But imagine,' Darren said, pointing out at the water, 'going out there on a big Kawasaki or something. No roads. No cars to worry about. Gunning it. Jumping the waves. Flying along. Just you and the water. Nothing else to worry about.'

'Kawasaki?' Troy said, peering up at Darren and shading his eyes with his hand. 'You've actually been looking at them, have you?'

'Just in the magazines at the newsagent's. But I'm serious about it. I think I'm going to do it.'

Curl wandered up to the foreshore and started going through a bin piled high with discarded fish-and-chip wrappings. He pulled out a two-litre Solo bottle, brought it back and tossed it to Troy, who took a deal bag out of his pocket and slapped it down on Darren's lap.

'Present from Floyd,' he said. 'Says he's sorry he couldn't make it.'

'Nah,' said Darren, handing the bag back to him. 'No way am I going near that stuff again.'

'You'll be all right,' said Troy. He took out a cone and a metal stem and stabbed it into the bottle. 'You're off the Largactil now, aren't you?'

'Fuck yeah,' Darren said. 'That was bad stuff. Bad, bad stuff.'

'Told you. Told you you'd feel better once you'd gone off it.'

'Yeah, but I was scared of stopping,' said Darren. 'I was scared of losing it again.' He shook his head. 'I can hardly remember a thing from the whole time I was on it,' he said to Roland. 'Nothing. It's just blank. It's lost. Like, Curl said you and him came to visit me at Larundel.'

'We went a few times,' Roland said.

'Yeah, see, I don't remember that at all.'

He looked out at the water, where a man was trying to stand up on a sailboard, a struggle to lift the sail as it swivelled and billowed in the wind.

'But thanks for visiting me, anyway. I appreciate it. Even if I can't remember it.'

'Yeah, so stay on the natural stuff,' said Curl. 'It'll do you some good.'

'I said no.'

Curl shrugged. He and Troy got up and took the bong to the caravan park, where they filled it with water at a tap. They disappeared somewhere among the trees.

'I still don't believe it was the mull, to be honest,' Darren told Roland. 'It's just that if the doctors were right, you know, no way I'm going to take the risk. I don't know what it was. Just, the whole situation maybe.'

'It was bad,' said Roland. 'Things were bad.'

'Yeah, they were, weren't they? You probably remember it better than me. It's got all mixed up in my head. It was good times, though, wasn't it? Before that. Sitting around in my mum's backyard, just talking and that.'

He spoke of it wistfully, as though it had all happened a very long time ago.

Roland nodded. 'It was.'

'So how's Cassie?'

'I don't really know,' said Roland. 'Her family's moved house.'

'Well, that's no surprise,' Darren said. He took a battered pack of Peter Stuyvesant out of his pocket and shook out a cigarette. 'You know, I really wish I'd done things better. All that stuff with Cassie. What happened between me and her. I think about it all the time now. I wish I'd done things differently, but I didn't.'

'I know what you mean,' said Roland.

'I look back and I think, well, that was my chance to show what sort of a person I was. You know, you always assume you're the good guy and everything, that you're going to do the right thing. But I just ran away from it. I suppose maybe I'm just not such a great person after all. Not who I thought I was, anyway.'

He shaded his eyes with his hand and stared out at the waves. The sailboarder was well down the beach now, gliding towards the headlands past the dark dots of swimmers' heads as they bobbed in the sapphire depths, a wake of spume like a tail. Nearby, some boys were throwing a tennis ball to each other, trying to make it bounce off the water. Their exclamations were songs of the purest joy.

'Anyway,' Darren said. 'I won't get all miserable on you. How's things with you? You back at school yet?'

'No,' Roland said. 'I start in a couple of weeks.'

'You ought to come and stay down here sometime. You'd like Len and Pat. They've got a whole lot of stories. From the war and that. If you can get them talking about it, which isn't always easy. When I first started fishing with them, I used to sit there and talk away, you know, just trying to be friendly, make conversation. Asking them stuff. Then one day, Pat goes, "You know why we like it out here?" and I go, "Why?" and he says, "The peace and quiet."' Darren grinned. 'So I took the hint. No, but they're good guys, though. And it's true, it's nice to just sit there and be quiet. Listen to the waves. Let the world go by.'

He butted his cigarette out in the sand and put it in his jeans pocket, looking at Roland with his pale, almost colourless eyes.

'It's not a bad way to be, I suppose,' he said.

There was laughter behind them and they turned to watch Troy and Curl as they came back towards the beach, stumbling along the path through the scrub. Roland and Darren stood up, wiping the sand off their legs, and went to join them.

ROLAND DIDN'T SEE Cassie again until late in the summer, when his family went to visit the Nobles at their new house in the more prestigious suburb of Hawthorn. The house was an elaborate old Federation structure that sat hidden behind an ivy-shrouded wall, a roof with peaks at all angles like the sails of a boat. A bay window bulged in a broad half-decagon at the front, flourishes of leadlight above the transom, and terracotta gargoyles snarled down from the gable ends and dormers. Colleen showed Joyce around, while Reg led Graham, Roland and Lily out to the backyard. The two fathers drank a beer standing by the pool. Cassie was floating on a lilo, supine, her fingers trailing in the dappled water. She was wearing her Ray-Ban sunglasses and no one was sure whether she was asleep or awake until Reg leaned over and splashed her and she cried out angrily and paddled away. Lily, shy in this unfamiliar place, stood close to Graham and watched Cassie, who quickly became lifeless again in the sun.

Joyce and Colleen came out and they sat at the table on the deck. Reg opened a bottle of pink champagne.

'It's such a lovely house,' said Joyce. 'I would love to live in a house like this.'

'It is smaller than our old place,' said Colleen. 'But really, we didn't need all that space. Just for me and Reg. And Cassie. This is more than enough for us.'

'I suppose you can have your Australia Day parties out here, can't you? Are you going to put in another bar, Reg?'

'I don't think so,' said Reg, lighting a cigarette. 'I'd say my bartending days are over.'

'Yes, I don't think we'll be having any more of those parties,' said Colleen. 'I didn't miss not having one this year at all. They were Glenella people, anyway. I never invited any of my friends from around here.'

'Do you know many people in this area?'

'Well, of course!' Colleen crowed. 'That's the whole reason we moved. All of our friends are from around here. Cassie's friends, too. And her school's only five minutes' drive away. Reg takes her there on his way to work and I pick her up in the afternoons. It's so much easier. No, it's wonderful for Cassie here. No more of those long train trips every day. I honestly don't know how we ever put up with being stuck all the way out in Glenella all those years. We're *so* much closer to every-thing here. And Cassie loves that pool. Just loves it. Cannot get away from it. She spent every day of the holidays out here. I said to her, "You're in for a rude shock when school starts. No more lying around in the sun." Well, I was wrong, wasn't I? Because as soon as she gets home from school, she's out here. Straight away.'

'She's been very quiet today,' Joyce said, watching Cassie as she drifted sullenly in the water.

'She's becoming a typical teenager. I wondered when that was going to happen. She used to be so well-behaved, but now it's sulking and tantrums and goodness knows what else. She's very angry at me and Reg. She resents us.'

'Oh?'

'She certainly does. We've become very strict with her after what happened last year with that Darren Wilson boy. We were too easy on her before. We trusted her too much. But we've laid down the law this time. No hanging around with boys after school or any of that nonsense. Reg was perfectly right about that. You know how sneaky these teenage girls can be. They're manipulative. They'll play you for a fool if you give them half a chance. Well, she already has, hasn't she?'

They looked at Cassie, who remained motionless, one leg bent on the lilo, her skin tanned and her hair gone white from the sun. She was inscrutable behind the dark lenses of her sunglasses.

'It's the hormones,' said Colleen. 'I don't think she knows *what* she's doing half the time.'

Reg turned on the spa. It heated up quickly and they all changed into their bathers and got in, except for Cassie, who continued to drift in the pool. The adults talked loudly over the bubbles, another bottle of champagne in an ice bucket at Reg's elbow. He pulled it out periodically, wiping off the cold beads of water, and topped up the glasses until the froth spilled over the sides, making Colleen shriek.

'Once I was sitting here for so long,' Colleen yelled. 'I was right up against one of the jets, practically sitting on it. And when I got out I had this big red bruise on my bum!' She cackled with laughter. 'Didn't I, Reg?'

When the spa got too hot for them, they got out and dived into the pool, shaking their heads as they came up and exclaiming with the shock and relief of it before swimming lazily to the steps. Reg ducked under the lilo and dumped Cassie into the water, her composure lost as she toppled, arms and legs flailing. Cassie hoisted herself out of the pool and stormed off into the house, screeching, dripping, pulling at her bikini bottoms, her wet feet slapping the flagstones. She slammed the French doors shut behind her. Reg guffawed, fishing her sunglasses out of the water and holding them up. When she came back outside later, she was calm, talking politely to Joyce and Graham and smiling at Lily, who beamed back at her. The two girls went into the house.

As the afternoon dragged on, as the ashtrays filled, as the sunlight climbed the sweeping roofs and struck the fluttering leaves of the elm trees, Roland was beset by that familiar Sunday afternoon melancholy. Cigarette smoke, salt-and-vinegar chips, the smell of spilt alcohol: all the Sundays of previous years came back to him at that moment and he was aware of things that had passed and could not be returned to, of things changing. Reg ordered pizza and they went back to the table, wrapped in towels, suddenly starving. The girls came chattering out of the house. They ate in silence, hands and mouths greasy, and leaned back in their chairs when they had finished. Graham patted his stomach and blew out his cheeks. Lily giggled. The adults talked groggily. Reg produced a bottle of whiskey and Joyce and Colleen groaned, holding their hands over their glasses. Graham winced as he held his out.

'All right then,' he said to Reg. 'Do your worst.'

At dusk, as the mosquitoes began to hum around them,

Roland sat in the spa again. He looked up at the sky as it paled and darkened. Cassie came over and joined him, ducking her head under the churning water and coming up sleek and dripping, her hair plastered over her neck, her face rosy from the heat. She peered at him through the steam.

'So, how are you?' she asked, speaking over the hum of the motor.

'All right,' he said. 'How are you?'

'All right, I suppose,' she said, blinking as the water ran down her forehead and into her eyes. She wiped it away with her fingers. 'Yeah, I'm all right.'

The evening ended with many farewells as the two families went drowsily out onto the street, the houses turned to the black shapes of pillars and steep-pitched roofs, cast iron and fretwork scribbled against the blind-drawn windows. The rush of traffic and life could be heard somewhere not so far away. Graham wound down his window and waved to the Nobles, honking the horn as the car began to move. Roland glanced back and caught a glimpse of Cassie, stretching and yawning, arms above her head as she raised herself onto tiptoe.

This is how he would remember her in years to come, that moment after the goodbyes, as she stood between her parents under those sulphur streetlights that seemed to bleed all colours into grey and to both starken and soften the faces like aging Kodachrome: the slight ungainliness of her movement that he would recognise anywhere, the particular slouch of her slim figure, that flourish of her hair as she turned and walked back towards the house. And it would not be until all those years later that he would realise, thinking back on that moment, how young she had been—still, he would think, really a child. How young they both had been. And he would remember his own feelings also. Perhaps it was love, first love, he would think, but so unlike the complicated loves of later years, unspoiled by that need to possess, by voluptuousness, by even the knowledge of it, the disappointment at its edge, by the impossibility of minds: something that was there only in that feeling of numinousness, of promise, and the delicateness of the yearning. It was part of that time, he supposed, when everything was new, every moment resonant with meaning, when fleeting glimpses, the meeting of gazes, a single word, felt as though they held more than the passing of entire later years.

The Arthursons drove home through the gracious old post-codes, past the terraces of splendidly facaded shops with their scrollwork and mouldings and urns, the grand stuccoed houses, bluestone churches, the streets of elms that met and tangled overhead like the endless vault of a cathedral. Trams glided past, jangling, weary faces within the glow as the family made their way towards rises that revealed the twinkling city, the iron curve of the river twisting through swathes of rustling trees in the darkness below. Then it all turned concrete, buildings like giant crenellations staggered across distances, a bright spot here and there, like some aquarium or bell jar—a restaurant with neon in the window, diners inside, steaming bowls—a glimpse of life that quickly ebbed into that long stretch of changelessness as they continued east past the shopping centres and petrol stations and through the endless maze of brick veneers. Far off, they could see Reg Noble's face lit brighter and larger than the moon above the static car yard, the long rows of warehouses and the narrow streets off the highway. It was deserted at this late hour, apart from the occasional low growling sedan that accelerated madly along the empty road, its engine howling as if in despera-tion or defiance as it sped through the quiet of the suburbs.

ACKNOWLEDGEMENTS

I want to thank my editor, Penny Hueston, for her continued encouragement over the years, her willingness to listen to my perennial self-doubt and her guidance as this novel took shape. I doubt it would exist were it not for her efforts. Thanks also to my publisher, Michael Heyward, for his ongoing support.

Nikolai Gladanac read an early draft of this novel as well as the final manuscript, much of the reading done, I suspect, while pulling all-nighters at the factory. His insights and suggestions during our many discussions about the book were invaluable. As were Grantley McDonald's thoughts and meticulous corrections. I knew I could make use of his pedantry one day!

I am very grateful to Sarah Taylor for her advice and percipient observations, to Vikki Pollard, whose impeccable memory and understanding of the world I have tried to describe were of enormous help, to Ben Cas for his extensive comments on the manuscript and to Geordie Williamson for his correspondence and his always generous and thoughtful words, which I have often found myself turning to when in need of solace.

The Australia Council awarded me an Arts Project grant for the writing of the final draft of this novel. This was much appreciated.

Special thanks to Bill Henson for allowing me to use the untitled work from his sublime *Untitled 1985–1986* exhibition for the cover. It was after seeing the exhibition that I decided to have another go at this book about the suburbs.